The Mid-life Trials of Annabeth Hope

Alice May

Other books by Alice May

Memoir
The House That Sat Down

Children's Non-Fiction
How to Draw a Giraffe – the Alice May Way
How to Draw an Ostrich – the Alice May Way

The Mid-life Trials of Annabeth Hope

Book 1 in The New Forest Families Series

Alice May

The Book Guild Ltd

First published in Great Britain in 2024 by
The Book Guild Ltd
Unit E2 Airfield Business Park,
Harrison Road, Market Harborough,
Leicestershire. LE16 7UL
Tel: 0116 2792299
www.bookguild.co.uk
Email: info@bookguild.co.uk
X: @bookguild

Typeset in 11pt Minion Pro

Printed on FSC accredited paper
Printed and bound in Great Britain by 4edge Limited

ISBN 978 1835740 590

British Library Cataloguing in Publication Data.
A catalogue record for this book is available from the British Library.

For
Gill and Nigel
with love
Thank you for always believing in me.

Chapter 1

Southampton

Beth paused in the doorway of the counselling room. A waft of lavender air freshener caught in her throat. The cramped room with peeling paint couldn't be more uninspiring if it tried. Yet it was a vast improvement on the waiting room, where the smell of damp and despair had seeped into her bones.

A slim woman in a neat blue suit looked up and smiled. 'Annabeth Hope?'

'Everyone calls me Beth.'

'I'm Jane Montgomery. Do you understand why you've been referred for counselling?'

Beth nodded.

'Come in and grab a seat. We'll get started.' The orange plastic chair she gestured to jarred with the dingy room.

A bumper box of budget tissues lurked on a low table. *That's a bad sign.* Beth's feet refused to move her any closer. Someone as young and perky as Jane couldn't possibly understand the shitstorm that was her life. If she started crying, she'd never stop. And she didn't have time for that.

She should be back in the forest seeing a man about the roof, not navel-gazing in a repurposed semi on the seedier side of Southampton.

'I just need another prescription.'

Jane glanced at the papers in her hand, the ends of her glossy brown bob swinging forward to graze her chin. 'I'm sorry. Doctor Sharma says no more sleeping tablets until you've given counselling a try.' When she looked back up, there was steel behind the sympathetic, puppy-dog eyes. 'Come in. Please. Let me help you.'

Beth sagged against the door jamb. 'I'm fine... I'm just... I'm...' Her cheeks burned at the wobble in her voice. *I'm a mess.* She glanced down at knackered body parts stuffed into frayed jeans and a faded hoodie; the naturally pale skin of a redhead leached grey by exhaustion; hair that was limp and lifeless. Fifty wasn't even that old. She felt closer to ninety. Her mobile pinged. Diving into her bag, she checked the screen.

'It's clinic policy for mobiles to be switched off during consultations, Beth.'

'Sorry. It's just Grace only started preschool last week and there isn't anyone else to... uh... never mind, I'll put it on silent. And...' She scanned the message as she fumbled with the handset. 'Oh no.'

'Problem?'

'The head of sixth form wants to see me. My stepson, Jack, has been in a fight.'

'Do you just have the two children?'

'No. Four.'

'What ages?'

'Rose is nineteen, Jack and Daisy are sixteen – they're twins – and Grace is three.'

'Gosh! That is quite a gap.'

'The older three are my husband's – he's called Paul. Grace is ours.'

Jane made a note. 'And Paul, is he supportive?'

'Not so you'd notice.'

'I'm sorry?'

'Believe me, I'm the one who's sorry.' The back of her eyes gave an ominous prickle.

'We can do this in the doorway if you prefer, Beth, or you could sit.'

Beth took a deep breath. Poor, sweet Jane had no idea what she was letting herself in for. *Perhaps I should sit, just for a minute.* In an uncharacteristic snap decision, she marched over the stained carpet, tugged a tissue from the box and planted her backside on the waiting orange plastic.

'Go on then, Jane. Fix me.'

Jane closed the door. 'Can you tell me why you feel Paul isn't supportive?'

'Because he buggered off.'

'I see. When you say he buggered off—'

Beth groaned. 'It's such a cliché it's embarrassing. He went out for a pint of milk six months ago and never came back.'

'You're sure he didn't have an accident?'

'Oh, I'm sure. He's not actually a missing person. He's just a waste of space.'

'So you have heard from him?'

'Once. But once was enough.'

The sound of Jane's pen scratching away in the otherwise silent room, officially documenting Paul's treachery, made Beth ache inside.

'What support do you have, Beth? Do you have family nearby?'

'My parents emigrated to Australia after my sister settled out there. We speak on the phone all the time.'

'What about friends?'

'Most of them are in London. I used to work there.'

'What about your stepchildren's wider family? Uncles and aunts? Grandparents?'

Beth really didn't want to get into Isla, the most perfect biological mother on the planet. 'Paul hasn't been in contact with his adoptive family since he left home at eighteen. And the children's grandparents have all passed. There is only this annoying woman in the village. She used to help Paul look after the children before we met. Barbara Trenchard. She hates my guts.'

Jane pursed her lips. 'You can't do everything on your own. You need a support network. What about neighbours?'

'I don't need people. They just let you down. What I need is sleep and a roof that doesn't leak.'

'Oh dear. It rained a lot last night.'

'It did. And the leak blew the electrics. Believe me, searching for buckets at 1am with a hyperactive three-year-old skipping around with a torch making ghost noises isn't fun. The only reason I'm functioning today is industrial-strength coffee.'

'So, the roof is a problem?'

'The whole farmhouse is a problem,' said Beth.

'Farmhouse? You live on a farm?'

Beth shook her head. 'It was a farm, years ago; now it's just a crumbling farmhouse with a bit of land. I grow vegetables. We have a few animals.'

'Like what?'

'Chickens, a duck, a donkey, llampaccas—'

'Lam-whats?'

Beth winced. 'Sorry, that's what Grace calls them. Llamas and alpacas.'

Jane grinned. 'Cute. Anything else.'

'No, that's it. Well, apart from Paul's ancient fox terrier, Paddy. The grumpiest dog on the planet.'

'And where is this farmhouse?'

'In the New Forest. A couple of miles outside the village of Ambleford.'

The consultation continued in much the same vein, with Jane asking questions and making note of Beth's replies, until eventually a ripple of light chimes rang out. Jane glanced at the clock. 'We've covered a lot of ground, Beth. Well done. Time's up for now. We'll pick this up in the next session. Meanwhile, I'll send you a link for a meditation app I want you to try. It should help you to relax before bed. Remember the importance of fresh air and exercise. And try to switch all that coffee for a decaffeinated alternative. Yes?'

Huh! Why didn't I think of that? Some organic veg, a herbal teabag or two, a quick trot around the park and a spot of deep breathing. Simple. 'I'd rather have tablets.'

'You need a long-term, healthy solution, not medication. I'll see you next week.'

Chapter 2

Meanwhile, in London

On any normal day, Dr Rick Mahon of Five Oaks Surgery would never contemplate jumping from a first-floor window. Especially not in the middle of clinic. Today was not a normal day. Today had gone pear-shaped in a bizarre, alternate-reality type of way. For once, the thought of seeing patients in the traditionally accepted manner – one after another, while nodding and listening, and then trying his damnedest to find a way to help them – was beyond him.

Hell, even skipping naked through Trafalgar Square handing out random prescriptions might be on the cards today. *On second thoughts, maybe not naked. I'm not that young anymore.*

His phone pinged several times from the inside pocket of his blue woollen jacket. Ignoring it, he opened the sash window. Traffic sounds, sirens and the hectic fug of city life spilled in. He leaned out and eyed the raised flower bed between the foot of the building and the car park. *Can I make it down in one piece?*

He glanced over his shoulder at the door. It was locked

from the outside. Surely no other doctor on the planet had ever suffered the indignity of being locked into his own consulting room? Were this a movie, he would merely throw a shoulder at the door, splinter the wood with ease and escape.

Huh! Writing on the floor in agony with a fractured collarbone, more like. Then again, two broken legs from jumping out of the window wouldn't be any better. Rick wasn't hero enough for either option. *Damn it all to hell.* He hated not being in control. And having nothing to do was even worse. Too much time to think. Keeping busy was the only thing keeping him sane. Another flurry of muted pings called out from his pocket, just as a click sounded and the door opened.

Abandoning the window, he crossed the room. 'Gita, thank God.'

'Calm down.' Gita – short grey hair and brisk mannerisms – shot him a look that would stop a herd of charging bison. What she lacked in height, she made up for in sheer force of will. It was one of the reasons he'd known she'd make such an excellent business partner. But she wasn't supposed to use her superpower on him.

'I am calm. Or I'm as calm as I'm ever going to get, given that you locked me in.' He stepped towards the door. She blocked his path. Unwilling to use his physical size against her, he stopped. A crash reverberated along the corridor from the waiting room. Gita didn't move. 'Let me past, Gita. Sam needs help.'

'He's fine.' She closed the door behind her and leaned against it. 'You know as well as I do, he considers himself practice security as well as reception manager.'

'That's not the point.'

'It's exactly the point.'

'But what about the patients?'

'Apart from Mrs Clutterbuck and her dodgy hip, there aren't any patients out there. And she's opened popcorn. She's thoroughly enjoying the sight of reporters baying for blood.' She sighed and pushed her small round glasses further up her nose. 'I'm trying to protect you.'

Rick slumped back against his desk. 'I know, I just don't know what's going on.'

'You're all over social media, for starters.'

That explained the insistent pinging. 'But I haven't posted anything.'

'You didn't have to.' Gita gave a bitter laugh. 'Turns out Dean Markwell's mother is Cora Diamond.'

'Who?'

'Cora Diamond. Z-list reality TV star.'

'Never heard of her.'

'Well, she's heard of you. And first thing this morning, she announced on all her channels that she's suing you.'

Nausea puddled in his belly like molten lead. Every doctor knew they were one consultation away from a lawsuit these days, but you could never tell which one. Rick closed his eyes. His heartbeat thudded in his ears and the room began to spin.

How the hell has it come to this?

Five years at medical school, two as a house officer, three more as a GP trainee, followed by twenty more as a community practitioner had taught him a lot, but he must have missed the session on how to handle rabid paparazzi chasing a story. The two reporters who'd hammered on his apartment door last night – no, hang on… not reporters… what had they called themselves? Social media commentators. That was it. Bastards, the lot of them. Asking all those questions. How dare they? Dean's situation was none of their business. Rick had never broken patient confidentiality and he was damned if he'd start now. He pushed himself to his feet. 'I'll go and give them a statement.'

Gita planted her hands on her hips. 'Over my dead body.'

'I'll just say "No comment" a lot, then they'll go away.'

'They bloody won't. You need to keep your head down and let me handle it. *You* are not what's important here.'

'I know that. What do you take me for? The only important person in all this is Dean.'

Gita shook her head. 'All our patients are important. It's bad enough we've got the General Medical Council breathing down our necks, thanks to you. Now, you're splashed all over social media *and* the national news! This could destroy us as a practice. And if we close, what happens to our patients? None of the other local surgeries have the capacity to take on extras.'

Rick bowed his head. GMC investigations were a necessary part of medical practice. There had to be accountability. Even so, they were hard on all involved. If he'd known before what he knew now, he'd have handled that whole consultation with Dean differently. Balling his hands into fists to stop them shaking, he wrapped his arms across his chest. 'I can make this right.'

'No. You'll make it worse. I've already been in contact with the British Medical Association. Their support team suggest you take some sick leave.'

'Don't be ridiculous. I'm fine.'

'You're not. Seriously, Rick. Just look at you. You've lost

weight; your clothes are hanging off you. You're pale and jumpy as hell. The bags under your eyes are big enough to pack for a family of five on a trip to Lapland.'

'I said, I'm fine.'

'Do you think I don't see you working yourself into the ground? Or know that you've been giving up your weekends to help shift the waiting list for the dementia assessment clinic over at St Marks? You never stop.'

Rick kept his eyes lowered and his mouth shut. Gita wouldn't understand that, for him, seeing a new patient every ten minutes and helping other people to solve their problems kept him from dwelling on how empty his life was. Ironic that the solution to one dilemma could be the cause of another much bigger one.

'What happened with Dean... it... look, given the current situation and the pressure you're under, Rick, it's my opinion that you're not fit to work.'

'I disagree.'

She lowered her voice. 'I... no, *we* need you to go.'

'Go? Go where?' *Dear God, please don't say to go home.*

'I don't care. Anywhere that isn't here. Somewhere no one will expect you to be. Off grid. Under the radar. Whatever. Just lie low for a bit. A couple of weeks, at least, until we get the GMC report through. Then, depending on whether they exonerate you or not, we can take it from there.'

Rick rubbed his temples. There was somewhere he could go. Thanks to Uncle Charlie, God rest his soul, leaving him his house. What with work and everything, Rick had not had a chance to see the property since the will had been settled. Goodness only knows what state it was in. Who cares? A few days kicking his heels in the New Forest might be a good idea. Especially if the alternative was his apartment, where the emptiness and isolation were a permanent reminder of what a failure he was at the things most people could accomplish with ease, like relationships and families. 'If I go, I need to see Dean first.'

'Absolutely not.'

'There might be something I can do to help. Let me talk to his mother, at least.'

'No! What part of "she's suing you" don't you understand? Any lawyer worth his salt would tell you to stay away.'

'But—'

'I'm begging you to stay away. If you won't do it for yourself, then do it for the practice. Heaven help me, Rick; if you approach Cora Diamond, then it's all over. This place will be finished. The reputational damage alone... it doesn't bear thinking about.'

He stared at a stain on the carpet, his thoughts tumbling over themselves.

'Please go, Rick. Think of it as a vacation. Heaven knows you're due one. Get some sleep. And, for God's sake, eat something. We need you to look after yourself. Then, come back in a fit state to help us look after everyone else.' Her gaze softened. 'Michaela agrees.'

If Michaela – the senior partner – agreed, then there was no avoiding this. *I can't remember the last time I took a holiday.* 'Fine. I'll go. Two weeks. Then I'll be back.'

'Great.' Gita dug the key out of her pocket. 'Right. Stay in here, while I deal with the circus outside and, when the coast is clear, I'll come and let you out. You can disappear off somewhere quiet and keep your head down until the dust has settled.'

She was gone before Rick could move. The click of the key turning in the lock made his stomach lurch. His inside breast pocket pinged again and then buzzed. Pulling out his phone, he scanned the news headline.

```
Cora Diamond launches legal action against
 Dr Rick Mahon for malpractice, while son,
YouTube gaming star Dean Markwell, clings
       to life after medication mistake.
```

Ping, ping, ping. X was going berserk. #DrDeath, #DeanMarkwell, #malpractice – all accompanied by a photo of Rick, lifted from the Five Oaks Surgery website.

Bloody hell.

His stomach heaved again. The walls closed in. There was no air. *Got to get out. Now.* He stumbled to the window and plonked his backside on the sill. The drop didn't look that bad. Swinging both legs out, he wobbled briefly, feet braced against the wall, hands clutching the window frame. Without giving himself a second to think, his bum left the sill and he launched himself out into thin air.

Chapter 3

New Forest

The unwanted counselling session over, Beth struggled to escape Southampton. Two supersized cruise liners had arrived at the docks at the same time, generating a huge increase in traffic. Taxis and coaches queued everywhere and, combined with roadworks, caused a massive transport snarl-up in all directions. It took over an hour to break free of the city. She let out a huge sigh of relief as she darted onto a remote back road through the forest. *Home soon.*

Around a particularly sharp bend, a pheasant dashed across the road. Beth swerved to miss it, clipping a pothole. An ominous whomp, whomp, whomp of rubber against metal filled the air. Cursing under her breath, she pulled onto the verge.

It's fine. I can change a tyre.

The wheel nuts disagreed. An exasperating ten minutes passed, until she growled in frustration and dropped the wrench to the ground with a loud clang. A harsh clatter of wings erupted overhead as startled crows launched from the uppermost branches of the trees lining the road. As their angry cawing died away, a lone squirrel rippled over a fallen log and darted out of sight, leaving the forest eerily silent. The normal bustle of small animals in the undergrowth was absent. Even the smell of the forest, of wet earth, moss and bark was not as comforting as usual. Beth stared around, an icy shiver scuttling down her spine.

The deep voice came out of nowhere. 'Hello.'

Whirling around, dropping into an instinctive fight-ready stance, her weight balanced, she raised her fists. A large man stood a few metres away. Beth's heart performed an impressive drum solo finale that almost crashed through her ribs.

Where the hell did he come from?

He was tall and slim, too slim really, with very broad shoulders. He gave every appearance of being innocuous, even though the trouser leg of his three-piece suit was torn at the knee. He smiled. 'Can I help?'

Swamped with panicked adrenaline, Beth's immediate thought was, *It's Hugh Jackman.*

He wasn't Hugh Jackman. His thick head of hair wasn't black, for starters. *Mind you, neither is Hugh's these days.* More of a polished chestnut, silvered at the temples. Even so, he definitely had the look of a mature, if slightly battered, Wolverine. A faint scar ran across the bridge of his nose and through one eyebrow. None of his features individually fit the classically good-looking mould, yet, somehow, they worked.

He waited for her to finish examining him, then lifted both hands palm out in the universal sign of surrender. 'I'm not an axe murderer. Honest.'

'That's what all axe murderers say.'

A smile ghosted across his face. 'I wouldn't know about that. Not being an axe murderer.'

An air of sadness lurked in his eyes. She resisted the urge to offer him a comforting cup of tea. Mainly because she didn't have one, but also because you couldn't be too careful with strangers on secluded forest back roads. *Don't be ridiculous. He isn't dangerous.* Her hormones, like overzealous regency mamas, had already booked the church, invited too many guests and eaten cake. They had only ever reacted this way once before, but Beth and her hormones didn't speak about Paul anymore.

'It's in the guidebook. Axe Murdering for Beginners. Page 1,' she muttered.

'I'll be sure to read it.' He nodded towards her car. 'In the meantime, do you need a hand?'

She relaxed her stance a fraction, her teeth chattering as the February wind blew through her. 'I know how to change a tyre. I just can't undo the nuts.'

'They've probably been put on with one of those power sprocket thingies at the garage.'

Beth raised an eyebrow. 'Power sprocket thingies?'

'It's a technical term.' That ghost of a smile returned.

Beth wanted him to keep smiling; it did nice things to his eyes. *What is wrong with me?* She gave herself a shake. 'I can manage.'

'Sure. Perhaps you can help me, then. I took a back road at Lyndhurst to avoid the traffic and now my satnav is on the blink.' He gestured further down the road. 'My car is way back that way. I started walking, hoping to pick up a signal on my phone. No luck so far. Can we do a trade? How about I change that tyre – assuming I can without a sprocket thingy – and you tell me how to get to Brockenhurst?'

'Your satnav is probably fine. The New Forest has mini Bermuda Triangles all over the place. No phone signal, no 5G, nothing.'

'I didn't think such a thing was possible in this day and age.'

'Most of the towns and villages are fine, but the more remote sections might as well not exist. It's all part of the façade of idyllic, rural charm that brings the tourists in.'

'Façade?'

She shrugged. 'You know. The general perception that everyone here is rolling in money and life is perfect. It's not true. Anyway,' Beth blew on her hands to warm them, 'if you want to trade changing a tyre for directions that suits me.'

He approached the car, his gait uneven. The leg with the torn trouser was giving him trouble. He shrugged out of his jacket and held it out. 'Here, put this on. You're shivering.'

'I don't—'

'Please. It's making me feel cold just looking at you.'

She stared at the soft blue fabric.

He twitched the jacket towards her. 'I get that you are super independent, but my life is currently falling apart. Believe it or not, helping you will help me.'

Beth rolled her eyes and took the jacket. Spicy cologne teased her nose. Slipping her arms into the sleeves felt like being wrapped in a warm hug. From a cautious distance, she watched the Wolverine twist the first wheel nut free, his shirt stretching tight across his shoulders, and racked her brain for something to say. 'Does your life falling apart have something to do with the hole in your trousers?'

The laugh he gave was short and bitter. 'Yes and no. An unplanned encounter with sharp shrubbery.'

'And what's in Brockenhurst?'

'Nothing. I'm not stopping. I just know the rest of my way from there. Geographically speaking, I mean. As for the rest of my life, that's anyone's guess.' He pulled the wheel from the hub and looked up. 'I have no idea why I told you that. Total overshare. Sorry.'

She shook her head. 'Forget it. If anyone understands life falling apart, it's me.'

'Really?'

'Yup. My husband left me. My step-teens hate me. They live with me full-time, by the way, and don't yet know their dad has no intention of ever coming back. My daughter and the dog are not far behind them. And don't get me started on the donkey.' *That was astonishingly easy to say out loud. Counselling, huh, who knew?*

He gave a low whistle.

'Exactly. Jane, my counsellor, seems to think that all I need is some herbal tea and a bit of meditation.'

'Herbal tea and meditation can accomplish a lot, but maybe not that much.' He wiggled the tyre at her. 'I'm assuming you have a spare somewhere.'

Beth opened the boot and hauled out the spare.

He eased the damaged tyre into the space left behind. 'If you're lucky, that might be repairable.' He took the spare, his hands brushing hers. Static electricity sparked. Beth's skin tingled. Her eyes jumped to his. Unable to break with his gaze, her pulse raced. All he had to do was lean in and…

'Did she suggest anything else?'

Beth stepped back. 'Who?'

'Jane.'

She leaned against the car. 'That I should get out more and stop overthinking things.'

'Sounds like good advice.'

'Ha! Maybe. She also said I need to stop being defensive and let people help me.'

His eyes danced. 'She might be onto something there. And you're already taking her advice.'

'Complete strangers don't count. She meant I should make friends with people in my village.'

He tightened the last wheel nut and stood up. 'How come you don't have friends? You seem… nice.'

'I have friends. They're just not local. I moved here because of my husband. He was born here. I'm his second wife. It's complicated.'

'Ah.' He leaned on the car next to her. 'Maybe Jane has a point. Single parenting is tough enough with support. Is your step-teens' biological mother on the scene?'

'She's dead. If she wasn't, I wouldn't be in this mess, because she'd still be married to Paul and… oh.' Beth's lower lip wobbled. 'Sorry. That makes it sound like it's her fault and I didn't mean that. It isn't, of course it isn't. I… I just…' She willed away the tears prickling behind her eyes. 'I'm the only parent those poor kids have and I'll be damned if I let them down.' Her voice dropped to a whisper. 'It's hard.'

'My dad always said that when stuff is hard, it helps to focus on the small stuff. You know? Just keep doing what you can and eventually things sort themselves out.'

Silence fell.

Beth sighed. 'Now I've overshared.'

'Nah. Don't worry about it. Your problems have put some of my crap into perspective. And it's not as if we know each other. We'll never meet again after this.'

'True.' The idea of not seeing him again brought with it a tsunami of sadness.

'Now.' He stood up, brisk and business-like. 'Brockenhurst.'

Beth's hormones got down on their knees and begged her not to let him go. 'Yes. Brockenhurst. It's down this road, second on the left and straight on until you hit the green. You can't miss it. Watch out for the ponies. They're gorgeous, but a total menace. The deer, too. Other than that, you should be fine.' She shrugged out of the jacket, already missing its warmth, and held it out. 'Thank you and good luck.'

Chapter 4

Beth spent the afternoon indulging in a series of what-if scenarios featuring the stranger from the road. All of which led to a happily ever after in one form or another. It was a brilliant distraction from the alarming fact that she was standing on the roof of her house.

'I do wish you hadn't followed me up here, Mrs Hope,' said Owen, the roofing contractor. 'It's not safe.'

The look of horror on his face would have been comical if the circumstances hadn't been so serious. George Botley in the village hardware shop had recommended him as cheap and reliable, but Beth had not expected him to be quite so elderly. *If one of us is a liability up a ladder, it isn't me.*

She shuffled away from the edge. 'I need to see how all that rain is getting into my kitchen without coming through upstairs first. It makes no sense.'

Owen pointed a shaky finger. 'There. That's how. Rain goes in through there, drops down the wall cavity between the old bit of the house and the new, until it hits the lintel above the kitchen door. It pools there and soaks through the plaster. Simple.'

Beth stared at where the thatched roof of the original eighteenth-century farmhouse met the slate section over the extension at the back. A wide strip of lead covered the deep gully between the two pitches. It was in a shocking state. 'That's pretty bad, isn't it?'

He pulled a face. 'I've seen worse.'

'Really?'

'Well… no. Not really. Not on a house someone's still living in.' There was a pregnant pause. 'You do realise that's a supporting wall down there, don't you?'

'Meaning?'

'Meaning you need to dry it out. And quick. The only way to do that is to fix this roof, otherwise…'

Beth didn't want to hear what the otherwise option was. 'How much to fix it?'

He sucked his teeth. 'Don't reckon you'll get much change from ten grand, depending on what else crops up. Never can tell for sure with these old buildings.'

'Ten thousand?'

'I can do you a temporary patch for a couple of hundred. A bit of felt and some strong sealant. It might hold for a few months, if you're lucky.'

'I'm never lucky,' muttered Beth, unable to tear her eyes away from the cracks in her home as she mentally rummaged through her finances. Since Paul had left, with Grace being so young, she'd been unable to work and look after the family at the same time, other than picking up the odd freelance online admin job. To make ends meet, she'd been selling off small parcels of the Merrill shares she'd inherited from her grandfather. Gramps had been so fond of that big old department store, but he'd never have dreamed what a lifeline his investment would be for her. The only problem was the shares weren't going to last forever and she was running out of money. But Grace was at preschool now. *I could look for a proper job locally to make up the shortfall.*

'Ten thousand max, you say?'

He shrugged. 'If we get onto it soon, yes. But if you wait… well…'

She turned and headed back down the ladder. 'I'll see what I can sort out and get back to you.'

*

That evening, after school pick-up, half of Beth's mind wondered if her Wolverine had made it to Brockenhurst. The other half locked the car door, grabbed Grace's little hand in hers and hurried after Jack and Daisy as they stomped across the gravel towards the house.

'Don't walk away from me, Jack,' she said. 'I've just gone three rounds with the head to stop her expelling you. What were you thinking?'

Jack pulled his hoodie up over short, spiky blond hair, stuffed his hands in his pockets and stared at the ground in sullen silence. Beth unlocked the front door and stood back to allow the children to go ahead. Her gaze fell on the bare wisteria branches clinging to the red-brick exterior wall. During the summer months, a pretty waterfall of purple and white flowers hid the poor state of the pointing.

'Why punch Aled? I thought he was your friend.'

Excited barking announced the arrival of Paddy, racing from his bed in the kitchen faster than should have been possible on arthritic canine hips. The terrier skipped around Jack's feet as if the boy had been gone for a month.

'You must have had a reason. Did he say something?'

Jack made a fuss of the dog. 'Drop it, will you?'

'No. Tell me.'

'Alright.' Jack shoved his hood back and rounded on her. 'He called Dad a loser. I said he wasn't. Then he said the forest was a big place to hide a body and that maybe Dad isn't coming back because he can't.'

Beth went cold. 'What do you mean?'

'Don't be thick. He's saying you've done him in. So, I thumped him. Happy now?'

'You defended me?'

'In your dreams. I was defending Dad.'

'Of course,' Beth whispered.

'Whatever.' Jack kicked his shoes off, dumped his school bag on the floor and clomped through to the kitchen.

Beth picked the post up from the mat. A seed catalogue, bills, a bank statement and a postcard, the back covered in familiar, spiky, capital-lettered, black ink. *Oh great!* She'd forgotten about that.

'Is that from Dad?' Daisy reached over and snatched the postcard from Beth's hand and waved it at Grace in triumph. The two girls scampered ahead of Beth into the kitchen, narrowly avoiding tipping over the bucket of water beneath the leak from the night before. 'Maybe this'll tell us when he's coming home, Grace. It's been ages since the last one came.' Pulling out one of the mismatched collection of chairs that huddled around the central table, Daisy sat and lifted Grace onto her lap. 'Let's see what he says.'

Beth yawned, pushed the kettle onto the Aga hotplate,

grabbed a mug from the cupboard and dug right to the back of the shelf to find a battered box of decaf teabags.

Rose appeared in the doorway, hair straighteners in her hand, long dark ringlets swinging around her shoulders. 'Ethan called. He can't give me a lift to work tonight, so I need the car, yeah?' Without waiting for Beth to reply, she left the room.

Daisy gave an outraged yelp. 'Dad's had his contract extended again.' She cast an accusatory glance at Beth. 'Did you know about this?'

'How could I?'

Daisy scowled. 'He'd have been home months ago if certain people weren't so difficult to live with.'

'Or maybe,' muttered Jack, 'he heard about the mega tantrum you threw when you found out he'd gone. Anyone with a brain can see why he wouldn't want to come back.'

Daisy's mouth dropped open for a second before snapping closed. 'Shut up, Jack.' She sniffed and returned her attention to the card. 'Listen, Grace, this bit is for you. He says he hopes you're enjoying preschool.' Daisy hugged her sister. 'You are, aren't you?'

Grace grinned from ear to ear.

'And he wants you to make sure Paddy's behaving.'

Grace giggled.

Beth shuddered at the memory of how distressed Daisy had been when she'd realised Paul was gone. The fridge door slamming behind her brought her back to attention just in time to see that Jack had liberated a plate of cold roast chicken.

'Not that.' Beth pulled the plate from his hand. 'That's for supper.'

Jack scowled. 'But I'm hungry.'

'You're always hungry. Here, have this.' Returning the chicken to the fridge, she passed him a bowl of leftover pasta. 'Grate cheese over the top and micro... oh, okay, you can eat it cold, too. That works.' Beth frowned, watching Jack shovel huge mouthfuls into his face, barely chewing before swallowing and then ramming in the next forkful. 'You did eat the packed lunch I made you, didn't you?'

'Yup.' He set the empty bowl aside and started rummaging in cupboards. 'Ate Benji's, too.'

'Did he say you could?'

'Yup.'

Beth nudged him away from the shelf of cereal boxes. 'Leave those. You'll want them for breakfast. Look, sit down and let me make you a sandwich.'

'Nah. Bread's fine.' He grabbed a slice of bread from the breadbin, folded it into four and posted it into his mouth in one go. Then, he pulled out four more slices.

Beth produced a plate.

Jack ignored it.

'Did you want to see Dad's card, Jack?' asked Daisy.

'Meh.' Jack swallowed and shook his head. 'If you ask me, there's something hinky about those. How come he doesn't ever call us?'

Beth held her breath.

'Don't be horrid, Jack,' replied Daisy. 'Where he is... it's like... I dunno... it's, like, well remote.'

'It's well remote here,' muttered Jack.

'No way. It's way worse there than the New Forest. And there's the time difference, too.'

He raised a sardonic eyebrow. 'Is there?'

'Yes. Abroad is always a different time. What he is doing is like Doctors Without Borders but for lawyers. He's a hero.' Daisy looked at Beth demanding confirmation. 'Tell him, Beth.'

Beth hesitated. Jack pinned her with a steady stare.

'Dad's a hero, isn't he?' Daisy's lips pressed into a grim line.

'Your dad is very special. Now, come on. I need to make supper. And Jack needs to leave me enough food to do it with.' She waved both hands. 'Shoo, all of you. Go do homework or something.'

Jack pulled headphones from his pocket, grabbed an apple from the fruit bowl and left, Paddy trotting at his heels.

Daisy rolled her eyes. 'Boys! Come on, Grace, let's go watch telly.'

'Yeah. Boys. Boys are yucky.' Grace tucked a cuddly unicorn under her arm and followed her big sister from the room. 'Not Daddy, though. Daddy's not yucky.'

Beth chopped onions, mushrooms and a pepper and added them to a wok on the Aga.

Rose came back, coat and handbag over one arm, and rummaged around on the Welsh dresser. 'I'm off,' she said, pouncing on the car keys. 'Justin's got me in the main bar tonight. Quiz night at the Crashing Boar – lucky, lucky me. It's all go in Ambleford.' She turned to breeze serenely from the room, but tripped over the bucket lurking in the doorway instead. Water slopped everywhere. 'Oh, for fu—'

Beth snatched a bath towel from the dirty laundry basket dumped by the door and chucked it over the spreading puddle. 'I'll do it. Go to work. You'll be late.'

The front door slammed. The sizzle and smell of sautéing vegetables filled the room as Beth mopped spilt water. Her mind drifted to her Wolverine and, somehow, she felt less alone. Even though she was never going to see him again. Which was a good thing, because that way he could stay perfect. She'd never have to learn that – like all men – he had feet of clay. She examined the damp patch of plaster over the doorway. Dark and menacing, it loomed like a vulture waiting for its next meal to hurry up and die. She hugged the thought of her Wolverine close. What was it he'd said?

Just keep doing what you can and eventually things sort themselves out.

Dashing away an exhausted tear, she grabbed her laptop. She could arrange to sell that last bundle of shares. And first thing tomorrow, she'd look for a job.

Chapter 5

The barn

Rather than focus on the interior of Charlie's barn conversion, Rick's thoughts were full of the red-haired woman with the flat tyre. It was a long time since he'd met anyone he could really connect with. He'd been tempted to ask for her name and number, but then thought better of it. *The last thing she needs is me complicating her life any further. I can't risk adding my problems to hers.* It was better that they not see each other again.

Shaking free of his thoughts, he examined his surroundings. In terms of location, tucked away at the end of a pothole-strewn gravel track in a remote part of the forest with only one other property in sight, the barn was perfect. There was small kitchenette and a main living area. A central open staircase rose up to a mezzanine level. Pools of sunshine poured through skylights onto the cluttered remains of a stranger's life. Eighty-one years' worth of Uncle Charlie's memories lurking in forlorn clusters. Charlie wasn't really his uncle. He was dad's best friend, someone who sent occasional Christmas and birthday cards. Rick had never expected to inherit his home recently and hadn't had time to come and see it until now.

Rick and the deceased Charlie had vastly differing tastes. Rick preferred sleek, modern minimalism. In contrast, Charlie had collected a cluttered mash-up of random possessions from multiple decades. The most up-to-date item in his home was a large cast-iron log burner in the centre of the living space. A metal flue rose up to exit through the vaulted ceiling. A tatty sofa and a scratched leather armchair with a matching footstool loitered before a boxy pre-millennium television set. *Could such an antique pick up a digital signal?*

He took a step towards it. The muscles in his left leg screamed. Cursing, he massaged his knee and thigh, his fingers catching on the rip in his trousers. That raised flower bed hadn't broken his fall quite enough. *Winter roses are vicious little buggers.* He still couldn't believe it. Firstly, that he'd jumped at all, and secondly, what had happened before he jumped. Before Gita locked him in his consulting room. Two people he had assumed were patients had stalked into the consulting room as if they owned it. He replayed the scene in his head for the millionth time, trying to see how he could have handled the whole situation better.

*

The woman perched on the chair next to his desk and flicked long dark hair over her shoulder. Her pointy teeth reminded Rick of the velociraptor in Jurassic Park and her red-lipsticked smile didn't reach her eyes.

'Hashtag Dr Death,' she said.

'I… I… uh. What?' Was that supposed to mean something? Rick's eyes darted from the woman to the skinny youth who'd trailed in behind her. Sporting an oversized black leather jacket, jeans and biker boots, the young man resembled a twelve-year-old playing dress-up. He pulled a phone from one of many zipped pockets. Pointing it at Rick, he said, 'Right, Sal. It's recording.'

'Wait. Stop.' Rick's hand shot out to shield his face from the camera lens. He hated having his picture taken. He always had, even before the scars. 'You can't film a consultation.'

Sal ignored him, her focus on the camera. 'Cheers, Abe. Hi guys. Sal and Abe are back with our latest Dean Markwell, aka the D-Man, update – and guess what? We're here with Dr Death himself.'

'This'll go viral,' Abe muttered.

'So, Dr Death,' Sal turned towards Rick, her tone hardening, 'tell all our lovely followers how it feels to kill the hopes and dreams of an entire generation.'

The skin on the back of Rick's neck prickled.

'You must have something to say,' Sal insisted.

He tugged at his collar and scanned the dark mahogany surface of his desk as if expecting to find an answer. Neither the computer, blood-pressure cuff, stethoscope, nor his rapidly cooling cup of coffee had anything useful to contribute. 'Uh… no comment.'

'What about the D-Man's fans?' demanded Abe.

Bile rose in Rick's throat. 'I said, no comment. Please leave. I have patients waiting.'

'You haven't, mate,' scoffed Abe. 'For sure, your waiting room's full. It's bursting at the seams. But not with patients.

They're all paps and commentators like us. Only we got here first. This is our scoop.'

'So, go on,' insisted Sal. 'Tell us what happened to the D-Man.'

The door crashed back on its hinges. Sam, a balding, middle-aged man of West-Indian heritage with a penchant for obsessive filing and dreams of being the security chief for Beyoncé, burst into the room. 'Sorry, Rick.' He growled. 'My bad. No idea how these scrotes got past me. Oi! You two!'

Rick watched in bemusement as the normally mild-mannered receptionist morphed into a short, but no less intimidating, version of Dwayne "The Rock" Johnson and made short work of hustling the intruders out.

*

The sound of a news alert on his phone echoed around the barn and brought Rick back to the present with a start. The stealthy fingers of an early-stage migraine tiptoed across his forehead. He popped two tablets from a blister pack in his jacket pocket and swallowed them dry. *Better get organised, before the pain really kicks in.* Limping out to the car, he retrieved a sports bag from the boot and his laptop from the back seat. Something soft landed on his foot. He looked down into the single remaining button eye of David's bear. His son had left it as a joke, when Rick had given him a lift to the airport. 'Boo's going to keep an eye on you, Dad,' he had said. 'to make sure you don't work too hard.'

Rick scooped the toy off the ground. 'Come on, Boo. Let's go inside.'

There was no power, but, given that the place had stood empty for six months, it wasn't surprising. Rick shivered and pulled a thick fleece from his sports kit, cursing the journalists outside his apartment who had stopped him getting home to pack properly. As he dragged it over his head, his eyes lit on a framed photograph on the wall. A younger version of himself stared back, dressed in his medical school graduation gown. Mum and Dad stood on either side, beaming with pride. One of the few times they'd been civil to each other since the divorce. Sadness stirred in his stomach. It was strange seeing them all so happy, none of them realising that Dad would be dead a month later.

A sudden urge to ring David slammed through him. They'd not spoken for a while. A twenty-two-year-old man working his dream job as a sous chef in an award-winning restaurant abroad didn't ring their dad very often. He checked the time on his mobile. No. Not a good time. He'd be prepping for evening service.

Seeing an alert from his voicemail, he slumped down onto the saggy sofa and listened to the automated voice.

'You have thirty-three messages.'

Bloody hell.

Ten twenty-three: 'Rick? It's Gita. Look, I'm sorry if I sounded harsh before, but it's for your own good. It's better this way. Call me when you're settled.'

Ten forty: Sam's gravelly south London tones grated down the line. 'Rick. Gita says you're on holiday for a bit. Best thing if you ask me, mate. Give us a bell if you need anything, right.'

Ten forty-five: 'Hi, Rick, Michaela here. Gita has let me know the situation and, as the senior partner, I have to agree that this is the best way to deal with the current situation. I think it's important to—'

Rick tuned out. They had written him off. Life without him would be easier. That much was clear. He dashed a hand across his eyes. If making him the scapegoat saved the surgery, he could cope with that. But what about Dean? While everyone was focused on blaming Rick, what was being done to help Dean?

Michaela's message ended and the voicemail beeped with the start of another one.

Beep. Eleven fifty-nine: 'Hello, is this Dr Rick Mahon's number? Oli Short from the Daily Metro here. I'd like to ask some questions about the recent article in The National Dispatch? How about giving us your side of the story? Call me back on this number.'

Beep. Twelve-oh-five: 'Dr Mahon, Ali Neera from Star Magazine. Cora Diamond says she's suing you. What's your response? Our readers would like to know. Call me.'

Beep. Twelve ten: 'Tam Parham from Newslite, call me.'

Beep. Beep. Beep.

Rick stopped listening. A buzzing sound filled his ears. Someone started swinging a heavy anvil around inside his head, crashing it against the inside of his skull. He crumpled in on himself. This was so much worse than he'd thought. For the first time in his life, he felt hunted.

How did they get my number?

Can they track me?

Might they turn up here?

He ripped the back from the phone and yanked out the battery and sim card. He only just managed to stop himself from throwing it on the floor and stamping on it, like some desperate movie character on the run from a sinister organisation.

Dropping the pieces of phone on the coffee table, he lay back, dragging the dusty throw from the end of the sofa up over his shoulders. Hunching down, he closed his eyes. Images of Dean, Cora Diamond, a pack of baying paparazzi and poor old Mrs Clutterbuck with her dodgy hip swirled and danced inside his head.

He was right. The beautiful red-haired woman with the sparkling green eyes was better off without him. Everyone was. A single hot tear leaked from the corner of his eye and trickled into the hair at his temple. He cursed himself for giving in to self-pity, as the migraine that had been lurking ramped up and swallowed him whole.

Chapter 6

The farmhouse

'There's a shedload of cows outside!' Jack's bizarre statement filtered into Beth's unconscious mind. As a wake-up call – an alternative to the usual light birdsong interspersed with strident cockcrows, sharp barks from random dogs and distant drumming of hooves from passing herds of deer – it was very effective. She struggled to open her eyes. Having lain awake most of the night worrying, she'd finally fallen into a bizarre dream in which George Clooney sat on a sun lounger in the back garden. He was being served a cup of coffee by a waitress, who, weirdly enough, was a cow – an actual cow, not a person with a bad attitude. Meanwhile, Hugh Jackman pulled himself from an azure-blue swimming pool and patted his tanned, muscular torso dry with a towel.

'Hey – Beth – did you hear me? There's, like, a million cows outside.'

She peeled one eye open. Jack's head, plus his bony shoulders clad in a frayed sweatshirt, poked through the half-open bedroom door. He was looking right at her, which was odd. He never usually looked at her, just vaguely off to one side.

'The herds were sold off years ago, Jack. Fields, too. There are no cows.'

'You reckon? Go see.' His mobile phone was glued to his right hand as usual, but she saw he'd removed an earbud from one ear. 'Cows,' he repeated, then re-inserted the earbud and left, as if – having informed her of the problem – he was now absolved of any responsibility.

Beth rubbed gritty eyes and listened. The audible signature of a sizeable herd somewhere nearby went a long way towards explaining certain elements of her dream. Sighing, she sat up, swung her legs out of bed and pulled a pair of jogging bottoms from a pile of other abandoned clothes. Hastily shoving her legs into them, she hooked a hoodie off the same heap and stumbled from the room and down the stairs, one hand on the rickety banister rail, one on the wall to steady herself. The sound of mooing was much louder from downstairs. The grey flagstones chilled her toes through the threadbare rug in the entrance hall as she hauled the heavy front door open.

Shit. Cows. At least thirty... no, forty... probably more. They must have taken a wrong turn on the main road and poured down the lane to come to a dead end when they'd reached the farmhouse and barn. There was nowhere else for them to go and, more importantly, no one with them. Since moving to the country from the city, Beth felt she had adjusted to rural life really well, but this situation pushed her way out of her comfort zone. *What the heck do I do?*

'You were wrong, Wolverine,' she muttered. 'Things aren't getting better.'

The animals stopped milling about. Countless massive black-and-white heads swung towards her. Ducking back inside with undignified haste, she slammed the door and leaned against it. Cursing, she looked up to see Jack clomp down the stairs, swing around the newel post and carry on towards the kitchen, as if oblivious of the herd of heifers outside.

'Oh no you don't, buster.' Beth dashed after him and pulled the white cable that snaked from his ear to dislodge the earbud. 'C'mon, Jack. Help me. What do we do?'

'We? This ain't my beef. You're in charge.'

When it came to cows, Beth discovered she wasn't averse to begging. 'Please, Jack. You know you're good with animals.'

Jack retrieved his earphone and re-inserted it. 'Have fun.'

The smirk that accompanied his words was a mistake. Something snapped inside Beth. She snatched his phone, pulled the headphones from the socket and shoved the handset deep into the central pocket of her hoodie.

'Hey!' Jack's eyes darted in horror from her pocket to her face. 'Give that back.'

'After you help.'

'No way.'

'You owe me.' Beth's nostrils flared.

'How come?'

'Suspension. Yesterday. Remember?'

'Oh man! You're, like, so extra.'

'Maybe so, but you need those cows gone as much as I do. Think about it. I can't get the car out. Do you want to walk the three miles to the village? Better leave now if you do or you'll miss your bus. If you help with the cows, I'll give you a lift and there'll be time for breakfast.'

Appealing to innate laziness and a growing teenage stomach was a dynamite combination. Confident she'd won her point, Beth hurried back up the stairs, calling over her shoulder, 'Get dressed and be quick. We haven't got all day.' Not stopping to see if he complied, she hammered on Daisy's bedroom door before walking in. 'Daisy.'

A low growl emanated from the bed.

'Daisy.'

The covers moved a fraction.

'Daisy. Wake up.'

The top section of duvet was thrown back and a rumpled blonde head emerged, along with a venomous hiss. 'What?'

Early mornings and step-parent issues were familiar dangers, so Beth kept things brief. 'There's a herd of cows on the drive. They need rehoming.'

'Don't look at me. I don't do animals. Not this early in the morning.'

'Can you babysit Grace?'

'Your kid, remember, not mine. You look after her.' Daisy pulled the duvet back over her head with a huff.

'For God's sake, Daisy, I—' Beth took a steadying breath. Demanding that Daisy get her bony backside out of bed wasn't going to work. She crossed to the window and yanked back the curtains. The surging mass of cattle outside in the half-light made her stomach heave. Averting her eyes, she forced a calmer tone to her voice. 'Please, Daisy, either look after your baby sister or help your brother move the cows. I can't do both.'

'Baby half-sister,' came Daisy's muffled correction.

'I'm not a baby!' Grace's outraged howl from the doorway made Beth jump.

'Sweetheart, I thought you were asleep.'

Grace's gaze bounced from Beth to Daisy and back, keen eyes sizing up the stalemate. Then the youngster hoppity-skipped over to the bed and lifted up a corner of the duvet. ''lo Daisy. Come play wiv me. Pleeeaase.'

Beth held her breath.

The mound under the bedsheets harrumphed loudly. ''K, kid. Gimme five and I'll be down.'

'Thanks, sweetie,' said Beth. She left the room, Grace hard on her heels.

Daisy erupted from the bed. 'Don't… you… ever… call… me… *sweetie!*'

'I was talking to Grace.' Beth ducked, pulling the door closed on the seething cloud of teenage emotion. Something heavy hit the wood with a bone-shaking thud. Beth gave Grace a wink. 'Well done, baby.'

'Not a baby, Mummy. Amember?'

Beth bent to hug her. 'No, you're not, are you, my love? Sometimes, you're wiser than all of us. Now, pop your dressing gown on, it's cold. Mummy's got to go and sort the cows.' Grateful that at least someone in the house still did as they were told without arguing, Beth jogged down the stairs to dig out her boots.

'I love cows,' declared Grace, arriving at her side a moment later, wearing a fluffy dressing gown and unicorn slippers. 'Can I come?'

'They're too big, Grace,' came Jack's deep voice. Dressed for the outdoors, he clattered unsteadily down the stairs, reminding Beth of a baby giraffe trying to stand for the first time. He'd grown so quickly in recent months it was as if his brain was still undecided about taking complete responsibility for his extra-long, scrawny legs.

'It's dangerous, Grace. Stay inside with me. Yeah?' said Daisy, stomping down behind him and peering out of the window. 'What do you reckon, Jack? Nick's herd from Hilltop Farm take a wrong turn on the way to milking, maybe?'

'Maybe,' said Jack. 'I bet he's got Ned out looking for them already.'

'Can we ring him?' asked Beth, handing him back his phone. 'Tell him they're here?'

Jack glanced at the screen and shook his head. 'No signal.'

Daisy checked hers. 'Me neither.'

'Blast.' Beth sighed. *If only I'd kept the landline.* 'What do we do?'

'Oh, for goodness' sake,' said Daisy. 'It's easy enough. Just get them moving back up the lane.' She opened the door and gestured outside. 'Go over to the mounting block by the stable doors and get up nice and high.'

Beth looked at the milling cattle in horror. 'Is that safe?'

Jack examined the herd. 'Looks like this lot are mainly young ones. Bullocks and that. They can be a bit jumpy, so no sudden movements, yeah?'

There was a wicked gleam in Daisy's eye. 'Don't be a wuss, Beth. Use your common sense and go slow.'

Beth couldn't believe she was actually considering this. 'So, I get up high. Then what?'

'Make a noise that annoys them enough to make them shy away.'

'What sort of noise?'

'Well, nothing too loud or too sudden, obvs... you don't want them to panic.' Daisy looked around her. 'Uh, Grace, go get a big plastic bowl from the kitchen and a wooden spoon, will you?'

Grace dashed off, returning seconds later.

Daisy passed them to Beth. 'Bash these together. Quiet to start, then get louder. They'll move away from the noise and once one of them turns, the rest will follow.'

'Where?'

'There's only one way to go, Beth.' Daisy shook her head, making Beth feel stupid. 'Jack can run out the back way, across the field to the main road. If he can get there ahead of them, he can make sure they head up to Hilltop Farm.'

'And if he doesn't?'

Daisy tutted. 'Look, just don't make them stampede. It'll be fine.'

Beth felt faint. *Stampede? Shit.*

'Or are you too chicken?' Daisy crossed her arms, the light of challenge glittering in her eyes. Beth swallowed and shook her head.

'I'll come with you, Mummy,' said Grace.

'No way,' said Daisy, grabbing her little hand.

'Sorry, kid,' said Jack. 'Not happening.'

'Watch from the window, darling,' said Beth. 'Keep Paddy safe indoors.'

As if mentioning his name conjured him up, Paddy arrived, throwing Beth a malevolent stare.

Grace scrambled onto the sofa by the window so she could see outside and Paddy followed. She took a firm grip of his collar. 'I'll keep you safe, Paddy. Look at all the cows.' She bounced on the cushions with excitement. Beth took a step closer to stop Grace accidentally choking the poor little dog to death, but Daisy beat her to it.

'Guess what's more interesting than cows, Grace?' Daisy asked.

Grace stopped bouncing. 'Err… unicorns?'

'Yes, obviously unicorns. But what else?'

'Oh, umm…'

'Pancakes, silly.'

'Yay!' Grace dropped the collar to clap her hands. 'I love pancakes! Can I help?'

'Sure can.' Daisy coaxed her sister off the sofa and towards the kitchen. 'And afterwards, we'll get dressed for school, okay?' Grace charged off down the hall and Paddy scampered along behind. Beth rolled her eyes. The dog might be old and grumpy, but he wasn't daft. Daisy was a casual cook at the best of times and food always found its way to the floor.

Beth stamped her heels into red wellington boots, grabbed a battered blue Barbour jacket and shoved her arms into the sleeves, before cramming the bobble hat she found in the pocket on her head. The bright red wool clashed with her hair but would stop her ears freezing off.

'Ready?' she asked Jack and reached for the door.

Chapter 7

Awake early the next morning, the red-haired woman still on his mind, Rick reached for another dose of medication. With luck, the worst of the migraine was over. His stomach rumbled as he limped into the small bathroom. He averted his gaze from the hideous brown sink and bath. A dishevelled pirate stared back at him from the mirror.

Sounds of a disturbance outside filtered into the room. A wave of stomach acid burned his belly and the awful memory of feeling hunted the day before resurfaced. If there were paparazzi outside, he was trapped. He staggered down the stairs, crept over to the front window, staying as low to the ground as possible, and peered through a narrow gap in the curtains.

What the...?

That was a heck of a lot of cows. The clumsy great beasts were shoving each other around, spilling across from next door's driveway as they mooed and stamped at the ground. A gnome in a long blue coat, red hat and wellies was skipping about on a raised block and bashing some sort of drum. What the hell were they up to? Some bizarre rustic milking rite?

Rick rubbed the back of his neck and groaned. *Why can't the world just leave me alone?* Leaning his forehead on the glass, he watched cows jostle his car. The tenuous grip on his legendary self-control snapped. He erupted from the barn with all the sophistication of a grizzly bear dragged from hibernation far too early. Waving his arms at the gnome doing the weird dance, he yelled, 'Get your bloody cows off my property.'

A gust of wind caught the door behind him, slamming it shut with a sharp bang. One fraction of a second later, the alarm on his Land Rover Discovery registered rough handling from the cows with an ear-piercing shriek.

Damn it.

Rick scrabbled in his pocket for the keys to shut it off and watched in horror as the frightened cows barged each other aside, desperate to escape the noise.

The entire herd turned as one and cantered up the lane out of sight.

Silence descended.

*

Perplexed at the sudden appearance of a stranger from the empty property next door, and shocked at the distress of the retreating animals, Beth felt a volcanic rage bubble inside her. She jumped down from the mounting block and stormed across the potholed gravel. Each fury-filled step hit the ground with such force that the brim of her hat started creeping down over her eyes. Anger overrode any thought of caution. Starting a fight with someone so much bigger than her was never going to be a smart move.

'You idiot! You scared the shit out of them.' She pushed him hard in the midriff with both hands. 'Why? Why would anyone do that?'

The idiot staggered but managed to stay upright.

Shoving her hat back up her forehead so she could give him the full force of her glare, she froze. 'Oh my God! It's you!' Just as her hormones recognised him and rolled out a welcome mat, her brain brought down the portcullis. *How typical! I've spent the best part of twenty-four hours dreaming about Mr Perfect only to find out he's Mr Not-So-Perfect.* 'Don't you know not to make sudden noises around young cows?'

His eyes widened with shock. 'I… I didn't mean to. I didn't know they'd… they'd—'

'What? Stampede? Is that the word you're looking for? It's the one thing I was trying to avoid. A sodding stampede. Someone could have got hur… oh no! Oh! Shit, shit, shit!' She gazed up the empty lane. 'No, no, no, no, no… Oh, please no… not Jack.' She pointed her wooden spoon at the Wolverine. 'I swear by all that's holy, buster… if my Jack's hurt, I'll… I'll… God, I don't know what I'll do, but it'll be bad. Really bad.' The spoon clattered to the ground and she broke into a run as fast as her welly-clad legs would carry her.

*

The dust settled. The rhythmic scrunch of retreating boot soles on gravel faded. The woman Rick had been dreaming about disappeared out of sight around a bend in the lane. How could he have mistaken her for a gnome?

She's a warrior queen; small and scary, but pretty damn awesome.

Rick limped in her wake, half afraid of what he might find. Hoping against hope that no one had been hurt as a result of his actions, yet again. He rounded the corner and slowed to a stop. In the distance, the warrior queen was in deep discussion with a slim, blond youth and a burly farmer-type. An irate arm was waved in Rick's general direction. With no obvious casualty in sight, Rick slunk back to the barn and paced up and down, mentally kicking himself.

You pillock! Any fool knows to be careful around animals. And warrior queen or no warrior queen, pissing off his new neighbours wasn't the smartest way to stay under the radar. Damn it. Being under that bloody GMC investigation for so long had out-and-out mashed his brain. It was like living with a huge storm cloud permanently stapled to his head, casting grim shadows over everything. It made him question every decision he'd ever made. Doubt things he'd always known were true.

He could do better than this. If he was going to stand any chance of going back and helping Dean, he had to do better. Second-guessing yourself in medicine was an insidious pursuit. The stakes were too high. Get things wrong and people died. Self-doubt, once seeded, multiplies exponentially. Rick was a case in point. He couldn't trust himself. Work had become swamped with worry about what the next patient through the surgery door might present with. Every day, he'd stared at his list of appointments, no longer seeing patients who needed his help. Instead, they were a quagmire of medical legal complications lying in wait to trip him up. Every day, a voice had whispered in the back of his mind, *You might get it wrong.*

Doubting himself was a short step from doubting the patients and that was an even bigger problem. Martin, his old training mentor, always said, 'A GP consultation is a collaboration, Rick, a partnership of trust between you and the patient. They need to believe you can help them. And you need to believe that they've given you the information you need to put the pieces of the puzzle together.'

It was true.

Shivering in his barn hideout and hating himself for making a stupid mistake with a herd of cows, Rick suddenly realised the exact moment that had started this whole fiasco.

When Dean Markwell had walked into his consulting room, looked him in the eye and lied, that was the day the foundations of everything he believed in had crumbled.

Now, Rick couldn't trust anyone, least of all himself.

His warrior queen hated him. Good for her. She was better off without him.

Chapter 8

Beth arrived back at the farmhouse exhausted. Her brain shut down all entreaties from her heart to go next door and see if the Wolverine was all right. *Stuff him!* Shucking her wellies, she scuttled over to stand on the warm bit of floor by the Aga. 'Gosh! It's cold out there.'

Paddy yawned, struggled to his feet in the dog bed on the flagstones, turned his back on Beth and sank back down with a loud huff.

'Well?' Daisy demanded.

'The cows stampeded.'

The teen's eyebrows disappeared up under her fringe. 'Oh my God. Is Jack alright?'

Beth's jangling nerves made her reply sharper than necessary. 'Honestly, Daisy, do you think I'd stood here, if he wasn't? Of course he's alright! He's feeding the chickens.' She glanced around the kitchen. 'Where's Grace?'

'She's upstairs getting dressed. Why? Don't you trust me? You're the one who dragged me out of bed to look after her.'

Beth put her hands up in submission. 'Sorry. Sorry. I've just had a scare. Plus, I'm still fuming. I can't believe that awful man over at the barn—'

'What man? You mean over at Charlie's place?' Daisy leaned over the sink to peer out of the kitchen window, craning her neck so she could peer past the side of the stables. 'There's a car. Someone moved in? What's he like?'

Beth hesitated, the Wolverine hovering in her mind's eye.

'Beth?'

'He's scruffy. And a right prat.'

'Huh. Figures. If I inherited a house, I'd be there, like, yesterday. I wouldn't wait six months.'

Rose sloped into the room, rubbing sleep from her eyes. She slumped onto a chair, draped her arms across the table and rested her head on top. 'What's a girl got to do to get any sleep around here?'

'Late night, was it, Rose?' asked Beth.

Rose rolled her head to one side and opened one eye. 'Duh! It's a pub. Of course it was late.' The eye closed and the head rolled back.

Daisy made a cup of strong coffee and shoved it in her big sister's direction. 'You were saying. The cows stampeded. Then what?'

Beth leaned back against the sink. 'I was convinced Jack was a goner, but, when I got to the junction, Nick was with him and—'

'Uh… cows?' Rose lifted her head, eyes leaping from Beth to Daisy. 'What cows?'

Jack burst through the back door. Paddy launched himself from his bed and skipped around the teen like a naughty puppy. Beth averted her gaze. The ungrateful creature never appreciated the one person who actually remembered to feed him.

Jack dumped his coat, hopped over his adoring four-legged buddy, and hurried to the cupboards in search of breakfast. Watching him pour nearly a pint of milk over a huge mound of cereal, Beth suppressed a wince. Such a lot being consumed by only one member of the household in a single sitting hurt. Was it any wonder the food bill was astronomical? She mentally added "buy more milk" to her to-do list for the morning.

Mid-mouthful, Jack dragged his eyes from his phone and glowered at her. 'What?'

Beth flashed him a bright smile. The milk was already on the cereal, after all. 'You were brilliant this morning. Thank you for helping.' Jack grunted and raised an eyebrow. Whether he was suspicious of her smile, her thanks or the compliment, Beth couldn't be sure. 'Are the rest of the animals okay?'

'All except Pablo. Daft donkey has got himself wedged between the black shed and the back of the stables again.'

Beth groaned. 'Why does he do that?'

'I gave up trying to coax him out. Grumpy sod tried to kick me.'

'Poor Pablo,' said Rose, stretching. 'I'll sort him out, after I've had a shower.'

'If you're sure you don't mind.'

Rose gave Beth a pointed look, before answering, her tone blank, 'Why would I mind looking after my dead mother's donkey?'

Beth's cheeks burned. 'Sorry. I didn't mean—'

'Oh no!' Daisy looked up in alarm. 'What's going to happen to Bert, Ernie and the girls? They belong to the new guy, don't they?'

Beth sighed. 'Yes. The llampaccas belong to whoever inherited the barn. Now he's finally turned up, we'll have to hand them over.'

'Someone's living at the barn?' Jack was at the kitchen window in a heartbeat. 'Since when?'

Grace bounced into the kitchen, waving a pink sparkly hairbrush at Beth. 'Ponytail, please.'

Beth spun Grace around and started untangling curls. 'Yesterday, I think. And to answer your question, Daisy, I've no idea. Whoever he is, he's not exactly skipped over quick sharp to demand them back, has he? If his appalling behaviour towards those cows this morning is anything to go by, who knows what will happen?'

Grace twisted round to look at Beth. 'What happened to the cows, Mummy?'

'They're fine, sweetheart. It's just the man next door was a bit silly and made too much noise.'

'They ran like mad, Grace,' said Jack. 'But they weren't hurt. Honest. I just thought Daisy's daft plan had gone wrong when I saw them galloping towards me.'

Daisy poked her tongue out at him. 'My plan was epic. You're just jealous that I thought of it.'

Grace's lip wobbled. 'Will the man scare the llampaccas, too?'

'I'm sure he won't,' said Beth. 'But we'll keep them a bit longer until we can be sure he knows how to look after them properly.'

Jack scraped his breakfast bowl, then stood up and

tucked his phone into his back pocket. 'We going to school then or what?'

'Ten minutes,' said Beth. 'I need to change. I've got some jobs to do in the village this morning.'

Jack huffed, hauled his phone back out and sat back down.

'Is one of those jobs getting the roof fixed?' demanded Daisy. 'You do know there's, like, this mega storm on the way, don't you?'

'That's true,' said Rose. 'Tail end of Hurricane Harvey from the States. Two months' worth of rain in twenty-four-hours, they reckon. It's all anyone was talking about in the Crashing Boar last night.'

'When is it due to hit?' Beth glanced towards the bucket in the doorway.

'Friday,' said Rose.

Jack looked towards the window as if expecting to see black clouds already and muttered, 'We'd better make sure the animals are all under cover.'

'Beth needs to make sure *we're* under cover.' Daisy pointed to the ceiling. 'It'll take more than that stupid bucket.'

'I'll sort it, I promise,' said Beth and hurried from the room.

Chapter 9

Rick needed coffee. Cursing the lack of power at the barn, he scratched the heavy stubble that had sprouted overnight and examined the log burner. Could he warm a pan of water on it? He'd have to find some kindling first. Dad had taught him how to light a fire years ago – on that disastrous camping trip. After the divorce, Mum had moved back to live with her parents in Scotland, taking Rick with her. Rick remembered her bristling with anger when Dad had arrived for a visit unannounced.

*

'You can't just turn up like this, Alan.'

Dad waved an apologetic hand. 'Charlie lent me a car and I—'

'I don't care if he lent you a coach and horses. You should have called first.'

'Please, Suzie – oh, hiya, Ricky, how are you? Look! I got you something.'

From behind Mum, Rick watched as Dad pulled a large

stuffed bear from the back seat of the car. 'This is Boo. He'll keep you company when I'm not here.'

At six, Rick considered himself too old for teddy bears. Nevertheless, he squeezed past Mum's legs, snatched the bear to his chest and threw himself into Dad's arms. 'I missed you.'

'That bear isn't going to fix anything,' snarled Mum. 'If it weren't for the courts saying I have to let you see him, I'd not let you darken this door.'

'Please, Suzie. I'm here on my own. I thought we could camp at that site up the road.'

Mum gave a bitter shout of laughter. 'Now I know you're mad for sure. It's April.'

*

Back in Charlie's barn, sitting on the sofa with Boo, Rick smiled.

That trip was awful, apart from building that fire to cook sausages.

His stomach rumbled at the thought. The next time Dad had come, they'd driven to a small hotel instead, watched movies and eaten junk food. All future Dad visits had followed the same pattern. They'd even played video games on a portable console plugged into the television of whichever hotel they were at.

It's a shame I never met Charlie, given what great friends he and Dad were.

Rick vaguely remembered a man trying to talk to him at Dad's funeral, but Mum had yanked him away. In all honesty, Rick had been in no fit state to register anything and… well… then he'd thrown himself into work to escape the grief. Rick shook his head. Working too hard had led to his own divorce. After that, work was all he had.

Only, he didn't have it anymore.

Rick stared out of the window, fighting a dense, invisible fog of loss, his eyes roaming over the farmhouse opposite. It was in a worse state than the barn. Both driveways were in poor condition, with a preponderance of weeds and grass sprouting through gravel. The missing gates explained how the cows had been able to get so close to both houses.

I should sort something out to stop that happening again. A gate might deter other unwelcome visitors, too.

As things stood, the paparazzi could waltz right up to the door, unimpeded. A shiver ran down his spine at the thought of strangers invading his sanctuary. Rick's gaze tracked the likely route for trespassers across the yard and spotted a figure approaching the door. Striding to the door, he yanked it open.

The warrior queen managed a wooden smile. 'It seems we're neighbours.' She thrust a plastic tub the size of a shoebox into his hands. 'Welcome to Old Farm Lane. Sorry, I can't stop. We're late for school.' She didn't sound sorry. She turned on her heel and hurried away.

What can I say to repair this?

'Thank you,' he called, finding his voice far too late.

Intrigued, he carried the tub to the kitchen worktop and popped off the lid. Inside were half a dozen chocolate cupcakes. The enticing sugary aroma from the cakes made his head spin. An almighty growl from Rick's mid-section announced his belly's intention to crawl up his throat and eat *him* if he didn't hand over the cakes right now. Stuffing an entire cupcake into his mouth, he chewed and swallowed. Slowly, the world reassembled itself around him in a more recognisable order as his blood sugar level stabilised.

Three cupcakes later, he felt up to making some decisions. Basic ones, admittedly, but it was a start. Opening his laptop, he piggybacked off the nearest – rather feeble – Wi-Fi connection. No doubt something else to thank the warrior queen for. Tamping down paranoid thoughts about being digitally tracked, he searched up local power companies. A miraculously short time later, he received the good news that power at the property could be restored later that morning. Thank heaven.

In the meantime, he still needed coffee. And, while he was at it, some basic provisions wouldn't hurt. An online supermarket delivery to the barn was an option, but might give his location away. A local corner shop was a better bet. He searched up a map of the area.

*

Beth herded Daisy, Jack and Grace towards the door. 'Come on, guys. We need to move.'

'You're the one who kept us waiting,' grumbled Jack. 'Where the f… uh, where were you?'

'Taking a welcome gift next door.'

'Are you crazy? After what he did?'

'He's our neighbour. We need to get on with him. For the animals' sake, if not ours.'

Jack flared his nostrils at her. 'You're soft in the head, you are.'

Beth secretly agreed. Common sense insisted that a

placatory gesture was necessary and she didn't have the energy to argue with herself. What a shame her Wolverine was such a disappointment. He hadn't exactly welcomed her or her gift with open arms and there was none of the easy connection they'd had the first time they'd met.

It just shows dreams should stay dreams. More fool me for getting my hopes up.

'What's done is done.' Beth rattled her car keys. 'Let's hit the road. No. Hang on. Grace, you can't go dressed like that. Mrs Fintan will kill me. No, don't look like that... I don't mean she'll actually kill me... but she'll tell me off, again. You've got to wear your preschool T-shirt.'

'I am.' Grace pulled up her glittery jumper to reveal the blue T-shirt with the gold preschool logo.

'Swap the jumper for a cardigan, so the T-shirt shows,' said Daisy. 'But defo keep the sparkly tights and the tiara. You look epic.'

Grace did as Daisy suggested, glaring at Beth as she did so. Then she grabbed her coat and stomped outside, only to stop on the doorstep and gasp. 'Wow! Look! There's cow poo everywhere.' Grace skipped over to the car, waving her arms around and singing at the top of her voice. 'Poo, poo, poo. Everybody, smell that poo!'

The trail of mess left behind by the herd made Beth sigh. *Yet another job to do.*

Daisy, tiptoeing around a particularly large cowpat, yanked open the rear passenger door. Jack folded up his long legs and inserted himself into the front passenger seat along with a backpack and a stack of lever-arch files. Fortunately, the engine kicked into life without its usual objections and they were soon trundling down the hill towards the village.

Used to stony silence from Daisy on all car journeys, Beth was astounded when the teenager spoke.

'I'm going around Noah's after school today, yeah? Like, to study.'

'He's in the year above and you aren't doing the same subjects. How you going to study?' scoffed Jack.

'Shut up, Jack!'

'Hasn't Noah's mum just had a baby?' asked Beth.

'I love babies,' declared Daisy.

'No, you don't,' said Grace. 'You hate babies. You said so.'

'Well, maybe I do, but I love you, Grace – you know that.'

'Of course you love me. I'm not a baby.'

Beth met Grace's gaze in the rear mirror. A flare of alarm shot through her chest as she recognised Daisy's defiant attitude reflected in the younger girl's eyes. 'No. I want you home at the usual time today. No going to Noah's.'

'You're not my mother. You can't stop me.'

'I'm the adult responsible for you. You can see Noah at the weekend.'

'I heard he went clubbing last Saturday and got totally bladdered,' said Jack.

Daisy slapped the top of her brother's head. 'Butt out, Jack.'

'Stop it, both of you. Daisy, you're coming home and that's final. You need to study. Think of your future.'

Daisy huffed. 'At least I've got a future.'

Jack whistled. 'Savage.'

'I beg your pardon, Daisy?' asked Beth.

'Just because you're old and your life's over,' Daisy hissed, 'doesn't mean you can wreck mine. If I want to go out, I will. So there!'

'Yeah!' chimed in Grace. 'So there!'

Enough. Beth hit the brakes and swerved into a lay-by.

'Hey! Go easy,' protested Daisy. 'Why are we stopping?'

Jack shot Beth a look. He opened his mouth, then very sensibly closed it again and hunched down in his seat.

Beth gave Daisy a steady stare via the rear mirror. 'You've got two choices. Apologise and agree to come home at the usual time, or get out of the car.'

Grace's eyes ping-ponged from Beth to Daisy and back again.

Daisy frowned. 'You can't—'

'I can.'

'But…'

'Try me.' Beth crossed her fingers.

'There's no need to get salty. I was only saying—'

'I'm not remotely interested in what you were saying. Are you in or out?' *I'll feel so guilty if I actually make her walk.*

'In, okay? In. God! Sorry. Alright?' The defiance in Daisy was heavy enough to crush concrete. 'Can we go, already?'

Beth took her foot off the brake and eased the car back onto the road.

Silence reigned for a few minutes before Grace spoke. 'Mummy?'

What now? 'Yes, Grace?'

'Why is there a sofa in that field?'

'What?' Beth glanced over. Sure enough, in a field to her left sat a battered brown sofa, a similarly worn footstool and an old fridge-freezer lying on its side with the door hanging open.

'I have no idea, Grace. Let's just get to school, shall we?'

Chapter 10

Rick pulled into a small, deserted car park in the nearby village of Ambleford. Grabbing a pair of sunglasses from the glove compartment, he went in search of a ticket machine.

An older woman wearing layers of purple fabric was being dragged along by a dog the size of a small horse. 'It's free to park, pet,' she called.

The dog showed an alarming interest in Rick's crotch. He took a step back and held out a tentative hand to be sniffed instead.

The woman laughed and tucked a stray strand of silver hair back into her bun. 'For all her size, she's a chicken really. A rescue. Mastiff crossed with a Great Dane, I think. She's far too big for me, but I love her anyway. She's… Tiny. Stop it!'

Tiny ignored Rick's hand and licked his smart Italian loafers instead, leaving a shiny trail of slobber.

'I'm so sorry. I'm Reena. Are…' She dissolved into a fruity coughing fit suggestive of a forty-a-day habit. She composed herself, watery eyes peering over gold-rimmed spectacles. 'Are you new around here?'

'Yes. Just moved in.'

'You've timed it well, pet. This little car park was packed ten minutes ago.'

Rick glanced around at the empty spaces.

'Parents dropping kiddies off at the preschool, over there.' She gestured across the green. 'They fight tooth and nail to park at eight-thirty every weekday, but they're all gone by nine. Off to work or Pilates or some such, one supposes. We're very proud of our preschool, but ever since they got an outstanding from Toffsted, it's been bedlam.'

Toffsted?

A glimmer of amusement in the old woman's eyes told Rick she was as sharp as a tack. 'Wealthy incomers bring their little darlings here to avoid forking out for private nursery fees.'

'Ah.'

'It's one reason all our local shops survive.' She gestured out of the entrance to the car park. 'Rich customers, pet.'

The car park was adjacent to a pub with a painted swing sign announcing "The Crashing Boar". Across the road from it was a stone war memorial flanked by stone benches. Past that was the green – a large rectangle of lush grass edged with pansy-filled flower beds and encircled with a ribbon of tarmacked road. Quaint cottages lined the far side. On the nearside stretched a parade of shops with jolly rainbow paintwork and matching awnings. A wide stone pavement between the shops and the road encouraged customers to linger. In the distance, a sunshine-yellow Victorian schoolhouse sat squat and steady inside a fenced playground, adjacent to a traditional red-brick church with a small bell tower.

'Craft shop, bakery, hairdresser, pet shop. You name it. We're spoiled for choice,' Reena said. 'Are you after anything in particular?'

'Coffee.'

'Aha. Stacy in The Coffee Pot serves excellent coffee, although…' Reena glanced at a slim watch on her wrist and pursed her lips. 'Oh, dear me, no. It's Wednesday. The local businesswomen hold networking events in there on a Wednesday morning. It'll be packed to the gills. Best avoided.'

Damnit.

'Don't worry, pet,' said Reena. 'Barbara Trenchard does lovely takeaway coffee from the deli counter at the back of the general store.' She nodded at a sprawling store-cum-post office opposite the entrance to the car park, a shiny red postbox standing to attention outside.

'Thanks.'

'You know, pet,' Reena said, 'you look ever so familiar. Have we met before?'

Rick shook his head, the hairs on the back of his neck standing to attention.

Tiny whined and suddenly started moving. Reena grasped the lead with both hands. 'Looks like we're off again. No doubt I'll see you around, pet. Toodle-oo for now.'

Rick pulled the hood of his fleece over his head, took a deep breath and crossed the road to the general store.

*

Beth stood just inside the general store, scanning the noticeboard for local job vacancies, still reeling from the telling-off she had received from Mrs Fintan over Grace's flexible uniform choices. Several cards requested cleaners and pet sitters. She could do both, but they wouldn't pay much – and she had enough cleaning and animal care to do at home. A small pink card, tucked behind a larger flyer, caught her attention. Beth pulled it out for a closer look.

'I hope you aren't going to lurk there all day, Mrs Hope.'

That voice set Beth's teeth on edge. She swung around to see the short, well-upholstered form of Mrs Trenchard behind the deli counter. The second to last person in the world that she would ever choose to speak to – the first being Paul. Known to Rose, Jack and Daisy as 'Aunty B', Mrs Trenchard made her disapproval of Beth clear with every encounter. Today was no different. Unfortunately, as a stalwart of the WI and owner of the village store, the woman's opinions held a lot of sway in the local community.

Beth shifted from foot to foot.

'It's an inconvenient spot to grow roots, I must say.' Mrs Trenchard waved a pair of tongs at the crowded shop. 'You can see how busy we are. Might I encourage you to leave? Unless you're planning to spend money, of course.'

All the bored people in the queue for the post office counter turned to stare. Beth muttered an apology, darted for the door and barrelled straight into a man coming the other way.

Large gentle hands grabbed her shoulders and stopped her from falling. A voice she recognised said, 'Steady on. Are you okay?'

Electricity sang through her veins at the contact, making her hormones give a happy little skip as they instantly recognised the Wolverine.

Mrs Trenchard tutted.

Beth's cheeks burned. *Got to get out.* Her instincts took over. She thrust both arms up and out, breaking his grip. 'I have to… uh, I need to…'

He stepped back.

She dashed past, straight out onto the pavement where she almost tripped over the extendable lead connecting old Mr Whitely to his asthmatic pug, Peter.

'Watch where you're going, madam,' roared Mr Whitely, waving his stick in the air under her nose.

She reared backwards and grabbed the postbox to prevent an ungainly topple into the gutter. 'Sorry, so sorry.'

Peter whined, farted and then continued to propel his crumbly owner towards the war memorial, just as he always did at that time of the morning.

Beth wanted the ground to swallow her up. She staggered away from the shop door and leaned against a table outside The Coffee Pot. The little pink card from the noticeboard was in her hand. Pushing the Wolverine from her mind, she focused on the pretty lettering.

Do you feel crafty? Help wanted.
Inquire at Bits and Bobs for more details.

As a rule, Beth didn't have much truck with signs from the universe, but this one was practically smacking her in the face. Bits and Bobs, the craft shop at the far end of the parade, was a stone's throw from the preschool. A job there would be very convenient… well… apart from the need to be creative.

Beth's self-belief was at rock bottom. Worse than that.

It had chiselled a further fifty fathoms down through solid bedrock into whatever crud lay beneath. But desperate times called for desperate measures. She had to apply for this job. And even if she failed to get it, nothing could be more embarrassing than the last few minutes. Could it? She tucked the card in her coat pocket and marched along the parade to the craft shop.

A dainty bell tinkled overhead as she entered and a waft of hyacinth and geranium engulfed her, bringing with it a surreal sense of calm and positivity. Around her, textures and colours in a restful yet inviting arrangement drew her in. She couldn't resist touching a display of woollen shawls.

'Soft, aren't they?' An amused voice came from the back of the long, thin room, where a large wooden table was surrounded by ladder-back chairs with vibrant seat covers. A woman sat in a rocking chair, crocheting. She had smooth tawny-brown skin and black box braids pulled into a simple twist that cascaded over one shoulder. Jewelled pins were tucked into the braids at intervals – glittered accents of magenta that matched a silk scarf draped around her neck.

'Hi, I'm Lucy.' That Lucy was creative was obvious. She held up her crochet and a fuchsia-pink wrap, identical in design to the blue one that Beth had been stroking, draped into her lap. 'All-natural fibres, perfect for baby blankets.'

'You're very clever.' Beth moved closer to admire it. 'I'm Beth, by the way.'

'Hi, Beth. I'm obsessed with all things baby-related, for obvious reasons.' A complicated cloth-based sling secured a sleeping infant to Lucy's chest. 'This is Hazel.'

Beth's heart melted at the sight of candyfloss-soft baby hair and a chubby brown fist. 'Oh. She's adorable.'

'While she's sleeping, she is.' Lucy grinned. 'The blankets are a new line. We carry a lot of handmade stock by local artisans, as well as the materials to make your own. Very popular with the tourists.'

'I'm not surprised.'

'You're not a tourist, though, are you?' Lucy put her head on one side. 'Tom and I moved here last summer. It's taken every second since then to get this place up and running. I've not met everyone in the village, yet, but I'm sure I know you.'

'I come this way most days. My daughter, Grace, is at the preschool.'

Lucy snapped her fingers in triumph. 'That'll be it. My Hari's at preschool, too. He's always talking about a Grace. I only dash in and out at pick-up and drop-off, though. It's no wonder I don't really know anyone. And now I've got this little handful, I've even less time.' She patted the baby's bottom gently and shrugged. 'Anyway, enough about me. Are you looking for anything in particular?'

'You have a job advertised.'

'Blimey, that was quick. I only put the ad up this morning. Are you into crafting at all?'

Beth opened her mouth, scraping the inside of her skull in search of some way to dazzle Lucy with her creative prowess. 'Uh... No, not really. I just need a job. I... oh, blast! I'm sorry. Daft idea. I know nothing about crafting and I'm only available when Grace is at preschool, which is probably no good for you. Plus, I'm not exactly popular around here. I'll scare off all your customers.'

Lucy's eyes bugged. 'Woah! Hang on. Before I go back and unravel all that, let me ask you one thing. Do you understand that a job interview is the part when you try to convince a potential employer that they *should* give you the job? Listing all the reasons why it would be a terrible idea isn't usually considered to be the best approach.'

Beth studied her shoes, kicking herself for running off at the mouth. 'Yes. Sorry.'

'No need to apologise. Now, have you got time to make us both a cup of tea?'

Beth glanced up. 'Uh, yes. I do.'

'Good. There's a tiny kitchen through that door. I daren't move for fear of waking the monster from the deep.' Lucy stroked Hazel's back. 'Mine's milk and no sugar, thanks.'

Beth went to make the tea. *She'd be mad to offer me the job but there's no harm in hanging around for a bit. I'm desperate for caffeine and Jane said I needed to get to know people, so here goes.* She returned to the shop with two mugs. 'Here we go.'

'You are a lifesaver. Now, tell me why you think you're not popular.'

Beth perched on a chair. 'I married a local boy under less-than-ideal circumstances. The local grandma mafia are a tough crowd.'

'Oooh! Tell me more.'

'My husband was originally one half of a pair of childhood lovebirds. Paul and Isla. The entire village watched them grow up together, fall in love and get married. Real Mills & Boon stuff – or so I'm told.'

'That's sweet, but I'm assuming it didn't last, since he's now your husband?'

'Yeah. No, it's really sad. She died. Hit by a car on New Year's Eve seven years ago. Drunk driver.'

'That's awful.'

'Paul was left with three young kids. Rose was only twelve. The twins were nearly nine. Anyway, I met him about eighteen months later, at a work event in London, and… well, about six months after that I got pregnant, accidentally. I was getting on a bit. Forty-six is late to start having babies. So, for me, it was kind of a now-or-never situation. And I was in love. With him, with the children, with the forest.' Beth shrugged. 'We got married.'

'Hardly the crime of the century.'

'Not technically, maybe, and no one said anything outright, but… well, it was a bit soon. And you can tell when you're being judged. And Isla was the perfect wife and mother, of course. I've never quite measured up.'

'I sense an inferiority complex.'

Beth relaxed back into her chair. 'Maybe, but that's old news. Mrs Trenchard even talks to me these days, although I think I preferred it when she didn't.'

'Barbara? From the general stores? She's a sweetheart.'

'Sweetheart, my arse. She's a dragon.'

'She's one of my crochet circle ladies. Looks intimidating, I admit, but—'

'She had me too scared to go in the store for nearly a year after I first arrived.'

Lucy dissolved into giggles.

'I'm serious!' Beth struggled to keep a straight face. 'I made a right tit of myself in there only this morning.'

'I'm sure you didn't.'

'Trust me, I did.'

'I've clearly had a very tame introduction to village life in comparison, then?'

'You're not a jumped-up Mata Hari from London like me.'

'Nah! I'm only from Southampton.'

'Practically a local.'

'I'm sure your lovely husband and kids are worth it all,' said Lucy, stroking Hazel's back.

Beth grimaced into her mug. 'The husband? Not so much. He left. It's just me and the kids now. And no matter how challenging they are. Underneath it all, I know they're good kids.'

'Gosh. I am so sorry.'

'It's fine. I'm fine. Honestly.' Beth blinked back traitorous tears. 'I'm just rubbish with men. I'm going to swear off them.'

'Oh, don't do that.'

'No, I really should. I have no judgement whatsoever.'

'That's not true.'

'It is. I met this guy the other day.'

'Is he good-looking?'

Beth blew out her cheeks, an image of the Wolverine's craggy face floating before her eyes. 'Not in the traditional square-jawed and handsome sense, but there's something about him. Just being close to him scrambles my brain. It's intense.'

'I'm sensing a "but" coming.'

'Yeah. It turns out he's my new neighbour and… it's complicated.'

'Complicated doesn't have to be bad.'

'Trust me. This time, it is. I just can't go there. There's too much going on. I don't have the bandwidth.' Beth put her mug on the table and stood up. 'Sorry. I'm talking your ear off. This was supposed to be a genuine job application. You're far too good a listener.'

'Ah, that's not me,' Lucy replied. 'That's the crafting environment – it's more effective than the confessional. Don't look at me like that. It's true. There are studies that prove creative activities are good for building positive mental health and resilience. They're real stress-busters. You'd be amazed what people share during the crafty crochet session, for example. Not that I'd repeat anything. Confidentiality's vital. What happens in crafting stays in crafting.'

'I believe you. And I don't usually rattle on, I promise.' Beth gave a sheepish grin. 'I don't suppose you'll consider me for the job, will you?'

'I wish I could…' Lucy wrinkled her nose, 'but I really need someone with practical experience. I'm so sorry.'

'Don't worry, I expected as much. If only I were more like my stepdaughter, Daisy. She's doing a textiles A-level at college. She probably knows all sorts of useful stuff.'

'Does she want a job?'

'She might, actually. She's a bit of handful but only for me, because of the whole wicked stepmother thing. She's sweetness and light with everyone else. Mrs Trenchard adores her.'

'There you go, running yourself down again. You really should stop that. Listen, mention the job to Daisy for me. If she's interested, send her in and she and I can take it from there. Leave me your phone number, too. I'll let you know if I hear of any other jobs going.'

'That's kind. I've one teen who doesn't stop eating, two others with hot shower dependencies, and don't get me started on Grace and her obsession with unicorns and sparkly stuff.' Beth scribbled her details on a scrap of paper and said goodbye with a heavy heart.

Chapter 11

The general store was much busier than Rick would have liked. No wonder the warrior queen had been in such a hurry to leave. He tucked his chin down and lurked at the back near the door, the need for coffee singing in his veins. A lady of solid build and mature years was refilling trays of cold meat behind a glass display counter nearby. She was wearing a stern expression, a voluminous pink tabard and plastic disposable gloves.

She caught Rick's eye, then glanced around the rest of the shop, before her gaze settled back on him. Leaning forwards, she murmured, 'Can I help?'

'Are you Barbara?'

'I am.'

'Reena told me you make good coffee.'

The woman stripped off the gloves. 'I do. It's only traditional filter. If you want all that hot frothy milk palaver, you'll have to brave The Coffee Pot. Only it's Wednesday, so I wouldn't. It'll be rammed.'

'Filter's perfect. Black, please.'

'Coming right up.' She handed him a lidded paper cup.

'That'll be two pounds. And here…' She passed him a folded piece of paper the size of a credit card.

'What's this?'

'You're trying to keep a low profile, aren't you?'

Rick's scalp prickled. 'Why do you say that?'

Her eyes flicked to something behind him. 'I sell papers.'

Rick followed her gaze. A shelving unit laden with newspapers and magazines stood behind the door. *Flaming Nora!* Predictable, shouty headlines stalked across them all.

```
Dr Death on the Run.
Dr Death Disappears.
Where Will Dr Death Strike Next?
```

Every single paper carried that awful picture of him.

He put a steadying hand on the counter. 'It's not… I mean, I didn't… um…'

She waved a dismissive hand. 'Don't. I've seen it all before. Most of what's presented as news, these days, is horse dung. My Brian always says there are two sides to a spoon.' She snapped her plastic gloves back on. 'Let's face it – guilty or not, you're going to lose. The court of public opinion has already decided. Having said that, my Brian always says that until the law itself decides otherwise, you've as much right to live in peace as the next person. And I agree.'

Rick rubbed his stubble. 'Uh… thanks…' *Am I seriously having this conversation?*

'The way I see it, lots of folk come to the forest in search of privacy. It happens all the time. Celebrities and whatnot. We're used to it. You never know who you're going to bump into in the Crashing Boar on a Friday night. Half of Take

That are knocking around here somewhere. My point is, while I can't speak for the tourists because they're a law unto themselves, most of the locals won't give you any trouble.'

Rick's eyes slid to the slip of paper in his hand. 'And this?'

'That's my number. If you need supplies, text me a list. I'll get it ready for you to pick up when we're quiet. It'll cost you a bit extra, but it's… shall we say, it's a special service for private customers. You can get other deliveries sent here too, if you like. Just mark them for my attention with your initials afterwards. We're dead quiet in here between 6 and 6.30 every morning. Come and get your stuff then. It'll just be me here, oh… and possibly Elvis, but he won't say anything.'

'Elvis?' *Surely not.*

'The postie. Here.' She put a small paper-wrapped parcel on the counter. 'Soda bread, cheese and olives. They'll keep the wolf from the door 'til you know what you need. I'll add it to your first bill.' She glanced around the shop again. Rick did likewise.

The door opened. A middle-aged man ambled in; his vast beer belly only partially constrained by a faded Def Leppard T-shirt. He frowned at Rick and did a double take.

'You'd best get going,' said Barbara.

Rick was already halfway out of the door, his parcel tucked under one arm.

*

Back at the barn, encouraged by Barbara's suggestion that most locals wouldn't give him any trouble, Rick decided to thank the warrior queen next door for the cakes she'd given him. *I'll apologise for the whole cow-scaring thing, too.*

He scrunched across the patchy gravel towards the farmhouse porch, grateful that the ache in his leg was easing. A row of tubby sparrows on the pretty gabled roof scolded him as he approached, before flitting down to a lichen-covered stone birdbath set in a rose bed to the left of the door. Arriving on the worn welcome mat, Rick took hold of the shiny metal hoop in the centre of the door and beat a short tattoo. After a short wait, the ancient slab of oak groaned open, just wide enough for a slim, dark-haired young woman to peer out. It was difficult to tell how old she was. *Twenty, maybe twenty-two? A bit younger than David, for sure.* With heavily kohl-rimmed eyes beneath a wispy fringe, she was, quite patently, not the warrior queen he was looking for.

'Hi. Is your mum in?'

'Mum's dead.' The young woman's face was expressionless.

'Oh!' *Shit.* 'Right. I came to say sorry.'

'She died ages ago. I'm over it.'

'No, I… ah…' Rick scratched his head. 'I meant about the cows?'

'What cows?'

'This morning?' He pointed at the cowpat-strewn yard behind him.

'Oh, those cows. Nothing to do with me, mate.' She frowned. 'Were they yours? I thought they were Nick's.'

'No, I just…' Rick sighed. 'Listen. The lady with the red hair, is she in?'

'Beth? No.'

Beth. So, that's the warrior queen's name. Rick stepped back. 'I guess I'll try later.'

'Sure.' She started to close the door.

'By the way, can you tell her thanks for the cakes?'

The door stopped moving. Rick now had the young woman's full attention. From the look on her face, he was no longer sure he wanted it.

'What cakes?'

'Uh, she gave me half a dozen cupcakes this morning.'

'That's where they went! Bloody Beth.' A high-pitched beeping sounded from the depths of the farmhouse. 'Look, mister, I got to go, that's my timer. If you want to thank my darling stepmother for the cakes she stole from me, come back later. Right?' She started to ram the door closed again, but then paused and squinted at him. 'Hang on, haven't I seen you somewhere before? Wait a minute... It'll come to me... Yes.' She snapped her fingers. 'Yes! I knew it. You're that dude on X? The one that drove over that YouTuber?'

Rick backed away, shaking his head. 'No. No way. Definitely not me. I've never driven over anyone.'

'There's a video on X says different.'

'It's not something I'd forget.'

'Nah! Guess not. Anyway, you're way too old. What are you? Sixty? Seventy?'

Rick stiffened. 'I'm fifty-four!'

'Whatever. The video guy, he's some posh doctor fella from London with pots of money. Near as killed some gamer, apparently.' She ran a disdainful gaze over Rick's scruffy hoodie and crumpled suit trousers. She shrugged. 'Like I said, I've got to go. Cakes. Oven. Bye.'

The door slammed shut.

Rick stumbled away as fast as he could. He hadn't ever

run anyone over, but once, very recently, he'd come close. Back in the barn, he opened his laptop.

There's no way I actually hurt her.

It took mere minutes to find the clip. A short film on a repeating loop. Grainy footage of him and Sal – no doubt shot by Abe. Heavily edited to create the worst possible impression. It was brutal. No one who saw that could think he was anything other than a monster. Rick pushed the laptop aside and rushed to the loo to throw up.

Chapter 12

Beth's mind was full of the Wolverine when she left the craft shop to pick up Grace. Telling Lucy that he was a no-go wasn't the same as believing it. Like teenagers in the grip of their first crush, her hormones capered about with excitement at the mere thought of seeing him again. It was ridiculous.

She drew level with the immense stone plinth outside the preschool playground and paused to stare up at the statue of the fourth Lord Astley. Immortalised in stone, the old man glowered across the village green much as he'd done in real life nearly a century before. From all reports, the sixth Lord Astley wasn't much better. Beth had driven past the grand gates to the Astley Manor estate often enough and seen countless plaques on local buildings, all bearing testimony to historic Astley benevolence. But rumours about the current lord told a different story. As she had never encountered him in person, Beth preferred to keep an open mind. Shivering, she dug her hands into her pockets for her gloves and her fingers brushed against the pink card.

Blast. It's only fair to Lucy to put it back on the noticeboard.

She checked her watch. There was just enough time. Plus, she needed milk.

Outside the general store, a minor game of car Tetris was underway. A green Mini, a white van and a tractor edged past a gleaming Land Rover that had been casually abandoned and was sticking out into the road near the postbox. A gaggle of onlookers offered well-intentioned but contradictory advice to the struggling drivers. Skirting the chaos, Beth slipped into the shop and repositioned the card on the noticeboard. She tensed at the sound of Mrs Trenchard's voice from the far end of the shop.

'Perhaps you could park with more consideration, next time, Lord Astley?'

Curiosity got the better of Beth's good sense. Despite the fact that the best course of action with Mrs Trenchard was always to slip away unnoticed, she wanted to know what Lord Astley looked like. She peered past a tower of baked beans at the only other person in the store, half-expecting to see a stereotypical bumbling aristocrat in tweeds and a flat cap. Instead, a tall, middle-aged man in a double-breasted grey suit stared at his phone, ignoring Mrs Trenchard.

Mrs Trenchard glared. 'Do you not think that, as local gentry, you should set an example and obey the rules of the road?'

He looked up. 'Do you have those Spanish olives Lady Astley ordered?'

'But… oh, never mind. Yes, I do. And the prosciutto and aubergine. It's all packed and ready to go.' She brandished a medium-sized box. 'Let me just ring it up.'

'Send an invoice to the house. Maria will settle it.' Lord

Astley pocketed his phone and reached for the box. 'Why she insists on buying from you is beyond me.'

Mrs Trenchard held on to the box, forcing his lordship to look at her. 'Maria understands the importance of supporting the local community. She's not a nouveau riche snob. You're no better than me, you know, Bobby. I remember you from primary school.'

'It's Lord Robert Astley to you.'

'If a plane crash and cancer hadn't seen off your cousin and his boy, it wouldn't be, though, would it? You'd be the poor distant relative still. Not poncing around in snazzy suits and a posh car. But seeing as you are Lord Astley, you could make a real difference around here. Be a force for good.'

'What exactly do you suggest I do?'

'For starters, you could have a word with your people about the mess they leave behind after your shooting parties. All that rubbish isn't good for the environment.'

'If you wish to complain, drop a line to the estates team, but...' He towered over the older woman like a serpent preparing to strike. All trace of bored condescension disappeared as genuine menace crept into his tone. 'I wouldn't if I were you. People who cause trouble for me find they get more trouble back.'

Mrs Trenchard didn't flinch. 'So I've heard. You tried to force Justin out of the Crashing Boar.'

'So?'

'You have fingers in a lot of pies, but you're only out for yourself. I, for one, am glad Justin managed to find the money to keep you out.'

'You'd be wise to stay out of my business, Barbara Trenchard.'

'I'm not scared of you.' The faint wobble in the older woman's voice said otherwise.

'You should be.'

Beth had heard enough. Without giving herself time to think, she reached for the open shop door and nudged it with enough force to make the bell at the top dance a merry jig. Then, grabbing a couple of random tins from the nearest shelf, she marched over to the counter and plonked them down, forcing a bright smile to her face. 'Good morning. Lovely day, isn't it?'

Mrs Trenchard and Lord Astley froze.

Lord Astley moved first, snatching his box and marching out. A waft of overpowering cologne rolled over Beth as he passed.

Mrs Trenchard blinked. 'Mrs Hope. I... uh... you came back.'

'I forgot something.'

Not at all her usual bombastic self, Mrs Trenchard picked up the tins. 'Cranberry sauce and artichoke hearts in brine. Are you sure?'

'Oh no. Silly me. Actually, I just need milk. Jack gets through it like there's no tomorrow.' She hurried to the fridge and returned with a large carton of semi-skimmed.

Mrs Trenchard rang it through the till. Her hands trembled. She fumbled with the card reader. Beth found herself in the unusual position of wanting to stick around to provide distracting chat, until she could be certain the older woman was alright. Casting around for a subject, she asked, 'Are Lord Astley's shooting parties really responsible for rubbish in the forest?'

'Oh yes. They bring city people here, which might be

good for the economy, but they never clear up properly afterwards. It's a disgrace.' Mrs Trenchard looked directly at her. 'You're from London, aren't you?'

'I was brought up in Cardiff, actually, but I worked in London for several years.'

The older woman frowned. 'You don't sound Welsh.'

'That doesn't stop me being Welsh.'

'Huh! I suppose you got used to lots of rubbish in a city.'

A muscle clenched in Beth's jaw. 'Not especially. And the shooting parties aren't responsible for all the rubbish in the forest.'

'What do you mean?'

'There's all manner of junk dumped in a field near Old Farm Lane.'

'What?' Mrs Trenchard gasped. 'Since when?'

'Oh, I… uh… I don't know. Grace spotted it all this morning.'

'Don't tell me the phantom fly-tipper is back. That's all we need.'

'The who?'

'A few years back, some blasted crim saved a fortune in local tip fees by dumping random junk all over the forest. It caused so much damage. They were never caught.' Mrs Trenchard placed an urgent hand on the counter between them. 'Tell me you've done something about it?'

'Like what?'

'You can't ignore it – it's not right. Have you rung the council? Logged it on their website? You have to get it removed. Preferably before the storm comes through on Friday. Or who knows where it'll end up?'

'It's the tail end of a hurricane, Mrs Trenchard, not a full-on tornado. I don't imagine the wind will be strong enough to shift a sofa or a fridge-freezer.'

'That's not the point. It needs to be sorted before the rain starts. You may not be from around here, but you should do your civic duty and report it.'

Beth supressed an eye roll. Her job here was done. Normal self-important Trenchard services had been resumed.

'You've made it abundantly clear that you don't like me, Mrs Trenchard, but I'm not completely incompetent. Now that I know the rubbish can be reported to the council, you can rest assured I will do so.' She scooped up the milk and stalked towards the door. 'And another thing: I may not be from around here, but I do care about the forest. It's my children's heritage. I'll do whatever is necessary to protect it and them. Don't ever think I won't.'

Chapter 13

Later that afternoon, Rick took advantage of the fact that power had been restored to the barn and took a long, hot shower. Afterwards, he changed into jogging bottoms, a T-shirt and a thick sweater from his gym kit. That awful video was still playing on his mind. He pushed it aside and logged onto his work email. His heart sank when he saw the sheer number of messages waiting for him. Gita had sent several, two of which had subject lines that stood out – and not in a good way.

He double-clicked on the first, headed "Legal Papers".

Rick,

I hope you're okay. These arrived for you. I took the liberty of opening them and scanning the contents for you – attached here – because I don't know where to redirect your post and this way is probably more secure anyway.

Long story short, Cora Diamond is definitely suing you for damages on Dean's behalf.

Please DON'T try to contact Cora.

DO contact your Professional Indemnity Provider. (I

can't do it for you. You have to ring them.) There's no point in you paying for insurance all these years and then not using it now that you need it. The number is below.

Ask for Mark Freeman. He's good.

You will have to come back eventually to go to court and fight this. But not yet.

Stay where you are and keep your head down.

Things will settle.

Gita.

Rick shook his head. *Is there any point fighting it?* Civil cases were based on successfully demonstrating a loss and – thanks to Sal and Ade and social media – the whole world knew Dean had suffered a loss. No wonder Cora was suing the person she thought was responsible for her son's situation.

He opened the next email.

Rick.

The GMC report is back.

I've attached a copy.

You need to read it.

Please don't overreact.

You haven't been struck off.

A warning isn't the end of the world.

Let me know if you need anything.

Take care.

Gita.

A warning! Damn. Rick closed his eyes and fought an urge to throw the computer across the room. The investigation had started months ago and he'd cooperated fully. He'd given a written statement. He'd even agreed to be interviewed in person, which wasn't strictly necessary, because he had wanted to be open about what had happened. And he'd desperately hoped to be exonerated. A warning wouldn't stop him practicing medicine but it would remain on his GMC record moving forward. Until that moment he hadn't realised how much having a clean record meant to him. He'd always believed that he was a good doctor. But… maybe he wasn't. Maybe this was a sign. Or, *maybe* he was overreacting and maybe he should just be grateful that he hadn't been struck off.

Damn it.

He'd followed the National Institute of Health and Care Excellence guidelines to the letter. He was sure of it. The medicine he'd practised was sound. Yes, he'd made mistakes, but not… He couldn't face reading the report. It made no odds, anyway. If that was their decision, the damage was done. There was no way he'd be allowed to help Dean now. Or anyone. Bile rose in his throat.

Don't think. Just walk.

He lurched to his feet and hurried outside, blundering down the lane. At the main road, he turned off into the forest, head down, hands deep in the front pocket of his sweatshirt. It was getting late. He kept walking, ignoring the dusk as it morphed into the blackness of night, and focused on putting one step in front of the other. His mind chewed over that one critical consultation with Dean. It replayed in front of his eyes as if he were back there, right now, and not stumbling around the forest.

*

It was a normal morning in clinic. He'd just ushered the Clutterbucks from the consulting room and saw that the next patient on his list was someone he'd not met before. He pressed the intercom. 'Dean Markwell to room 3, please.' Taking a swig of almost-cold coffee, he pulled up a fresh consultation template on the computer. There was a strange popping sound and the screen went blank. Strange. Rick frowned. The printer was dead, too.

The door opened. 'Am I in the right place?' A stocky young man in black leisurewear, with short, dark hair gelled into stiff spikes, stood on the threshold.

'If you're Dean, then, yes, you are.' Rick smiled a welcome. 'Come in. Grab a seat. I think we've had a power cut.'

'Yeah, the telly in the waiting room just went off.'

'Did it? We'll have to do this the old-fashioned way, then.' Rick rummaged in his desk drawer. His fingers closed around some blank Lloyd George patient notecards – the sort used before NHS notes went digital. Just the job for situations like this. 'So, what can I do for you, Dean?'

'Well, thing is, Doc. I just moved here, yeah? And I've run out of my anxiety meds.'

'Have you officially registered with this practice, yet?'

'Nah. No time. I've been busy. The move and all. Mega stressful.'

'Not to worry. I can see you as a temporary resident until you register properly.'

'That's what the fella on reception said.'

'Sam? Did he give you a temporary resident form to fill in for me?'

Dean nodded and handed it over.

'Great. Now, I just need to run through some basic questions about your health and then we'll get on to your medication.' Dean's answers helped Rick piece together a picture of his general health. He seemed to be a relatively fit twenty-one-year-old man with a history of mild anxiety and depression. 'That all sounds fine. Which medication are you on?'

Dean reached into his pocket. 'I brought the empty box.'

Rick checked the label. The box was battered and the printing was smudged, but he could just about make out Dean's name, the drug – a standard anxiety medication – and the dose. Everything else was illegible. 'What happened to this?'

Dean's cheeks flushed. 'Dropped it in the bath, didn't I.'

'And you've run out completely?'

'Yup.'

It wasn't the sort of drug a patient should go cold turkey on. The side effects of sudden withdrawal could be nasty. There wasn't much time to waste. Rick bit his lip. 'Hmm. I'd prefer to do a full assessment before prescribing more and I'd like you to see a counsellor.'

'Oh man, that'll take ages. I need those tablets.'

'Look, I'll issue you a two-week supply, but, in that time, you must have a follow-up consultation. I'd like to review where you're at and have a think about what else we can offer you. Does that sound fair?'

'Sure, Doc. Whatever.'

'Good. By then, the power will be back and I'll have access to your notes.'

Dean's eyebrows twitched. 'You mean, like all the stuff my old doctors have said?'

'Yes. Don't worry. It will be on the system. The only reason I can't see it today is… well… technology, eh? Great when it works.'

Dean sat back in his chair. 'Uh, yeah. I guess.'

Rick grinned. 'Apart from your tablets, are you looking after yourself? Making sure you eat a healthy diet and getting plenty of exercise?'

'Yeah, man. All of that.'

'Do you drink alcohol?'

'The odd pint at the weekend.'

'What about recreational drugs?'

Dean shifted in his seat, stretched and shook his head.

Rick jotted Dean's replies onto the Lloyd George form.

'Is that the prescription?'

'No,' said Rick, laughing. 'I'm making a record of what we've discussed. Normally, I'd type straight into your computer notes, but, for now, I'll use these instead and transfer the information later when the power is back.'

'Oh, right.'

Rick observed the young man. He was well presented, had no obvious signs of addiction and he'd produced evidence that he'd been prescribed the drug before. There was no reason not to issue a temporary script. Rick pulled a blank prescription form from the tray of the powerless printer and filled it in by hand. 'Take this to the chemist and, remember, you absolutely mustn't mix these tablets with any other drugs.'

'I said, I don't do drugs.' An exasperated edge had crept into Dean's tone.

'I believe you, but I have to say it. It's in the rules.' Rick signed the script and then added a sentence to the Lloyd

George record. 'Look, I've documented that I've warned you. If you just initial that to show you understand, then the script is yours.' Rick held out a pen.

Dean gave him a long stare, before taking the pen and placing a squiggle where Rick indicated.

*

The forest floor was uneven. Tree roots and ditches lay in wait, ready to trip anyone not paying attention, and Rick's leg was aching. He slowed his pace, forcing himself to pay more attention to his surroundings. Getting injured out here wasn't a good idea. But he couldn't stop thinking about what had happened in the weeks after that consultation.

GMC investigations were hell, but they were a necessary evil. Patients needed to know they were getting good care and a formal route for them to report concerns was essential. Even so, it was a nightmare process to go through as a doctor – relentless questions and the sensation that you were guilty until proven innocent. And he hadn't been proven innocent. Yet Rick knew in his heart that he hadn't made a mistake.

He hated getting things wrong. Acid burnt his stomach. *Why didn't they exonerate me?*

There was only one thing to do. Read that whole damn report. He stopped walking and squinted through the trees. Where exactly was he?

A long, mournful howl rose into the icy night air.

Rick shivered, his skin tightening under a thick crop of goosebumps. Convinced something was moving in his direction at speed – something big – he broke into a run. His foot caught on an exposed root. Suddenly, he was falling, the world spinning. He threw his arms up to protect his head and rolled down a steep slope, coming to a halt on a thick carpet of fallen twigs, moss and desiccated leaves. Gasping for air, he stared up at stars winking through bare branches that reached overhead.

Heavy panting sounded nearby. It was getting closer. Before he could regain his feet and escape... oomph... a solid weight landed on his middle, forcing what little breath he had left from his lungs. Expecting sharp teeth to descend any second, Rick opened his mouth to yell, but his cry was cut off when a rough, wet tongue rasped his cheek. The creature on top of him whined, gave an apologetic woof and snuffled at his ear.

Fending off slobber, Rick sat up and pushed the big dog off. 'Tiny?'

Tiny gave an answering whine, creeping back to lean against Rick.

'You scared me.'

The answering woof was subdued.

Rick slumped down onto his back with a short laugh. 'Are you lost, too? Never mind, stick with me and you'll be alright.' It was fairly sheltered where he'd landed and he didn't have the energy to get up. 'Let's stay here for a bit. I need to rest this leg.'

The dog wriggled closer and a waft of meaty canine breath mingled with the rich smell of fresh earth. Rick put an arm around the furry bundle and lay still, listening. Light rustles sounded from small, unseen creatures in the bushes and gentle gurgles suggested a nearby stream. An owl hooted way up high. Warmed by the dog, Rick forced himself to relax. To be nothing more than himself; an emotionally broken human, lying on a forest floor. Soon enough, he drifted off to sleep.

*

Something soft tickled Rick's cheek. It wasn't Tiny. The dog was on his other side. Staying very still, he opened his eyes and saw a big pair of twitchy pink-and-grey nostrils mere inches from his face. Behind the nostrils loomed a pair of large, brown eyes fringed by the longest eyelashes he'd ever seen. Beyond them was a mass of shaggy white fur and two long, banana-shaped ears that stood to attention.

The strange animal inspected Rick. Rick returned the favour. Tiny whined, lifted his head and wagged his tail in greeting. A noise sounded in the distance; the huge shaggy head pulled away and the creature was gone. Rick sat up, his back stiff from a night on the ground.

Did that really happen?

Tiny headbutted his chest for attention.

'Morning.' Rick rubbed the dog's ears.

The noise came again, closer. Someone was calling.

Rick scrambled to his feet. 'Reena?'

Reena's voice spilled down the slope before she came into view. 'Oh, thank goodness. I've been worried. I woke up and Tiny was gone.'

'I was lost. Tiny found me.' Rick brushed twigs off his sweatshirt.

Reena picked her way down the slope and clipped a lead to the dog's collar. 'I'm glad you're both alright.'

Rick looked around. The stream he'd heard the night before skipped through the sheltered hollow, edged by flat silver-grey boulders and gnarled oak trees with squat, knobbly brown trunks wrapped in dark layered skirts of green ivy. 'Where are we?'

'One of the oldest parts of the forest. Proper ancient, broadleaf woodland. Locals call it "King's Spring". Rumour has it, Charles II hid here after the Battle of Worcester, on the run from the Roundheads. Superstitious folk would have you believe the spirit of the forest kept him safe until he could escape to France.'

'Do you believe that?'

'Meh. It's a load of codswallop. Although, I can't dismiss it entirely.'

'It does feel kind of special.'

'Most folk don't take their eyes off their electronics long enough to see the true beauty of the forest. Like the fabled white stag. Now that's a sight to behold, I can tell you.' She turned to scramble back up the slope.

Rick hurried after her. 'I saw a white stag the day I arrived.'

'Did you, now? It's considered good luck, you know.'

'It stepped out in front of my car and damn nearly killed us both.'

'Then you're lucky to be alive, aren't you?'

Rick laughed. 'I can't argue with that.'

'Anyway, you said you were lost. Where do you need to be?'

'The barn on Old Farm Lane.'

'Charlie's old place? Are you a relative?'

'No, but my dad, Alan, was a friend of his.'

'Alan, yes. Gosh, I knew you looked familiar.'

'You knew my dad?'

'Of the two of them, I knew Charlie better. Such a big

character. Alan was quiet, more reserved. Poor Charlie was devastated when he died. But that was more than twenty-five years ago. You must have been young to lose your father. I'm so sorry.' Reena put a gentle hand on his arm. Then her manner changed, becoming brisk. 'I have to go past the barn on my way home. Come on. I'll show you the way.'

'Thanks.' Rick fell into step beside her.

'Are Beth and the kids helping you settle in?'

'Beth? The warri... I mean, the woman next door with the red hair?'

'That's the one,' said Reena. 'Look out for her, won't you? Only, don't say I said so. She's got a lot on her plate and refuses to ask for help.' Tiny whined. Reena patted the dog. 'Thanks for looking after my baby. She must have been terrified.'

Rick laughed. 'She wasn't the only one. I heard her chasing me and couldn't run fast enough. I thought I was a goner.'

Reena stopped and gave Rick a steady stare. 'It just goes to show that not everything we run from is as bad as we fear.'

Chapter 14

Beth stood by the Aga waiting for the kettle to boil, scrolling through local job adverts on her phone. Perhaps she should apply for an overnight shelf-stacking position at the supermarket. The kitchen door banged back against the wall.

Rose stalked in and pointed an accusing finger at her. 'You stole from me!'

'Pardon?'

'The guy from next door came over yesterday. Wanted to *thank*,' Rose made little bunny-ear speech marks in the air with her fingers around the word, 'you for the cakes you gave him.'

'Oh. I meant to say. He got so cranky about the cows. I thought one of us ought to behave like a grown-up.'

'You should've asked me.'

'About the cakes? There were so many, I didn't think you'd miss them.'

'They were mine.'

'From ingredients I paid for.'

'Don't be tight. You can afford it.'

'Can I?' *How come she thinks I'm made of money?* 'Rose, the grocery bill for this family is astronomical. Have you seen how much your brother eats?' Beth already bought budget brands for most things, secretly decanting stuff into high-end packaging in the utility room, banking on the fact that none of the children would ever go near the washing machine of their own accord.

'Stacy wanted four-dozen frosted cupcakes for The Coffee Pot,' Rose grumbled. 'I had to make another batch.'

'Why did Stacy want them?'

'Duh. To sell, of course.'

'Cakes you've made here?'

'Yeah.'

'I admire your initiative, but don't we need a licence for that? I mean for the kitchen.'

'It's only a few cakes. Why are you making such a big deal?'

'Rose, there are laws about selling food for public consump—'

'You see? There you go, moaning again. Dad would say I could.'

Beth gritted her teeth. With Jack as the only son and Daisy such a daddy's girl, Rose, with her quiet, sensible nature, had often been overlooked by Paul. Then she'd discovered the alluring power of butter, sugar and flour and things had changed. 'Well, your dad's not here, is he?'

'Because you've driven him away.'

'That's not fair. Anyway, if you listen to what I'm saying, you'll see I'm not actually telling you to stop.'

'Eh?'

'You're nineteen, Rose. If you want to sell cakes, go ahead. I bet you could sell to other outlets, too. You make amazing cakes. Only, do it properly. Get a licence. Don't get us fined or sued or whatever. We can't afford it.'

Rose levelled an unblinking stare at Beth. 'You really think I could sell to other shops, too?'

'Yes, but you'll have to start bulk buying your own ingredients and work the cost of them into your prices.'

Rose chewed on the inside of her cheek, deep in thought. 'If I apply for a licence, you need to sort that roof out – or else they'll never sign this place off.'

'I'm just about to call the roofer,' said Beth. 'And after that, I've got some fly-tipping to report before Mrs Trenchard finds out I haven't and puts a hit out on me.'

'Don't diss Aunty B. And don't give any more freebie cakes to, what's his face, the psycho next door.'

Beth tutted. 'You can't go around calling people psychos.'

'I can. You should see what's on X about him.'

'X?'

'Get with it. Twitter is now X.'

'Is it? Well, you know what I think about social media. You shouldn't make judgements about people based on a few random posts.'

'Watch this and then tell me I'm wrong.' Rose tapped at her phone and shoved it in front of Beth. 'He says it isn't him, but it is.'

'Oh.' The figure in the video, driving away from a hit-and-run, was the spitting image of Beth's Wolverine.

'See? Psycho. Anyway, I'm off to work. Laters.' Rose flounced from the room with the dramatic flair of a whole troop of Taylor Swift backing dancers.

Her mind in freefall from that video, Beth tried to remember what she'd been about to do. *Oh yes. The roof.*

Time to check that the money from the sale of those Merrill shares had arrived in the account. She logged into her account, frowned and then phoned the bank, getting straight to the point as soon as she was connected.

'Hello, yes, can I ask about a recent transaction, please? I can see that £10,000 arrived in my account, as expected, about an hour ago. The problem is it looks as though it went back out again, almost straight away. Is that a glitch?'

A flurry of keystrokes rattled down the line, before the man on the other end spoke, 'No glitch, madam. The money arrived at 11.39am but was transferred out again at 11.45am.'

Beth went cold all over. 'Transferred where?' But she knew where – or, at least, who. There was only one other person with access to the account.

More keystrokes and the bank teller confirmed her suspicions. 'It's gone to a savings account in the name of Paul Hope.'

'He can't do that. It's not his money.'

'This is a joint account, madam.'

'I know that, but—'

'This is a legitimate transaction. Mr Paul Hope is a named account holder.'

Blood buzzed in Beth's ears as she put the phone down.

She glanced at the time. She was late to pick up Grace. Grabbing her bag and keys, she hurried down to the village in a hazy fug of shock. It wasn't until they were on their way back, with Grace singing a less-than-musical version of "The Wheels on the Bus" from her booster seat in the back while kicking Beth's seat with enthusiasm but no rhythm, that the trembling started. Hot, fat tears welled in her eyes, making the world go wobbly.

Unable to see the road, Beth pulled into a lay-by to calm down and stared out of the windscreen at an old washing machine lying on its back with the door torn off its hinges.

Bastard. How had he known? Had he been watching the account? A shiver ran down her spine. *You stupid, stupid woman. You should have known better than to risk using an account he had access to.* A thought occurred to her. Perhaps he'd only married her for her inheritance in the first place. Well, it was all gone now. She was a fool for trusting him. Could she trust anyone? The Wolverine sprang to mind. What if Rose was right and he was a hit-and-run driver? He'd admitted that his life was falling apart the day they met. No matter how much her thoughts kept returning to him, she'd be a fool to trust him. The space around her heart hardened as if a defensive shell were forming. Stuff Paul. And stuff the Wolverine. He'd already put Jack at risk by scaring the cows. If that didn't show he could be careless with other people, then what did? She was better off without a man and always had been.

A wail rose up from the back seat of the car. 'Mummy, come on!'

Wiping her face on her sleeve, Beth squared her shoulders and restarted the engine. For the first time ever, she wondered how much more she could take.

Chapter 15

Rick was in the kitchen making coffee when he heard a car door slam. A flare of alarm shot through his chest like a nuclear warhead, setting his pulse racing. He peered out at the drive from behind half-closed curtains, sagging against the windowsill with relief when he saw the noise had come from next door.

A child skipped from a small blue car into the house. The driver stayed behind the wheel, slumped over, unmoving. Rick scratched his head. Perhaps he ought to check on them. Reena had said Beth was struggling.

He limped across the gravel and tapped on the driver's side window. 'Are you alright?'

The car door was thrust open, forcing him to jump back or be knocked over.

Beth leapt out, her eyes flashing sparks. 'What?'

'Umm…'

'Seriously. What do you want?'

Rick raised both palms in surrender. 'Hey, hey, calm down. I—'

'Don't "Hey, hey" me, buster. Who the hell do you think

you are, telling me to calm down?' She punctuated every word by ramming a pointy finger into Rick's chest. Her breath was coming in great heaves that rocked her tiny frame.

Retreating from the jabbing finger, Rick stumbled, his left thigh muscle going into spasm and throwing him off balance.

'Are you drunk?' she demanded.

'No.' Outraged at the suggestion, Rick drew himself up to his full height. 'It's barely lunchtime.'

'Oh, so it's okay to be drunk by supper, is it?'

'What? No, I… Look—'

'No, you look. I've had it up to here, see?' She jerked her hand up, pointing to the top of her head. 'With men. Men like you. Men like Paul, taking stuff from me.'

'Paul?'

'Taking money I don't have. Wanting things I can't give. There's nothing left, see? It's all gone. So, whatever it is you want from me, you can't have it.'

'I don't want anything.' That wasn't true. For some strange reason, Rick wanted to pull her into his arms and hold her close. To tell her that everything would be alright. That whatever she needed, he would find it for her, no matter what it was, what it cost or how far he had to go.

A flurry of agitated barks heralded an elderly terrier, who lumbered out of the farmhouse door towards them. The young woman he'd upset the day before called the dog to heel. She stalked up to Rick, hands on hips, her eyes bouncing from him to Beth.

'What's going on?' she demanded. The dog wheezed and sneezed, before parking his bum on the girl's foot and leaning against her, panting hard. 'Beth? What did he do to you?'

'Rose, I—'

Rick stepped back again. 'I didn't do anything.'

Rose rounded on him. 'You must have done something.'

The dog growled in agreement.

'I only asked her if she was alright.' To his horror, he heard Beth sob and turned to see her face crumple.

'Nothing's bloody alright. It's all a big, fat mess,' she whispered, dashing a sleeve across her face before glaring at Rick. 'And you should be ashamed of yourself… putting people at risk. He's only young. I can't believe that you'd be so… so… thoughtless.'

Rick blinked. 'I'm sorry?'

'So you should be. He could have died. You don't seem to care. I shouldn't be surprised. I've seen what you're capable of. That video… You're reckless and… and… Oh!' Beth turned on her heels and ran into the house.

Rose followed Beth. The terrier gave him a menacing stare before padding after them.

Rick rocked back on his heels. She'd said, 'He could have died.'

She must mean Dean.

So much for Gita's brilliant "escape to the country and lie low" plan. And so much for Barbara Trenchard telling him the locals wouldn't give him any trouble. And as for Reena telling him to look out for Beth – fat chance of that happening.

Reena was wrong about something else, too. The things you run from in life *are* as bad as you fear. Given how hostile Beth and Rose were, how long would it be before they sold him out to the paparazzi and this little idyllic hideout of his was overrun? Images of swarming journalists crowded into his mind faster than he could push them out. He raced back to the barn, frantically working though his options.

Should I go somewhere else? But where? And would it make any difference?

If people in a remote community like this knew who he was, everyone would know, everywhere. It was only a matter of time before this happened again. He hurried to the window to double check no one was lurking on the driveway and yanked the curtains closed. With a few unsteady paces to the sofa, he sank into the saggy cushions next to Boo, his limbs trembling.

Think, damn it. Think.

A strange calm descended. It was pointless running. There was nowhere to go. He'd cope. He'd have to. If the paps were on the way, he needed to be as resilient as possible. To do that, he needed to look after himself. The irony wasn't lost on him. He'd spent his whole life telling other people how to look after themselves. And all that time, he had worked too many hours, hadn't taken any holidays and had eaten whatever junk food he could grab on the way home after a late-night surgery.

Ha! No wonder I'm a mess.

He'd have to start with the basics. Try to relax, eat some decent food, get some sleep and do some exercise. If he did, perhaps he could survive whatever was coming.

Rick dug the pieces of his phone from the kitchen drawer and reassembled them. He sent a text to Barbara requesting a list of healthy groceries, then browsed through a few budget clothing websites. He only had a couple of outfits; he could do with some more some walking boots at the very least. Plus, he needed a razor. No point looking like the wild man of the woods if he was going to have his photo splashed everywhere again. If he looked like he'd lost the plot, it wouldn't help his credibility in court. He placed an online order of non-food essentials and requested that they be delivered to the village store. As he did this, his phone beeped with multiple incoming messages. He ignored them all and then dismantled the phone again. No point making it too easy for the bastards to find him.

Right. Next step. Read that GMC report. All of it.

He needed to understand. He paused and rubbed the back of his neck. He should probably send an email to David, too. It wasn't fair not to let his son know what was going on. He wasn't going to dump all his problems on him, just let him know that he was taking a break from work and that he was fine. Problem was, what to say? Sighing, he reached for his laptop.

Read the report first. Worry about David later.

Rick downloaded the report and started reading. Half an hour later, he got up to switch on the kettle and stare out of the kitchen window. Then, he took a strong cup of coffee back to the sofa, where he scrolled through the whole document again to re-read the final section.

In conclusion, this investigation finds that Dr Mahon acted in good faith when prescribing anti-anxiety medication to Dean Markwell. The recommended course of treatment was appropriate to the history presented.

Vindication of a sort.

He'd known the medication was correct.

But it wasn't enough for exoneration.

He thought back to the lengthy grilling he'd had from the harassed GMC examiner. That was soon after the initial investigation had been launched, but before the wider story connecting Rick to Dean had gone viral. Before Cora Diamond, Sal and Ade, and #DrDeath.

Remembering the GMC inquiry process made him flinch. He'd been interrogated down to minutiae and, medicine aside, the process had revealed that Rick had made one mistake. Not a huge one in the grand scheme, but still a mistake. And his only defence was unprecedented circumstances.

Pathetic.

In his mind's eye, he could see the GMC examiner sat in his consulting room in the same chair Dean had used. He remembered the man's white handkerchief that he had mopped his brow with and then tucked back into his inside pocket. It was as if it were playing out in front of him right now.

*

'You're saying that as a result of an unexpected power cut, you were forced to take handwritten notes of the consultation. Is that right?' the examiner lisped.

'Yes,' replied Rick.

'Dr Mahon, why didn't you transfer these notes onto the computer the instant power was restored?'

'By the time the system was back up and running, all of the paper records I had for Dean were missing,' said Rick. 'Both the temporary resident form and the notes I'd made.'

'Missing how?'

'Right at the end of the consultation, we were interrupted by Sam Maddoc—'

'Your head of reception?'

'Yes.'

'Why?'

'A patient, Mr Shah, had collapsed in the waiting room. I grabbed the defib and ran to help. When I got back, the power was back on, but my notes were gone.'

'You're saying confidential patient information just disappeared?'

Rick shrugged. 'That's what happened.' He shifted in his seat and lowered his voice. 'I can only assume Dean took them.'

The examiner frowned and made a note on his clipboard. 'That's quite an accusation.'

'Perhaps he didn't realise they were supposed to stay with me.'

'What you're saying is that you allowed a patient unsupervised time in your consulting room, aren't you?'

'But I—'

'You gave a patient free access to a printer tray full of blank scripts, which goes against all best practice guidelines.'

'I was dealing with an emergency. And, anyway, he didn't take any blank scripts. They have all been accounted for.'

'It doesn't matter. It's your responsibility to keep your consultation space secure.'

Beads of sweat formed on Rick's brow. 'I know, but I thought he was right behind me. And if I'd taken the time to see him out of the room ahead of me and Mr Shah had died as a result of the delay – which he genuinely might have, and in full view of a waiting room full of patients – that would be wrong, too, wouldn't it?'

'I don't make the rules.'

Rick slumped back in his chair. 'I couldn't win, either way.'

'It's not about winning. It's about finding the truth.'

'The truth is, I did my best. I've always done my best for my patients, but it isn't enough.'

The examiner sucked his teeth and made more notes. 'Were you aware at the time of the consultation that Dean Markwell had a well-known history of drug dependency?'

'I had no idea. I made my judgement call based on the facts as they were presented to me. And I stand by that decision. Dean denied taking drugs. I specifically warned him about the dangers of mixing that particular prescription medication with anything. I even asked him to initial where I'd written in my notes to confirm that he understood the warning.'

'Why did you do that?'

'Because it rams the message home to patients that I'm not kidding around about side effects. I always did it before everything went digital. It was second nature to fall back into old habits on a paper record.'

The examiner sniffed. 'What did you do after you realised the paperwork was missing?'

'There wasn't much I could do. Without Dean's personal details – his address, date of birth, etc. – I had no way of looking him up on the system. I couldn't be certain I had the right person. It turns out there are a lot of Dean Markwells about the same age out there.'

The examiner whipped out his hanky again, blotted more shine from his pate and stayed silent.

'I told our reception team that a Dean Markwell was

supposed to come back for a full assessment of his condition and that we needed to make sure we registered him properly.' Rick's shoulders slumped. 'But he never came. A week later, I saw his picture in the papers and found out that he'd overdosed.'

'The problem is, Dr Mahon, without a proper record of the consultation, we can't know for sure what did or didn't happen.' The examiner pursed his lips and wrote furiously on his clipboard. 'And, of course, in his current condition, we can't ask Dean.'

*

Coming back to the present, Rick groaned at the memory. Pushing it and the accompanying nausea aside, he forced himself to read the rest of the report's concluding paragraphs.

It is reasonable to assume that, as he claims, Dr Mahon did follow NICE guidelines and warn his patient about the lethal complications that might result if the medication prescribed was mixed with other drugs. However, as the consultation documentation is not available, this cannot be proved. We recommend Dr Mahon receives a warning and undertakes additional training with regard to documentation and confidentiality.

Rick gave a bitter laugh.

It sounded innocuous. It wasn't. He would willingly undertake whatever retraining they recommended. Yet the unfairness of the whole situation stuck in his craw. Talk about a rock and a hard place. He was damned either way. Yes, he shouldn't have rushed ahead of Dean, should have taken the time to escort him out of the consultation room, but then Mr Shah…

Head pounding with suppressed rage, Rick pushed the laptop aside and struggled to his feet. He had to find something else to think about. His gaze lit on Charlie's belongings dotted around the room. Clearing stuff out would be a good distraction. Much better than sitting around obsessing about things he couldn't change, mooning over the woman next door and wondering when the paps would arrive.

He opened the unit under the television set and immediately wished he hadn't. A tower of dusty VHS tapes tumbled onto the carpet.

Great! Obsolete technology from the eighties.

Stifling a sneeze, he grabbed a black sack from the kitchen and started chucking things in. Then, something caught his eye and he paused.

Surely not?

He hauled the box from the back of the cupboard out into the light. A surge of nostalgia warmed his belly. A Sinclair ZX Spectrum. Who'd have thought? The exact same model his dad had brought on all those weekend access visits. Games, too. Not discs; original reel to reel tapes – "Jetpac", "Horace Goes Skiing", "Manic Miner". *I had all of these when I was a kid. Talk about a blast from the past. Hang on a minute. No way.* Rick grabbed "Horace Goes Skiing" and looked at the back. That pen mark… The scratch on the case. He picked up the console, turning it this way and that. Yes. That dent, too. From when he'd dropped it that time, when he was about thirteen, trying to set it up. *Bloody hell, this is Dad's old machine. What the hell is it doing here?* Even the cassette player that plugged into the console, with the scrappy bit of masking tape on the cable, was there.

So many things about the barn that didn't make sense collided together in his head. Why was that picture of Rick with his parents here in Charlie's house? Why had Reena talked about "Charlie and Alan" as if they were a pair. She'd said Alan was the quieter of the two and... Rick got to his feet. Ouch! Pins and needles. He hobbled over to the bookcase where there was another framed photo. This one was of Dad and Charlie, each with an arm around the other's shoulders, beaming at the camera. A pair. A happy pair. Partners.

Rick wiped the dust from the glass with his sleeve. He'd been too busy feeling sorry for himself to see what was under his nose. It explained so much. The divorce. Mum's bitterness.

I wish he had told me.

Rick had always thought of his dad as alone, lonely even, but it wasn't true. With infinite care, he placed the frame back down and smiled. The barn didn't feel like a stranger's home anymore.

He returned to the console. After all these years, would it still work? He plugged the wires into the back of Charlie's... no... Dad and Charlie's ancient telly. Then, he inserted a game into the tape deck. A blast of opening music made him grin so wide his cheeks ached.

What are the chances of that?

Dad had always said life was full of surprises. Pulling some cushions off the sofa, Rick settled down to some virtual skiing – with Horace.

Chapter 16

Beth blasted into the kitchen. She stomped up and down the quarry tiles, hands clenched into tight fists, anger crawling through her veins like fire ants.

Rose was right on her heels. 'Beth? What's going on?'

'Nothing. I'm fine... I'm... I'm just cross with him.'

'Why?'

'For putting Jack in danger.'

'It's more than that.'

'It's... it's...'

Rose pulled out chair. 'Sit. I'll make you some tea.'

Beth sank onto the chair, arms folded, chin down. The sound of the kettle being filled and the clattering of mugs washed over her. A cup of tea arrived on the table and, to her surprise, a gentle hand squeezed her shoulder. Covering the hand with one of her own, she gulped and, against all insistent internal instructions to the contrary, her face crumpled.

Rose tutted. 'Oh, for goodness' sake.' She wrapped an arm around Beth's shoulders and pulled her close, murmuring the same sort of nonsensical nothings that usually soothed a tearful Grace. Stunned, Beth blinked furiously and dashed at her face with her free hand. Paddy sidled up and plonked his bony bottom on her foot in a rare display of solidarity. He'd never done that before.

Rose patted her shoulder one more time. 'Right. Stop crying. Here.' She placed a triple chocolate muffin on the table. Grabbing one for herself, she took a huge bite and sat down opposite. 'Come on. Spill. You don't usually lose your shit like this. Not even when Daisy's being totally rank.'

She scrubbed at her eyes with a manky tissue from her pocket. 'It's nothing.'

'Don't gimme that. You're usually all nicey-nicey and "let's give everyone the benefit of the doubt". Then, all of a sudden, you're giving him next door what for.' She gave a wicked little snicker. 'Both barrels and then some. Poor sod. The look on his face.'

Beth groaned. 'I'm going to have to apologise, aren't I?'

'Uh, you think?' Rose's words dripped sarcasm, but they weren't accompanied by the usual look of disgust for her that Beth had come to expect. 'So, go on,' the teen prompted. 'Why'd you flip out?'

What should I say? She couldn't tell Rose about the money. 'It was that video you showed me, of him running that woman down—'

'Nah, ah, ah. Don't give me that. You hate social media. No way would you go for him over something like that. And, anyway, I didn't mean it when I called him a psycho, I was just ranting. No. You've been off your game for, like, ages. 'Fess up, Beth. What's going on?'

Beth hesitated. Rose always got super-defensive when the subject of her father came up. 'I'm worried about money.'

'Why?'

Beth rolled her sodden tissue into a ball. 'I can't afford to fix the roof. I thought I could, but I can't. And if I don't fix it, the builder said the leak will do serious damage to that wall.' She nodded towards the doorway with the bucket.

'Well, speak to Dad. I mean… look, whatever's going on between you two, he won't want the house falling down. He can send you extra. On top of whatever regular maintenance he's sending, I mean. He must be earning a packet and—'

'I haven't received a penny from your dad since he left.'

The words fell into a puddle of shocked silence.

Rose shook her head. 'Don't be daft. Of course he sends money. Look.' She jumped up and rummaged through the postcards on the Welsh dresser. 'This one, no… no… this one. He says he got a promotion. See?' She waved the card, pointing at the irregular capital letters that were so typical of her father's erratic handwriting. 'Even if he can't be here, he wouldn't not send money.' Her voice cracked. 'What are you spending it all on?'

Beth didn't have the energy to pretend anymore. Fed up with constantly getting the blame for things that weren't her fault, she dug inside her handbag, right to the bottom, to the little hidden pocket, and pulled out a crumpled envelope.

'Dad's handwriting.' Rose snatched it and tore the contents from the envelope. 'It's dated six months ago. Oh my God! How could you keep this from us?'

'Just read it.' Beth stared down at her hands, picked at her thumbnail and waited.

The cuckoo clock ticked away in the otherwise silent kitchen. Beth didn't need to look at the paper to know what Rose was seeing. She'd read it herself, thousands of times.

BETH,

BY THE TIME YOU READ THIS YOU'LL KNOW I'M NOT COMING BACK.

WE WERE A MISTAKE FROM THE START.

I DON'T LOVE YOU

I LOVE ISLA. I ALWAYS WILL.

ROSE, DAISY AND JACK REMIND ME THAT SHE'S GONE. I CAN'T STAND IT.

I'M GOING AWAY. TO TRY TO BE HAPPY SOMEWHERE ELSE.

A LEGAL FIRM WILL SEND YOU A DOCUMENT TO SIGN THAT TRANSFERS OWNERSHIP OF THE FARMHOUSE TO YOU. IT'LL BE EASIER FOR YOU TO LOOK AFTER THE KIDS, IF YOU OWN THE PROPERTY OUTRIGHT.

DIVORCE ME.

UNDER THE NEW NO FAULT DIVORCE RULES, YOU NEED TO PROVE OUR RELATIONSHIP HAS IRRETRIEVABLY BROKEN DOWN.

USE THIS LETTER AND THE FACT THAT I DISAPPEARED WITH NO WARNING AS PROOF. IT GIVES YOU ALL THE GROUNDS YOU'LL NEED.

YOU WON'T HEAR FROM ME AGAIN.

PAUL

Typical bloody Paul, getting all legal with a goodbye letter. He didn't have the guts to stay and help manage the emotional fallout his decision had caused. *Selfish git.*

Rose's eyes grew big and round. 'It wasn't you that drove him away. It was us.'

'No, Rose, no, no, no. Sweetheart, you mustn't think

that. That's why I didn't show you this. I was afraid you'd think that, but it isn't true.'

'It's what he says.' Rose's voice was barely more than a whisper.

'Your dad can't have been well when he wrote this. Grief does strange things to people.'

'He's not coming back.'

Beth dabbed at her eyes and sniffed. 'No, I don't think he is.'

'And the postcards?'

'I sent them. If you look closely, the writing's a good copy but it doesn't quite match.'

Rose frowned, looking from the letter to the back of the postcard. 'But why? And how?'

'Remember how upset Daisy was, just after your dad left.'

Rose nodded, her face pale.

'I thought if she heard from him, it would help. I know people working abroad – it was easy enough to call in some favours. I send the cards out already written. They put a foreign stamp on and sent them back in the next post. I only meant to send the one. But it made her smile and I got carried away. I don't know how to stop. If… no… when she finds out, she'll hate me even more than she does already.'

'Don't tell her.'

Beth couldn't tell what was going on behind Rose's rigid expression. 'What do you mean?'

'I'm not saying I believe you, but if there's no money and the roof is as bad as you say it is, then we've got bigger problems on our plate. Daisy having a tantrum isn't going to help.'

Beth tipped her head to one side. 'So, you're saying I should focus on the roof first.'

'Yeah. We can deal with her and this,' she pointed to the postcard and letter, 'later.'

A little voice in Beth's heart sang out on hearing, 'We'.

Rose crossed her arms and gave Beth a calculating look. 'You must wish you'd never come here.'

'No, I don't. Honestly. I always wanted to be part of a big family.'

'You should have got married younger. Had lots of your own kids.'

A painful lump swelled in Beth's throat. No matter what she did, Rose, Daisy and Jack would never see her as a mother. Struggling to keep her tone light, she said, 'I tried. I was engaged once for nearly ten years.'

'No way.'

Beth smiled at the memory. 'Trent. I adored him. He was a musician. He played guitar in a band.' She sighed. 'There was always some big opportunity for the band on the horizon and the wedding kept being put off and… well, let's just say, it didn't end well.'

'How come?'

'He was a heavy smoker. As a way to wind down after gigs, you know? Only, it wasn't just cigarettes. He moved onto weed, lots and lots of weed, and then stronger stuff. Everything kind of went downhill from there. Eventually, he cheated on me with someone I thought was a friend.'

'Sounds like a right plonker.'

A gurgle of laughter took Beth by surprise. 'He was.'

'You're better off without him.'

'Maybe. A few years later, he discovered clean living.

He married a woman decades younger than himself, had a couple of babies and now posts nauseating pictures of his perfect family all over social media.'

'Is that why you're anti-social media?'

Beth nodded. 'And smoking. And drugs. The whole thing put me off relationships for ages, too, but then I fell for your dad and decided to give love another chance. Soppy cow that I am. The fact that he came with a ready-made family was the icing on the cake for me.'

'Yeah, right!' Rose snorted.

'I mean it.'

'I don't see why anyone would want someone else's kids,' Rose muttered.

'Well, my stepmother is amazing and—'

'You haven't got a stepmother.'

The look on Rose's face made Beth laugh. 'I have. You met her at the wedding. She came over from Australia with Sophie?'

'No. I met your mother, Isabella.'

'Isabella is my stepmother.'

Rose's jaw hung open, 'So, your real mum's…'

'My biological mother died when I was about the same age you were when…' Beth's eyes drifted to the photo of Isla on the dresser. 'Well, anyway, Isabella married my dad a few years later.'

'Oh, so Sophie is…'

'My half-sister.'

'Like Grace is to me. How did I not know this?'

'We don't do the half thing or the step thing. We're just family.'

'That's nice.' Rose tucked Paul's letter back into the envelope and slid it back across the table towards Beth.

'You'd better put that away. Are you sure you've not had anything else from him?'

Beth shook her head.

'No communication at all?' Rose suddenly stiffened as if a terrible thought had scampered through her mind. 'What if he's dead? Like Mum.'

'No. Please don't worry. He's alive. I've got proof. Sort of. Look, let me show you.' Beth reached for her laptop. She searched up her bank statement. 'See there? I sold the last of the shares my grandad left me to pay for the roof and that's the money arriving in the account. But six minutes later, it's gone.'

Rose squinted at the screen. 'I don't understand.'

'The money was transferred out again. And not by me,' said Beth. 'The only person who could have done that is Paul. This is a joint account and he's the only other person with access. The bank has confirmed that it went to another account in your dad's name.'

'So, you're saying he, like, stole it?'

'Well... um...'

There was a long silence.

Rose ran the tip of one bright-pink acrylic nail along the grain of the wood on the tabletop and scowled.

'What are you thinking, Rose?'

When she spoke, her voice was thick and wobbly. 'It's one thing to think that he's not well and needs to be away from us, but for him to steal from us, to actively make life harder... put us in danger?' She wiped her eyes, got to her feet, grabbed a jacket from the back of her chair.

Beth stood up. 'Where are you going?'

'Out.'

'Rose. Please, I—'

'Let it go, yeah? I need to think.'

The back door slammed.

Hot needles prickled at the back of Beth's eyes. She watched through the kitchen window as Rose jumped the stile at the bottom of the garden and disappeared into the forest.

Thank heaven I didn't tell her what else you've done, Paul. Wherever you are, I've never hated you more than I do right now.

Chapter 17

Daisy sawed her toast and marmite in half, making the kitchen table shake and tea threaten to slop over the rim of her mug. Her lip curled as she muttered, 'Sending kids out to work isn't legal. It's not Victorian bloody England anymore, is it?'

'It was only a suggestion,' said Beth, 'and watch your language.' Fortunately, Grace was busy chatting to her unicorn and tearing toast into little pieces to sneak under the table for Paddy and wasn't listening.

Beth squinted as she tried to force the blade of the kitchen scissors into the tiny stitches on the hem of Jack's school trousers. 'Oh, for goodness' sake! It shouldn't be this difficult to let down a hem. Ah, there, got it.' She snipped, releasing the fabric. 'There, Jack. That'll do for now, but try not to grow any more. These need to last until half term, at least.'

Jack's mountain of muesli was high enough to rival the Alps. He looked up and removed an earbud. 'What?'

Daisy huffed. 'There'll be proper stitch removers in that craft shop you're so fond of.'

'No doubt, but that'd cost money.'

'Don't be so tight,' muttered Daisy.

'Give it a rest, Dais,' said Rose, stacking plates into the dishwasher. 'Jack, thank Beth for sorting your trousers and go get dressed.'

Beth froze. Rose had never backed her up in a dispute with the younger children before.

'Eh? Lemme finish eating first.' Jack stuffed in a loaded spoonful and milk dribbled down his chin.

'Do you ever finish?' asked Rose, light exasperation in her voice, making Beth duck her head to hide a smile.

Daisy leaned towards her brother. 'Did you hear, J?'

'Hear what?'

'She,' Daisy pointed at Beth, 'wants me to get a job.'

Jack raised an eyebrow. 'Doing what?'

'Craft shop in the village.' Daisy got up to throw her uneaten toast in the bin.

Beth rummaged through the basket of clean underwear on the kitchen counter, looking for Grace's second pink sock. 'I just thought you might be interested. Forget I spoke.'

Jack leaned back, making his chair creak. 'But, Dais, I thought you liked all that crafty cra... um, I mean... well, don't you?'

'That's not the point. Mum would never say I had to get a job.'

'Be fair. I didn't say you had to—'

'She'll be sending Grace up chimneys next.' Daisy waved at the ornate brickwork over the Aga.

Grace examined the chimney breast with interest.

'No, I—' Beth shut her eyes and counted to ten.

Rose leaned both hands on the back of a kitchen chair. 'We've no idea what Mum would or wouldn't do. She might think a craft job would work well with your art and textiles A levels.'

'No one gets it, do they?' Daisy huffed. She slammed her plate down and left the room. Grace scrambled to follow, her unicorn under one arm. Paddy glowered at Beth before dashing after them both.

'Great,' said Jack, scraping his chair back from the table as he stood up. 'Well done. Now she'll be a pain in the butt all day.'

'That, brother dear,' muttered Rose, 'is the least of our problems.'

'What do you mean?'

'Nothing.'

'No, go on; out with it,' insisted Jack.

Beth's eyes flew to meet Rose's.

'Sorry,' Rose mouthed, giving a small shrug.

Jack put his phone away. 'What's going on?'

'Money is a bit tight,' said Beth, her voice low.

He frowned. 'How tight?'

'Very tight. I'm spending this morning putting up that second-hand polytunnel I got from the free ads. Growing more veggies will cut down the food bill.' Beth tried to sound jokey, but her voice shook. 'I just have to figure out how to rebuild the damn thing without any instructions.'

'Veggies? That's what this is about?'

'It's more than that.' Rose dried her hands on a tea towel and threw it on the table. 'It's like this. Dad—'

'Rose, no.' Beth shook her head. 'Please.'

'It's been going around and around my head all night.

If what you said yesterday is true, then we need to face this together. We agreed not to tell Daisy, yeah, and I get that, but Jack's different. He's solid. We should tell him.'

Jack growled in exasperation. 'Tell me what?'

Beth sank into a chair. 'Fine.'

'Here's the thing, Jack. Dad isn't working abroad for a charity.'

'Tell me something I don't know. I'm not stupid. What's he up to then?'

'He's left us. Like, for good. He's not coming back.'

Jack blinked. He looked at Beth. She could see the exact moment he put two and two together. 'You're sending the postcards, aren't you?'

Beth nudged a toast crumb along the table with one finger.

Jack gave a low whistle. 'Fucking hell. I knew they were hinky. How? No, scratch that. Why?'

'Thing is,' said Rose. 'Dad hasn't just not been sending postcards. He hasn't sent any money, either.'

Jack's mouth hung open. 'What? You're kidding. No way!'

'We've been living off money I inherited,' said Beth. 'Plus, a bit from whatever online work I've been able to scare up. It was enough to cover the basics.'

'I don't believe you.'

'Show him the letter, Beth.'

'No. I don't want to read any fucking letter. You're making this up.'

'I'm not, I promise I'm not.' Beth's heart started to thump. It was hard to swallow.

'Dad stole the money that Beth had ready for the roof and—'

'No! No. Stop it, just stop.' Jack slammed both hands down onto the table, making both Beth and Rose jump. 'Fuck's sake!' He spun on his heel, his shoulders set, and stalked from the room.

Rose's shoulders slumped. 'I'm sorry. I thought he'd handle it better.'

Beth got to her feet and put a tentative arm around Rose, fully expecting her to shrug it off – surprised when she didn't. 'It's fine. You're right. He needs to know. The question is, will he tell Daisy?'

'I hope not. She'll go off the deep end.'

'We'll have to tell her some time. You're right about facing this together. Let's give Jack some time to process things. Hopefully he'll come around.' Beth went over to look out of the window. 'I was going to ask him to take the llampaccas back over to the barn after school. It's one thing taking them in when there is no one to care for them, but it's another to keep paying for someone else's animals. We can't afford it anymore.'

Rose joined her at the window. 'Let me do the school run this morning. I could have a chat with him. Not about Dad. About the herd.'

'Would you? He'll listen to you over me any day. Warn him to be careful of the guy next door, though. I… I don't know what to think about him. And after I yelled at him, yesterday, a little distance might be a good thing.'

'Sure. Anyway, listen. I had an idea. What about renting space in the field for camping? Lots of places do it. I saw some stuff on Freecycle, old tents and the like. We could charge more if we offer facilities. Look.' She took out her phone and scrolled to images of tents.

'You mean, this is all free?'

Rose nodded. 'Stuff gets abandoned after festivals and things. You just go and pick it up before someone else does.'

'That's not a bad idea. Let me think about it.'

Rose grabbed the car keys from the side and called down the hall. 'Time to go, you lot. Big sis is in charge of the school run, today. Get your lazy butts in the car. Grace, lose the wings. You know how Mrs Fintan feels about fairies.'

'Oh, ship!' muttered a small voice.

Beth followed the direction of the voice to the alcove under the stairs, where Grace was trying, and failing, to do her shoelaces. 'Grace Louise Hope, did you just curse?'

Grace, all wide-eyed innocence, said, 'I only said "ship". You say "ship" all the time.'

'I don't.'

'You do,' insisted Grace. 'You say "shipshipshipshipship".'

Daisy stomped past. 'Nah, Grace. She's not saying "ship". She's saying "shi—"'

'Daisy!'

'Alright, alright. Keep your hair on.' Daisy stomped outside, muttering what sounded suspiciously like, 'Stupid cow!'

'Fine,' said Grace. 'I'll say "bucket", instead. Like Jack. "Bucketbucketbucket".'

Beth squatted down, leaning into the small space to help tie Grace's laces. 'Please don't. No ships and no buckets. Especially not with Mrs Fintan or the children at preschool… or anyone. Promise?'

'Whatever.' Grace rolled her eyes and made her way out to the car.

Jack barged past, refusing to look at Beth.

Rose gave her a reassuring smile. 'He'll come around.'

But what if he doesn't?

Chapter 18

Standing at the side of the road in the bright morning sunshine, Rick stared at an olive-green bath, a broken shower door, rusting pipework and shattered tiles. They weren't there when he'd left the barn for a walk. Yet now, on his return, here they were. It just showed what a city mentality he had that when he thought of the country, he pictured green fields and neat hedgerows, not fly-tipped bathroom suites chucked in ditches.

Puzzled, but not unduly concerned, he walked on. There was a spring in his step that had been missing for quite some time. An afternoon spent playing video games followed by a long walk in the fresh air had done him some good. Hence, he was out again today. Perhaps Gita had a point about him needing a holiday. He wouldn't go so far as to say that he was feeling positive about his situation, but the heavy shroud of desperation had lifted a fraction. Things were still dire. And they were going to get worse. But the GMC hadn't struck him off. And his medical decisions had been deemed sound. He would focus on those two pieces of good news and deal with the other crap later.

A rhythmic thumping, interspersed with a lot of cursing

coming from the front garden of the farmhouse, caught his attention. Peering through the beech hedge, he could see Beth wielding a sledgehammer.

Thump.

Thump, thump.

Thump.

She paused for breath, wiping a forearm across her brow.

Thump, thump.

Then she said something unintelligible and swung the sledgehammer again, slamming it down onto a metal pole.

Thump.

Rick was about to leave her to it, when she yelled, 'Stupid bloody thing. Just go in, damn you.' She swung the hammer even higher, bringing it down with a force that had minimal effect on the anchor but maximum impact on the tool itself. The shaft splintered and the hammer head bounced off, straight through the side of the greenhouse.

Broken glass tinkled to the ground.

'Oh no.' Beth dropped the remains of the handle and covered her face with her hands. 'Please no. No, no, no, no, no.' Her shoulders started to shake.

Rick stood rooted to the spot. No way was he risking another shouty encounter. He'd only just recovered from the last one. But... his warrior queen was crying. He hated people getting upset. Seeing Beth cry tore at his heart.

A grey donkey ambled over and nudged her in the stomach until she dropped her hands.

'Pablo!' she said, between sniffs. 'You're supposed to be out the back.' Wiping the heel of one hand across her eyes, she dragged out a hankie and blew her nose, before fondling the donkey's ears.

'Know what, Pablo?' she said, slinging an arm around the animal's neck. 'Daisy's right, I am a stupid cow. But don't tell her I said so. And poor Jack. What must he be thinking?' She waved a hand at the metal post. 'I don't know what to do. If I can't even put this stupid thing together, how can I sort anything else?' She released the donkey. 'Maybe I should just give up.'

Rick watched Beth and the donkey disappear together around the side of the house.

She sounded utterly defeated, a million miles from the impressive, if scary, woman he'd seen on previous occasions. The impulse to help her was overwhelming, even though she'd been so angry with him. It would be sensible to keep his head down. But where Beth was concerned, Rick didn't want to be sensible. He squinted through the hedge. *What exactly is she doing anyway?* Squeezing through a small gap, he went over for a closer look. *Interesting. Looks simple enough. Like a big 3D jigsaw.* He pulled out the anchor that had given Beth so much trouble. He re-sited it several inches to the left, where the ground wasn't so solid, and went in search of some sort of mallet from Beth's shed to drive it into place. He found other useful tools there, too, and, within half an hour, had almost completely assembled the plastic tunnel. There was one small section remaining. An essential piece of equipment was missing, but there might be something he could adapt to fit in one of Charlie's many sheds. He forced his way back through the hedge and jogged down the track, surprised to see a tractor and small trailer parked across the entrance to his drive.

Beth was leaning on a gatepost, watching a short, wiry man unload hay bales to form a wall that completely blocked

Rick's car in. A wave of panic crawled up Rick's chest. If reporters arrived, he might have to make a run for it. He needed his car. The tractor engine roared back to life and the wiry man gave Beth a cheerful wave before steering the vast machine down the track towards Rick.

'Wait. Stop.' Rick flapped an arm to get the driver's attention.

The man's crumpled, weather-beaten face broke into a broad grin. He waved back but didn't stop.

Blast.

Beth spotted him running towards her and took a step towards him. 'Hi. Listen, I wanted to apolo—'

'You can't leave that there,' Rick gasped, pointing at the hay.

'Oh, that's not for me.'

'Well, it's not mine, is it? And it's blocking my car in.'

Beth's face fell. 'Do you need your car, right this minute?'

'No, but… If it's not yours and it's not mine, why is it here? Oh!' A large, brightly coloured bird glided in to land on the fence near Rick's hand. Not terribly comfortable around large birds having been dive-bombed as a child by a seagull after his ice cream, he took a hasty step back. 'What the—?'

'I can ask Jack to move it when he gets home.'

'So, it *is* yours, I… Oh heck!' He jumped as two more birds landed near his feet.

'They're only pheasants. They won't hurt you. And, for the record, the hay is definitely yours. It's for the llampaccas. Grass isn't enough this time of year. It needs supplementing. They need saltlicks, too.'

What was she taking about? More birds back-winged overhead, dropping like fat, feathered missiles, followed by a dozen more. The air filled with squawks and fluttering. Having landed, each bird shook tail and wing feathers into place and set about pecking at the ground. Rick stared at them in amazement. 'What on earth is going on?'

'It is the final shoot.'

'The final shoot? I don't understand.'

'The final pheasant shoot of the season.'

'And...?'

'It's like this. The majority of the land around here, apart from yours and mine, is part of Lord Astley's estate. His staff run shooting parties throughout the autumn and early winter months. But the guns can only legally aim for birds that are on or over estate land.'

'Are you telling me these birds are here because they know they won't be shot?'

She gave him the sort of smile a teacher might give a dim-witted student who had finally understood something. 'Pretty much. I know it sounds far-fetched, but I'm telling you, that's what's going on here. Please don't stress. They'll all disappear as soon as the shoot is over.'

'This place is insane.'

'No more than anywhere else. And if you think the birds are bad, you just wait. This whole place will be swarming with people soon.'

A trickle of icy alarm ran down Rick's spine. Beth was still speaking, but he couldn't hear what she was saying over the whooshing of blood in his ears. He glanced back up the lane, fully expecting to see a TV van stuffed with rampaging paparazzi bearing down on him.

'Did you call them? Oh my god, you did, didn't you? Thanks a bunch. Kick me while I'm down, why don't you?'

Dizzy with panic and desperate to get indoors before he did something stupid like faint, Rick hopped through the shifting mass of feathered bodies littering the yard as fast as he could.

Chapter 19

The next morning, having dropped Grace at preschool, Beth walked back along the parade towards the car park, wondering how and why that last conversation with the Wolverine had ended so strangely. The sound of a baby crying filtered into her thoughts. The door of the craft shop banged open and Lucy stuck her head out.

'Tell me, Beth,' she demanded, her skin pasty with exhaustion, 'why does anyone have more than one child?'

'Don't ask me. Most of mine came as a package deal.'

Lucy shushed Hazel. It had no discernible effect. 'Have you time for a cuppa?'

'A quick one. I need to pop into the Crashing Boar later. Rose said they have a lunchtime shift going, then I'm dropping my CV into some places in Highcliffe.'

'No luck on the job front, then?'

'Not so far. What's bothering Hazel?'

'Teeth, I think. Not that I *can* think anymore.'

'That bad, huh?'

'Tom was on call last night and I reckon he had more sleep doing the whole casualty doctor thing than I did. Talking to you just might save my sanity.'

'Don't look at me for sanity.'

'Are your kids giving you grief, too?'

'Always, but no. It's the man next door.'

'Oooh.' Lucy wiggled her eyebrows. 'The good-looking neighbour you mentioned. What's the problem?'

'Let's just say, he has issues.'

'We've all got issues, darling.' She looked down at her wailing daughter. 'Haven't we, Hazel? Yes, we have.'

'Can I hold her?'

'Fill your boots.' Lucy handed the wriggling bundle over. 'Trying to run a business with a newborn baby was a daft idea. What was I thinking?'

'You're just tired. Go sit down.' Beth walked up and down the shop, gently rocking the sobbing child. 'Grace used to love it when I held her facing out, so she could see what was going on.' She turned Hazel around. Frantic sobs became gasps and hiccups, then Hazel belched like a beer-sodden football supporter and stopped crying all together.

'Sweet heaven above. Peace at last. Why didn't the little traitor do that for me?'

'Pure luck, I promise you. Anyway, how are the interviews going? Found a crafty whiz-kid, yet?'

Lucy snorted. 'Hardly, I've had three ladies apply, but none of them are right.'

'They can't have been worse than me.'

'I wish that were true. The first had the worst BO imaginable. I couldn't breathe the whole time she was in here. The second wouldn't stop talking. Honestly, she'd drive me mad in half an hour. Plus, I got the impression she had a problem with the idea of working for a person of colour.'

'No way! That's awful.'

Lucy pursed her lips. 'Meh! It happens. It shouldn't, but it does. Anyway, neither of them would have created the right atmosphere in here.'

'And the third one?'

'Ah, well, her I recognised. From that lot over past the railway tracks in the next village. Do you know the family I mean?'

'I'm not sure I do, but, then, I'm not in the loop with local gossip.'

'I avoid gossip as a rule, but I did hear she lost her job at the Crashing Boar because the till was light too many times.'

'Oh, yes, I do know. The Dixons, isn't it? I heard Rose telling Daisy. That's why there are some shifts going.'

'I don't suppose your Daisy is interested in the job here, is she?'

'She might've been if I hadn't been the one to mention it to her.'

'How so?'

'It wasn't a conversation that went well.'

Lucy yawned. 'Sorry. Not trying to be rude. Just cream-crackered.'

Beth tipped her head towards a wingback armchair tucked away right at the back of the shop. 'Why not have a rest? It's quiet in here. I can keep an eye on things. If you've got a sling for Hazel, you can give me a couple of jobs to do, too. But only idiot-proof stuff, mind.'

'Oh, thank you. If you're sure you don't mind. There's a papoose over that chair. Can you sort the wool in that box into baskets of different colour and then tidy the shelves on the far wall? That would really hel... oh, sorry.' Lucy stifled another yawn, settled herself down in the chair and closed her eyes.

Beth hummed, concentrating on sorting wool. Hazel stuffed a chubby fist in her mouth and dribbled. Lucy snored. The shop doorbell tinkled. Beth looked up. *Oh heck.*

Mrs Trenchard's steely gaze swept around the shop and zeroed in on Beth. 'Mrs Hope. It's you.'

Beth resisted the urge to look down and double check her own identity. She pointed to the baby strapped to her front and then to Lucy. 'Just lending a hand. Although, heaven help me if someone wants to buy something. The till looks very complicated.' Beth stopped, realising that Mrs Trenchard was a customer. 'Can I get you anything?'

The older woman shrugged out of her coat and scarf and bustled over to the little kitchenette to hang them on a hook behind the door. 'That till's the same model as the one in the post office. I'll operate it for you.'

'I couldn't put you out like that.'

'You're not. Crafty Crochet starts in twenty minutes,' said Mrs Trenchard. 'I always come early to get the teas and coffees sorted.'

'Crafty Crochet?' Horrified at the thought, Beth cleared her throat. 'Oh dear. I can't crochet to save my life.'

'We do the crocheting, Mrs Hope. You supply the wool.' She nodded towards the box of wool that Beth was sorting. 'You seem to have that covered. Ah, look, Reena's here.'

Outside on the pavement, Reena was tying Tiny's lead to a post.

*

An hour later, when Lucy finally stirred, the Crafty Crochet Circle were all creating away and chatting quietly. Beth watched as Morgan, the twenty-eight-year old mechanic from the village garage – all intense black eye liner and flawless beehive, with flowers tattooed down her right arm – demonstrated how to make delicate, lacy baby booties in sky-blue merino wool. Cathy, a young woman in her early twenties with Down's syndrome, had arrived with her two adoptive mothers, Liz and Stephie. She chatted away to everyone, while ball after ball of brightly coloured yarn spun off her hook into ornately patterned squares. George Botley, from the hardware store, had been a surprise late arrival. He slid into a seat next to Cathy, who gave him a big grin and showed him how to help stitch her woollen squares into a blanket. Beth focused on the yarn supply, surprised to realise she was enjoying herself.

Lucy yawned and sat upright. 'Oh, Beth, I didn't mean to steal your whole morning. Aren't you supposed to be at the Crashing Boar?'

Beth checked her watch. 'Yes, I am. Sorry, I'd better go.' She passed Hazel back to her mother, aware that Mrs Trenchard was frowning at her again.

What have I done now?

'Thank you so much,' said Lucy. 'I'd forgotten what a nightmare teething is. It'll be so much easier when she's older.'

'Don't you believe it,' muttered Beth, reaching for her bag.

'What do you mean?'

All eyes were suddenly on her. Beth shifted from foot to foot. 'Oh, nothing. Only that it gets more complicated when they're older. There's no manual and everything's subject to random change without notice.'

'That's true,' said a quiet voice. Beth was amazed to hear George speak at all, let alone agree with her. 'Whatever you do, they won't like it,' he continued. 'Parenting is about being supportive, but not too supportive. You've got to encourage, but, at the same time, appear completely uninterested. It's quite a skill.'

Beth laughed. 'Exactly. I've no idea what I'm doing half the time, although I probably shouldn't admit it. Anyway, I have to go. Don't want to be late.' She smiled a goodbye to the group and headed for the door.

Passing Mrs Trenchard, she heard the old woman mutter, 'With four children to look after, I should think you have enough to do focusing on them, rather than going galivanting to pubs at lunchtime.'

Beth stiffened. No way was she letting that slide. 'I'm applying for a job, if you must know. Someone has to keep a roof over the children's heads and put food on the table. The only person doing that is me and I'll do it the way I think best.' She was out of the door without giving Mrs Trenchard a second to respond.

*

Utterly seething, Beth stomped along the wide pavement towards the Crashing Boar. Wrapped up in her thoughts, she accidentally bumped into a woman leaving the pet store with an immense bag of dog food in her arms.

'I'm so sorry.' She steadied the woman before she toppled into the road. The shiny dark bobbed hair made Beth do a double take. 'Jane?'

The counsellor was barely recognisable in a tatty fleece

and dog hair-covered jodhpurs, and liberally shedding the scent of horses and Chanel in her wake. Beth wasn't sure it was her until she smiled.

'Hello, Beth. You look well. I was worried after you stood me up.'

'Stood you up?'

'You had a follow-up appointment with me at the clinic yesterday.'

'Did I?' Beth put a hand to her mouth. 'Oh my goodness. I did. I'm so sorry. I completely forgot.'

'I wasn't surprised you didn't come. You weren't exactly fully engaged in the first consultation.'

Guilt sloshed through Beth's middle. 'It's not that… Well… it is a bit, but I've got some major financial problems. I'm looking for a job.'

'I see.'

'But I have followed your advice.'

'How so?'

'You said I should open up to people. And I did. I made a friend.' She shut the image of the Wolverine out of her mind and concentrated on Lucy. 'And I've been trying to socialise more, too. I've just come from crochet club.'

'How did that make you feel?'

Beth tipped her head on one side. 'Good, actually. Barbara Trenchard is still pissing me off, mind, but that's nothing new. Everyone else was really nice.'

'I'm glad.' Jane jerked her chin towards a battered green Vauxhall estate parked at the side of the road. 'Would you mind opening the rear door of that car for me?'

Beth pulled the door handle. A chorus of excited yaps started. Two short, hairy dogs, looking remarkably like

Dougal from *The Magic Roundabout*, bounced onto the pavement and chased each other around in circles.

Jane dumped the sack on the back seat. 'Thanks. I've got an equine therapy session starting soon. Right, come on, you two. In.' She whistled and the dogs leapt back into the car.

'Counselling horses as well as humans?' asked Beth, impressed by the display of canine obedience.

'Not exactly. It's officially my day off. I teach vulnerable youngsters to ride. Looking after horses is good therapy and so is spending time with the dogs. I was hoping to start a session at the Astley stables, but Lord Astley refused permission.'

'I'm not surprised. He's a nasty piece of work.'

'The riding centre over at Bisley have said I can go there instead. Today's the first session.'

'I hope it all goes well. I'm sure it will. And...' Beth paused. She wasn't given to sudden impulses, but Jane's advice in that last appointment had genuinely proved helpful. 'Look. I really am sorry I stood you up. Is there any chance I could... well...?'

Jane pulled a jangly bunch of keys from her fleece pocket. 'Are you asking for another appointment?'

'Uh... I think... well, yes.'

'I tell you what. Given your current situation, how about a telephone consultation? It'll save you travelling to Southampton and give you extra time to find that job.'

'That would be amazing. Thank you.'

'Righto. I'll email you an appointment time for next week.'

Chapter 20

Stuck inside, waiting for a paparazzi invasion that never arrived, and replaying his last conversation with the warrior queen, Rick realised that he might have overreacted. By the time all the birds had gone, he felt very foolish and felt forced to indulge in another gaming session to take his mind off it. It didn't help. He'd fallen into bed with a thumping headache and vowed to get outside for some fresh air and exercise the next day.

After a tricky night, tossing and turning, he finally dropped off just before dawn and slept through until mid-afternoon. Kicking himself for wasting the best part of a day, he wrapped up warm and set off to explore the land behind the barn. Climbing over a gate into a field he thought was empty, he soon discovered his mistake. Five long-necked animals careened over in a blur of shaggy coats and dim expressions. They pushed and shoved each other aside to get close to him. Not sure if he was about to be crushed or licked to death, he backed up as far as he could. Pressed up against the hedge, sharp hawthorn needles pricking his backside, Rick cursed his decision to come to the New Forest at all.

The lead animal peered through curly tendrils of hair dangling from an unkempt topknot. Rick blew his own overlong hair out of his eyes and returned the intense stare. A memory stirred. He put a hand out for the animal to sniff, but jerked it back as one of the other creatures lunged at him.

A loud hee-haw filled the air, sending the animals into a confusion of random circles. A tall youth, whose pale face and forearms were a stark contrast to his black hoodie, stood silent and unmoving a few yards away. By his side was the old, grey donkey Rick had seen in Beth's vegetable garden. After more random jostling, the strange creatures returned their attention to Rick.

The donkey gave another hee-haw, threw his heavy head up and pranced on the spot. The youth shoved his hood back, pulled headphones from his ears and muttered, 'Give over, Pablo. You'll do yourself an injury.'

Rick wracked his brain. Beth had mentioned a name. What was it? 'Are you… Jack?'

'Yup.'

'Am I trespassing? If so, I'm sorry. I'm not sure of the boundary.'

'Nah. It's your field.'

'Is it? Oh. Right. Ah…' One of the creatures nudged Rick's stomach with its muzzle. He edged back further into the prickles. He covered a yelp of pain with a cough.

'Relax,' said Jack. 'They won't hurt you.'

Rick tried to move again and one of the animals lunged at him. 'They seem quite insistent that I stay here.'

'Stop it!'

'Stop what? I'm not doing anything.'

'Not you. Them.'

'Oh. Right.'

'Give them a shove – gentle, like – and they'll back off.'

Rick did as he was told and was rewarded with a little more room to breathe. 'What are they? Llamas or alpacas or something?'

'They're both.'

'A mixed breed? I didn't know that was possible.'

Jack shook his head. 'A mixed herd, not a mixed breed. It's not common for them to live together, but this lot seem happy enough. The two tall ones are llamas – see their long banana-shaped ears?'

Rick nodded.

'They're gelded males – Bert and Ernie.'

'Is there any chance I might have met one of them before? Out in the forest?'

'That'll be Bert.' Jack's grin transformed his face, making him look several years younger. 'Always running off, he is. The three small brown ones, they're alpacas. Charlie called them his angels after some crummy seventies' TV show.' Jack pulled a despairing "What can I say? Adults are weird" expression.

'Do they bite?'

'Nah! You're alright.' said Jack. 'The worst they'll do is push you over by accident. The smaller ones spit when they get grumpy. Then you need to duck, real quick.'

'If this is my field, why are they here?'

Jack squinted at him as if he'd grown another head. 'Because they're yours. They've been in our field for the last couple of weeks.'

'I don't understand.'

'They were Charlie's, yeah? Now, they're yours. They come with the barn. It's like a "buy one, get one free" thing.'

'But no one said anything about... Hang on... Llamas and alpacas.' The penny dropped. 'Is that what she meant by llampacas?'

'Beth call them that, did she?'

'I didn't know what she meant.'

'Grace mashed the words together when she was learning to talk. It stuck.'

'Grace?'

'Half-sister. Beth's daughter.'

'So, Rose is your sister, too?'

'Yup. And Daisy, except me and Daisy are twins.'

'That's a lot of sisters.' How many people had he potentially pissed off next door? 'Any brothers?'

Jack shook his head.

'Wait a sec,' said Rick. 'Charlie died months ago. Who's been looking after this lot?'

'Me.'

'All this time?'

'It's no biggie. I've been doing it for years, anyway. Since Charlie got too old to lift the hay bales.'

Rick groaned, several comments from the previous day's conversation with Beth started to fall into place. 'This is what all the hay is for.'

'Yup. I moved it for you. It's over there, next to the standpipe.' Jack indicated an area past the fence where two outbuildings stood, one either side of the boundary fence between the barn and the farmhouse. A large mound was covered by a grubby, grey tarpaulin weighed down with old tyres. 'There's enough for the rest of the winter. They'll need lots of water, too, so keep the trough topped up. The stream at the far edge of the field isn't enough.'

Rick let out a long sigh. 'They sound like a lot of work.'

'Not so much. They're good company. Pablo, here, will miss them.' Jack patted the donkey. 'He's neurotic at the best of times. On account of being a rescue donkey. He's better with company. The llampacas remind him to be nice.'

'Pablo isn't mine, then?'

'No, but it's been easier to look after them all in the same field. I've been moving them between your field and ours.' He swept an arm towards the field next door, separated from Rick's by the hawthorn hedge. 'Over there, see? Behind the stable block? It stops the pasture getting cropped too short and makes life more interesting for them.'

Rick examined the half-stone, half-brick stable block next door, not sure what to say.

Jack turned to go. 'Pablo and me will leave you to it.'

'Wait a sec. I don't suppose...' Rick's voice cracked. The last thing he needed was to be responsible for other living creatures. He could barely look after himself. 'Would you consider continuing to look after them for me? I'll pay you.'

Jack hesitated. 'Rose said that Beth said we're to keep away from you.'

Rick felt as if he'd been sucker-punched. People didn't usually tell their kids to stay away from him. He rubbed the back of his neck. 'I guess me trending as "Doctor Death" on X doesn't help. Stands to reason she'd want you to keep clear.'

'Is that why you look familiar?' Jack pulled out his phone. 'Let's see, hashtag what did you say? Doctor Death... Oh, right, yeah. I remember seeing that.' He glanced from his screen to Rick and back again. 'Is that you? No way. You're having a laugh.' He peered at Rick, tipped his head to one side and back before shrugging and re-pocketing the phone.

Rick felt obliged to say, 'I didn't do it.'

'Didn't do what?'

'What they're saying I did.'

Jack wrinkled his nose. 'None of my business, is it, mate.'

'I think that's why Beth doesn't like me.'

'I doubt it. Beth hates social media. Nah! She thinks you're a tool for scaring the cows. She thought you'd killed me.'

Rick slapped a palm to his forehead. 'That's what she meant about me being irresponsible. She said something about me risking a young man's life. I thought she was talking about Dean, but she meant you.'

'All I know is, she said you were weird about the hay. Look, if you want me to take care of the llampacas, I'll do it.'

'What about Beth?'

'Who cares what she wants? She's not my mother.'

Rick suppressed the urge to tell him to show more respect. 'We should at least consider her feelings.'

'Why?'

'Because it's the right thing to do. I tell you what, I'll pop over and speak to Beth and apologise for being weird. Hopefully, she'll be fine with you helping me out.'

Jack shrugged. 'Whatever. I've got to go.'

Rick watched the lad leave. Reena was right, Beth had a lot on her plate. The last thing she needed was someone with his sort of baggage adding to her troubles. The best thing to do was go and apologise and then make sure to stay the heck away from her.

Chapter 21

The last person Beth expected to see at her front door was Mrs Trenchard. Yet there she was, a determined expression on her face, a foil-covered dish clutched to her ample bosom. It was as if the older woman had been rehearsing what to say because all her words came out in a rush.

'Mrs Hope. I wanted to apologise for speaking out of turn at crochet club. It wasn't my intention to upset you. And my Brian always says the best apologies come with food. So, I brought you a cottage pie from the freezer. It's home-made, all organic veggies from the allotment. My Brian has a way with plants, I can tell you, and I... I... well... I'm sorry.'

A weighty silence filled the air. The people pleaser in Beth felt obliged to fill it. 'Would you like to come in?'

'Thank you.'

Beth fielded the pie dish thrust towards her and followed her visitor to the kitchen. Mrs Trenchard discarded several layers of outerwear onto one of the ladder-back chairs and plonked herself down.

Beth placed the dish onto the kitchen counter. 'This is very kind, thank you. Tea?'

'Excellent idea.'

Popping the kettle on, Beth racked her brain for something to say.

Mrs Trenchard tapped her fingernails on the tabletop.

The cuckoo clock ticked.

Mrs Trenchard cleared her throat. 'The other day, in the store, you were very kind to me.'

'I bought milk.'

'You did more than that and we both know it.' Mrs Trenchard stared off into the distance. 'I can handle Robert Astley, you know. He has always been a bit of a tyrant. I don't know what Maria, his wife, sees in him. Anyway, your support surprised me. Especially as we're not exactly friends. Why did you... you know?'

'I don't like bullies.'

'I didn't needed your help, you understand, but... well... thank you.'

'You're welcome, Mrs Trenchard.'

'Perhaps you should call me Barbara.'

A cessation of hostilities was the last thing Beth had expected. She pushed away from the counter and joined Barbara at the table. 'Only if you call me Beth.'

'Please forgive me, Beth. What you said about keeping a roof over the children's heads; was that just a figure of speech or...? Is everything alright? Money-wise, I mean.'

'Goodness, I forgot I was making tea.' Beth leapt to her feet and busied herself with cups.

'I only ask because I feel a responsibility towards Isla's... to the children. Isla wasn't just my goddaughter, you know. She was family, my second cousin's niece. She spent a lot of time with me when she was growing up.'

'I didn't know that.' Beth placed the tea on the table and sat back down. 'I'm sorry. It must have been hard to lose her.'

'Especially so young. She had so much to live for.' Barbara dug a handkerchief from her cuff, dabbed at her eyes. 'She had plans for this place. Did you know? She was going to turn it into a donkey sanctuary.'

'No, I didn't.'

Barbara nodded. 'She talked about it all the time. And then, one day, she was gone. It was painful to see Paul remarr… I mean, to see him moving on. I'm sorry. I didn't handle it very well. I was worried for the children more than anything else.'

Beth reached across the table, stopping just short of touching Barbara's arm. 'I do see how it must have looked.'

'My Brian always says I should keep my nose out and he's right.' Barbara sniffed. 'I can be a nosy old badger sometimes. I tried to talk to Paul about it.'

'Did you?'

'He and I never did see eye to eye. I always felt he was quite controlling.' Barbara blew her nose. 'I'm sorry, I shouldn't criticise your husband. Anyway, he told me to keep my big fat nose out.'

'I didn't know that.'

'He said not to ever talk to you or he'd stop me seeing the children. I couldn't take the risk that he'd actually do it, so I stayed away. I usually make a point of welcoming newcomers. It's part of my role on the Women's Council. I didn't do that for you. I regret that.'

'Don't beat yourself up about it.'

For some reason, it no longer bothered Beth that the children were fond of Barbara. 'I'm glad the children have you. I know they are always popping into the store to see you.'

'They're good kids.' Barbara smiled. 'Anyway, you didn't answer my question about money. Paul has been away a long time. He is supporting you all, isn't he?'

Beth felt something inside snap. The children were related to Barbara. She was matriarch to a massive family spread the length and breadth of the forest. Paul forcing her to stay away had made all their lives far harder than necessary. Why the hell should Beth protect him? If she were going to keep her precious little family together, she needed help. And who better to have on her side than Barbara.

'No, he isn't.' Beth was amazed what a relief it was to finally tell someone. 'Quite the opposite, in fact.'

The cuckoo announced 2pm.

Barbara's mouth fell open. 'Why?'

'You'd have to ask him that, but you'll have to find him first.'

'You don't where he is?'

'Not a clue.'

'Goodness. I know he left all of a sudden. And there were all those silly rumours, of course.' Barbara's face flushed.

'You mean the rumours that I'd bumped him off?' Beth snorted. 'I almost wish I had. If I'd buried him under the patio, at least I'd know where he was.'

'I never thought that. People can be very silly sometimes. Although, I was relieved when the postcards started arriving at the post office for delivery up here. Daisy is always so happy when they come. She tells me all about his work abroad.'

'He's not sending the cards. I am.'

'Oh.'

Beth reached into her handbag and slid Paul's letter across the table. 'He did send this, though.'

Barbara scanned it. 'Oh my.'

'I stupidly thought he'd come back.'

Barbara handed the letter back. 'At least he's done the gentlemanly thing and given you the house. Isla's life insurance paid off the mortgage after the accident, I know that much.'

'You're kidding.' Beth's head spun, a million thoughts crowding in at once.

'Why? What have I said?'

Beth opened and closed her mouth. There were no words.

Barbara's voice came from a long way away. 'You've gone ever so pale. Are you alright?'

'Paul must have remortgaged.'

'Surely not?'

'When I signed for the house, it came with a mortgage. £200,000.' Beth gave a bitter laugh. 'He didn't mention that little gem in his letter, did he? I had to sign. What other choice did I have? And he swanned off, leaving me in debt up to my eyeballs.'

Barbara tutted. 'My Brian always said he was a rat.'

The front door slammed so hard the whole house trembled. Daisy's angry voice echoed down the corridor.

'You cow! You nicked my job.' The teen erupted into the kitchen, stopping short as she saw Barbara. 'Aunty B!' She looked from Beth to Barbara and back again, her face flame red. 'I didn't see you there.'

'Why aren't you at school?' asked Beth.

'It's Wednesday. Half day. I was going to go see that lady

in the craft shop, but Sonja said she saw you working in there and not to bother.'

'I helped Lucy out, as a friend. Anyway, I thought you didn't want the job.'

Daisy scowled. 'I changed my mind.'

Barbara crossed her arms over her ample bosom and fixed Daisy with a stern glare. 'I think you owe Beth an apology.'

'Eh? Oh right. Yeah. Sorry.' She didn't sound sorry. She stuck out her chin and sidled towards the door muttering, 'I've got homework to do.'

Barbara shook her head, 'That girl reminds me so much of her mother. My Brian always says if Isla were still with us, there'd be fireworks between those two, for sure.'

'Really?' The idea that Isla might have struggled with Daisy's attitude intrigued Beth.

'Oh yes. Isla was quite a handful back in the day. Delightful, but hard work. Now, tell me what you are going to do about your situation.'

Beth leaned back. 'I've been job-hunting, but there isn't much out there.'

'There never is in the forest in winter. You might be able to pick up something for the summer at one of the caravan parks.'

'It won't be enough. Rose had this great idea to rent out the back field for campers.' Beth was surprised to see Barbara shake her head.

'Goodness no, Beth. You can't do that.'

'It's alright. I looked into it. All we have to do is to apply for permission from the council.'

'No, no. You can't. You are too close to Tara's place.'

'Tara?'

'She runs the campsite at the bottom of the hill. They are only just making ends meet as it is. Another campsite this close wouldn't be fair.'

'There are hundreds of campsites in the forest. One more won't make that much difference.'

'I disagree.'

Beth got to her feet, stony resolution settling on her shoulders. 'I'm sorry for Tara, I really am, but I have to do what I can with what I've got. So far, this is the only thing that might work.'

'There must be something else.'

'There isn't. And I have to put the children first. I am going to apply for permission this afternoon.'

Barbara stood and picked up her coat. 'If you've made up your mind—'

'I have.'

'Then there's nothing more to be said. I'm sorry, Beth. If you move forward with this, I'll have no choice but to register an official objection.'

Beth listened to the other woman's footsteps tip-tapping their way down the hall. The front door slammed. So much for burying the hatchet.

Chapter 22

The next afternoon, Rick knocked on the farmhouse door. Rose opened it, crossed her arms and leaned against the jamb without speaking.

Rick pinned what he hoped was a non-confrontational expression on his face. 'Hi there. Is Beth in?'

'You aren't going to upset her again, are you? Because Grace's in there, too, and she's only little.'

An inky pool of sadness settled in Rick's middle. 'I promise I don't make a habit of upsetting people. I just want to ask her something.'

'Beth doesn't usually lose her rag. Not like the other day. The thing is, a kid from the village died, a while back. It was a stupid accident at the skate park. And since then, Beth worries about us. When you set the cows off, she was afraid for Jack.'

'I'd like to say I'm sorry.'

Rose gestured for him to enter. 'Down the hall. She's in the kitchen.'

Stepping inside, Rick's nose twitched. 'Something smells good.'

'Cupcakes.'

The terrier at Rose's ankle whined. Rick put out a hand to be sniffed. 'Hello, boy.'

'Paddy doesn't like strangers.'

'Sensible dog.'

'This way. Watch the bucket.'

The air in the kitchen was thick with the sweetness of warm sugar. Trays of colourful cupcakes covered every available surface. At the table, wielding a piping bag, Beth stiffened the instant she spotted him. Knowing he was a source of tension for her really hurt.

'I'm sorry I put Jack in danger,' he blurted out. 'I was weird about the hay, too. I was having a really bad day. Not that that's an excuse, of course. Oh, and thank you for the cakes you left when I first arrived. That was very kind.'

The little girl at Beth's side glanced from her mother to Rick and back again.

Rick kept rambling. 'And whatever it was I did a couple of days ago, which made you yell at me out by the car, I'm sorry about that, too.'

Beth hid her face in her free hand. Her shoulders shook.

Oh heck. She's crying again.

She dropped her hand, revealing eyes that danced with laughter. 'Now I'm the one who's sorry,' she said. 'That last one was all me. Bad timing on your part. Bad behaviour on mine.'

A wave of relief washed through him. 'I'm Rick, by the way.'

'Hi, Rick. I'm Beth and this is Grace.'

'You have messy hair,' said Grace.

Beth gasped. 'Grace!'

'But he has.' The child dropped her voice to an earnest stage whisper. 'He looks like the llampacas.'

Rick laughed. 'I do, don't I? My hair has never been this long before. But guess what? I've heard that people can start to look like their animals and I've only just found out the llampaccas are mine. Maybe that's why my hair's gone mad.'

Grace giggled. 'You're silly.'

'I am, but it's a scientific fact. Honest. Ask your mum.'

'It's true, Grace. You'll have to be careful or you'll end up looking like Paddy.'

Grace looked at Paddy and hooted with laughter.

'Right.' Rose picked up a large Tupperware tub and started stacking cupcakes into it. 'Now that you two have made friends, is it safe to leave you to play nicely? I've got to deliver these cakes to The Coffee Pot. Can I take the car, Beth?'

'Go ahead. Jack and Daisy's bus gets in at three. Can you pick them up on your way back?'

'Sure. And later, Ethan said he'd give me a lift in his van to check out that stuff on Freecycle, yeah? If it's any good, we'll grab it and shove it in one of the sheds.'

'Good idea.'

Grace scrambled off her chair and bounced on her tiptoes in front of Rose. 'Can I come?'

'If Beth says it's okay. But remember, we're delivering the cakes, not eating them.'

Grace dashed out to fetch a pink coat. She returned stuffing her arms into the sleeves. 'Can I, Mummy? Please?'

Beth helped her do the buttons up. 'Pay attention to your sister.'

Rose thrust one of the boxes of cakes towards Rick. 'Give us a hand out to the car, will you?'

'Sure.'

Minutes later, Rick found himself standing on the drive with Beth as they watched the car trundle away down the track. He scuffed the toe of one shoe in the gravel. 'Thank you for keeping an eye on the barn after Charlie died. And thank you for looking after the llamas and alpacas. I had no idea about them. If I'd known, I'd have… well, I'd have done something. But I didn't, so I couldn't. You know?'

Stop wittering.

'Jack and Charlie had an arrangement.'

'I'm sure it wasn't all Jack. Do you mind if he keeps taking care of them? I'll pay him, of course. I'm clueless and I'm hoping he'll teach me. And you must let me pay you back for anything you've had to lay out for all that hay and stuff.'

The shadow of a frown flit across Beth's face. 'There's no need, Rick. Ordering in bulk for all the animals meant I got a discount.'

'All the animals? How many do you have?'

'I've never counted, let me see: Pablo and Paddy, then there's Percival the rooster and the hens, Priscilla, Penelope and Patricia… What?'

Rick raised an inquiring eyebrow.

Beth laughed. 'I know. It's a lot of Ps. But Paddy and Pablo were here before I arrived. Their names are nothing to do with me.'

'And the others?'

'They were Grace's idea. We adopted four bald, skinny chicks when a local battery farm was shut down by the RSPCA last year. She thought giving them names beginning with P would help them feel like they belonged.'

'Interesting strategy. Did it work?'

'You'd have to ask them. Percy was originally Persephone, but we had to change it to Percival when his feathers grew back and we realised he was a boy.'

'Any animal names not beginning with a P?'

'Only Genghis. He's a stray cat that adopted us last winter. He lives outdoors in one of the sheds and generally keeps himself to himself. Oh, and our latest arrival is Lady Muck, a wild mallard with a bad leg. Jack found her under the hedge a couple of weeks ago. She likes our pond.'

Rick felt drawn to this woman more than ever, with her crazy patchwork family pieced together from leftover fragments. 'Well, let me know if you need any help with anything.'

'Thank you, but we're fine.'

She's so defensive.

'Of course you are. So, can Jack help me out?' All of a sudden, she wouldn't meet his eyes. 'What is it, Beth?'

'Can I ask…?'

'Go on.'

'Here's the thing. Rose showed me this video of you and… um.' She bit her lip, her cheeks flushed.

'I know the one you mean. It's not what it seems. It has been edited. That's not what really happened. Honestly.'

'What did happen?'

'It's complicated.'

'If you're not prepared to try and explain—'

'No. It's just, I can't. Some of it is confidential.'

'It's simple enough. Did you run that lady over or not?'

'Not.'

'I want to believe you, Rick. I really do, but it's hard.'

'It's like this. Let's say I had a famous... uh... client, whose privacy I am bound to protect.' He waited for her to nod. 'There were these people after me, chasing a story about that client.' As he spoke, Rick could feel himself start to shake as the memories crowded in. His leg started to throb, as if he'd just landed in that flower bed all over again. 'I was so desperate to get away from them that I jumped out of a window.'

'You're kidding.' Beth's mouth dropped open.

'Unfortunately, there were more of these people waiting outside and they saw me. I got to my car but they were all running towards me. I don't know how many, but it felt like hundreds and hundreds of them.'

'What did you do?'

'I couldn't think, I just started the engine.' He dashed a hand over his eyes, trying to wipe the visual echo of those minutes away. 'I steered for the exit to the car park just as the woman in the video ran at the car. I braked. She had plenty of time to stop, too, but she didn't. She threw herself on the bonnet. I swear she wasn't hurt. She looked at me through the windscreen. She even winked. Then, she screamed, went all floppy and slid to the ground.'

'You're saying she was acting?'

'I am. And I reckon my dashcam footage would prove it, too. I can show it to you, if you like.'

Beth shook her head. 'I believe you.'

'Anyway, I checked she was clear of the wheels. She was conscious, too. Then I drove away. I should have stopped, I know. I panicked.'

Beth put a gentle hand on his arm. 'I'm sorry. Thank you for telling me. I only asked because I need to know Jack will be safe if he is working for you.'

A warm tingly heat radiated up Rick's arm from her hand. 'I promise. I won't ever put you or your family in danger.'

'Fine. If Jack wants to help you, he can.'

The smile she gave him triggered a warm fluttering in the centre of his chest. It was so long since he had felt anything like it that it took him a moment to recognise it as genuine happiness. 'Earlier, Rose said we'd made friends. Have we? I mean, your counsellor told you that you needed friends and I could certainly do with one.' His lips twisted in a self-deprecating grimace.

'I'd like that. Mind you, I'm not very good at the whole friend thing. I'm trying. Only, I have trust issues.'

Her eyes were full of worry. Rick fought the urge to sweep her into his arms and hold her close. He wanted to soothe those worries away. He wanted so much more than friendship. But he came with a truckload of crap. Friends was the best he could or should hope for – for her sake. Even as his body swayed towards her, his feet backed away.

She let go of his arm. 'I'd better get on. I have to do something about the roof before the weather turns.'

'Let me know if you need anything.' Leaving the words hanging in the air, Rick headed back to the barn, determined to do something practical to help.

I'll have a rummage through the sheds and see if I can find something to fix that polytunnel.

Chapter 23

Half an hour later, stood on the roof, in the lead gully between the thatch and slate halves of the farmhouse roof, Beth paused to get her breath back. The climb up had been more taxing than she'd expected. Her thoughts strayed to Rick. She liked the idea of being his friend, even though every cell in her body clamoured for more. She had to be cautious, though. There was clearly much more to his story than he was letting on. Even so, she had always told the kids not to make up their minds about people and things based on social media. She couldn't expect them to do as she said if she didn't follow her own advice.

So, friends it is.

A stern gust of wind from the forest buffeted her and she wobbled.

Oops. Better concentrate.

She examined the damaged lead, chose the longest crack and then tipped gloopy, black sealant from a large tin onto it, watching it slowly slop into place. Twisting the container to stop the flow of goo, she moved on to repeat the process at the next section of damage, and then the next. The stuff was a law unto itself, sticking to everything it came into contact with. With luck, it would prove an effective temporary solution to the leak. Buying it and some extra lengths of roofing felt from George in the village hardware shop had cost her a fraction of what Owen, the roofing contractor, was going to charge. Mind you, George would probably have refused to sell it to her if he'd realised she was planning to come up on the roof herself. She'd lied and said it was for the shed.

Standing up, she experienced a major head rush.

Woah! This is way higher than I remember.

It was cold, too. But the stunning view across the forest was worth it. Scudding clouds crossed blue skies over an intricate patchwork of woodland, fields and streams. Looking down, Beth's gaze caught on a lone figure near the vegetable patch.

What is he doing? Honestly! Just as I think he might be okay, he goes and does something weird again.

'You do know you're trespassing, don't you?' she called out. He didn't respond. She called again, louder. 'Rick. What are you up to?' A wicked smile tugged at the corner of her mouth as he spun around, searching for her, looking in all the wrong places.

Eventually, he looked up.

His eyes bugged. 'Blimey! I could ask you the same question.'

'I said I was going to fix the roof.'

'You didn't say you were doing it yourself.'

She shrugged. 'I'm quite capable, you know.'

'I never said you weren't. Why didn't you ask me to help? We're friends now, remember. Friends help each other.'

What would it be like to let him help? To relax for once and trust someone else to take the strain?

The thought was too tempting. She pushed it away. 'I'm fine.' Switching the tub of sealant from one hand to the other, she prayed her fingers wouldn't become totally bonded to the container by the fat drips oozing down the side.

'I can see you shaking from here.'

'I'm just cold.' She shivered.

'Stay there, I'm coming up.'

'Don't go all caveman on me, Rick. I can do this.'

'Hang on, there's no ladder. How in hell's name did you get up there without a ladder?'

'Magic,' she said with a grin, leaning a fraction too far forwards. 'Whoops.' Wobbling, she took a hasty step back from the edge.

'Be careful.'

'I am being careful – and I'm nearly done. Relax.' She tipped the last of the sealant over the last split in the lead.

The sound of a car chugging up the lane reached her.

Blast it. That's the kids.

The second that Rose spotted her on the roof was obvious. The car skidded to a halt on the track and shingle went flying like buckshot. All four children leapt from the car and pushed through the hedge to stand in the vegetable garden with Rick.

'What on earth is going on?' demanded Rose.

'I bet it's epic up there,' said Jack. 'How cool is that?'

'She's only on the roof, Jack. Not Mars.' Daisy huffed and crossed her arms.

'Mummy,' Grace called. 'You're so high up. Can I come?'

'No.' Beth and Rose spoke in tandem.

'And she says I'm irresponsible,' said Daisy.

'Shut up, Dais,' said Jack.

Daisy scowled and stalked off. 'I've got better things to do than this.'

'Are you okay up there?' asked Rose.

'I'm absolutely fine.' Beth crossed her fingers behind her back.

'I did offer to help,' said Rick, more to Rose than anyone else.

Beth could practically hear Rose rolling her eyes as she replied, 'I don't doubt it.'

'And I said there's no need,' said Beth. 'The roof is fixed. For now, anyway.'

'I can't believe you would do something so dangerous,' Rose grumbled. 'What sort of an example are you setting Grace?'

'Actually, Rose, I think I'm setting a great example. I'm not sitting around waiting for someone else to solve my problems. Facing stuff head on is the way to go. Getting off my backside and doing what needs to be done. And do you know what?'

'What?'

'It feels good. It's way better doing something, instead of wasting time worrying.' Beth laughed as she realised that every word she was saying was true. She suddenly felt invincible and waved the empty tub of sealant in glee. 'This stuff is disgusting, but it's supposed to be totally watertight. If we can get through the storm in one piece, then I'll know this patching method works. I can keep buying more if we need it and we'll have time to save up for a proper repair.'

'You can't keep going up on the roof,' spluttered Rick.

'Why not?'

'It's dangerous.'

'No more for me than it would be for you. And for the record, getting up here was totally safe. I just squeezed out of my bedroom window onto that single storey bit of flat roof. See?' She pointed to where the conservatory wrapped around the side of the house from the back. 'Then I just had to walk round to this bit and climb up. No biggie.' Beth looked at Grace, whose eyes were huge. 'But if you ever think about copying me, Grace Louise Hope, I'll confiscate all your unicorns. Forever. Do you hear me?'

Grace nodded.

'Good. Now, Rose, why don't you take Grace inside and put the kettle on. I'm gasping for a cuppa. I'll be down in a tick.'

Rose grabbed Grace's hand and went indoors – the militant set of her shoulders assuring Beth that words would be exchanged later.

As soon as they were out of earshot, Beth called down, 'Rick, that friendly offer of help you mentioned, were you serious?'

'Yes. What do you need?'

'I'm not convinced my clever route up will be quite so easy in reverse. I only came up that way because we don't have a ladder. Any chance you've got one?'

Jack stepped forwards. 'Charlie kept one in the old dairy over at yours, Rick. Shall I go and get it?'

'Seeing as Beth has agreed to let you work for me, I reckon that's a good idea.'

'She has?' Jack threw a questioning look up at Beth.

She nodded. 'As long as your schoolwork doesn't slip. Yes.'

'Ace.' He punched the air and dashed off, a huge grin on his face, returning minutes later with the ladder.

'Where do you want it?' asked Rick.

Beth wrinkled her nose. 'I can get back down to the flat roof safely enough, but if I can use the ladder from there, it would be easier.' She scrambled down the short drop from the main roof, stopping short when she saw Rick's head and shoulders poking up from the top of the ladder. 'You're determined to climb up here, aren't you?'

'Getting onto a ladder to go down is the trickiest bit. Jack is holding the bottom so it's rock steady. I'm just here as a bit of backup. If you slip, I'll catch you.'

'Come on, Beth, I'm hungry,' called Jack. 'Let him help. I don't want to have to clean up the mess if you go splat.'

'Fine.' She mock glared at Rick, but deep down the toasty warm sensation of being taken care of felt so nice that she had to swallow hard against the lump that came to her throat.

*

Later that afternoon, back at the barn, Beth's words kept going around and around in Rick's head. She was obstinate and infuriating and, at the same time, utterly incredible. Her strength put him to shame. Forget warrior queens. Up on that rooftop, with her red hair streaming out behind her, she'd looked like the empress of the whole damn universe. He should follow her lead and start facing stuff head on. Everything he'd ever worked for, his whole life, was in London and yet here he was cowering in the New Forest, worrying about Dean and doing sod all to fight back.

It's time to get a grip.

Riding a surge of positivity, he forced himself to re-read Gita's emails. Then, he pieced his phone back together and dialled Mark Freeman, who got down to business straight away.

'Rick, I'm glad you've called. Gita hoped you would. Have you seen the GMC conclusion?'

'Yes. A warning and a recommendation for additional training. What exactly does that mean?'

'Pretty much what it says. You'll have to do a course on documenting notes properly and general confidentiality, which you'll pass easily. It's the wider implications of their conclusion that are the problem.'

'Which are?'

'If you'd been completely exonerated, which you haven't, then Cora Diamond wouldn't be able to launch a legal case against you. As it is, the warning – regardless of the specific details of that warning – means a civil case for damages can go ahead.'

'She can sue me on Dean's behalf?'

'Yes. Don't forget; this isn't a case to say that you're guilty or not guilty. It's not really about the medicine anymore. It's about proving a loss, which, for Cora, under these circumstances, is going to be a skip through the bluebells. The only defence you can legitimately mount that might counter this is to prove categorically that you did document the consultation and that you definitely warned Dean of the dangers of mixing his meds, and that what happened to him was entirely his own fault.'

'But I can't do that without the missing consultation documents.'

'Exactly.'

'So, in your professional opinion, I'm going to lose.'

There was a pause. 'I'm sorry, Rick, but yes. Given all the publicity, it's highly likely that you will. And then it'll all be about awarding damages for Dean's ongoing care.'

'Do you know how he is?'

'Not good.'

Rick sighed. 'I've stopped reading the news; I can't cope with it.'

'It's a good idea to stay offline at the moment. There's so much rubbish being peddled and Cora Diamond is giving TV interviews left, right and centre. You don't need to listen to any of them. As far as we know, Dean is in a coma and showing no signs of recovery. And, to put it bluntly, therein lies the problem.'

'Meaning?'

'He's a young man. Ongoing care over many years could cost a fortune.'

'Hundreds of thousands, I expect.' Rick's voice cracked.

'Probably millions,' said Mark. 'And because you've not been completely exonerated, the court can find you liable – and they probably will.'

The silence in the room once the call was over was thick and heavy. Looking on the bright side, at least he was insured. And if... no, *when* he lost the case, at least Dean would be taken care of. The bright side didn't help. Booting up his laptop, he searched the news feeds for Cora Diamond. As he expected, she actively condemned Rick in the most strenuous terms, blaming him outright for Dean's condition. While he didn't like it, he could understand it. What did surprise him, though, was the compelling way she spoke about the growing crisis in young people's mental health and the urgent need for more focused and accessible resources. She was right and she appeared to be building one hell of a platform from which she might be able to do some good. If it weren't for the fact that she was denouncing him personally to do it, Rick would have been cheering her on. He shut the computer off, his spirits sinking to new lows.

A scuffling sound came from the window. A shadowy face peered through the glass and then bobbed down out of sight. Rick's chest tightened. His heart rate, already high, rocketed further and his blood started to boil.

Dammit. Why couldn't he just be left alone?

A burst of rage carried him to the door. Two jean-clad, hooded figures darted across the yard and disappeared behind the old dairy. Rick gave chase. He rounded the building and stopped short. Two scrawny teenagers leaned against each other, sniggering uncontrollably, while trying – and failing – to clap each other on the back.

'I told you so,' crowed the taller one, bending forwards, hands on his knees, gasping for air. 'Didn't I say the place isn't empty no more?'

The shorter one caught sight of Rick, giggled and nudged his friend.

The tall one glanced up. 'Shit.' He took to his heels, calling to his mate over his shoulder. 'Come on, you stiff. Run!' Both teens jumped the fence and disappeared into the forest.

There was a faint sweetness in the air. A small tendril of smoke curled up from the ground where the boys had been. He stamped it out and then bent to retrieve a roach from the flattened grass. That explained the giggling. Numerous cigarette butts littered the ground. *What a stupid place to smoke! Right next to a sodding great pile of hay.* He collected as many of the disgusting remnants as he could. A wave of dizziness forced him to pause. The heady cocktail of adrenalin, panic and anger receding to leave him emotionally exhausted. He rested a hand on the stone corner of the outbuilding to steady himself.

A voice called out.

A swimmy version of Beth approached.

Chapter 24

Beth took one look at Rick and knew something was wrong. 'What is it?'

'I'm fine,' he replied. 'Just dizzy.'

'Sit.' Beth jerked her head towards the oak bench outside the dairy. She tried not to stare at Rick's unsteady progress. It was this unpredictable condition of his that didn't add up. He seemed so healthy and solid one minute, yet the next he looked shaky and defeated. Almost as if he was two different people.

Perhaps he has an identical twin.

As soon as the thought scuttled across her mind, she dismissed it. Identical twins wouldn't have matching scars making them look like dishevelled, if sexy, pirates. She brushed an accumulation of cobwebs from the silvered wood and sat down. The whole seat heaved as Rick lowered himself onto the other end. She examined him surreptitiously. He might be heavy, but he was trim for a man his age. A solid wall of muscle. Dragging her eyes away, she cleared her throat. 'You fixed the polytunnel for me. Thank you.'

Rick's smile was faint, as if he'd had to dredge it out of his boots with immense physical effort. 'You're welcome. I enjoyed having something practical to do.'

'You say you're fine, but you don't seem very well.'

'I'm just really tired. And, for the record, I'm not drunk.'

'Why would I think you were drunk?'

'You accused me of being drunk before.'

'I'd forgotten about that.'

'I was tired then, too.'

Beth leaned a fraction closer. 'Is the tired and dizzy thing connected with your... um... head injury?'

'Eh?'

She gestured to her eye and nose.

'You mean this?' He pointed to his scar. 'No. That was ages ago. A legacy from the last rugby match I ever played. An illegal tackle put me in a coma for a month, just after my twenty-second birthday.'

'It looks nasty.' She cursed her tactlessness. 'I mean the injury looks like a nasty one... not that the scar is nasty... because it isn't... I... uh.'

'It was nasty. I only survived because I was playing for the university medics' team. If you're ever planning to have a major head injury, I recommend surrounding yourself with twenty-nine other doctors first, preferably before the after-match drinking starts.' He snorted in disgust. 'There was only so much the trauma surgeon could do. I wasn't stable enough to have a cosmetic procedure done for a long time afterwards. And by then, I couldn't face it.'

Beth patted his arm. An unexpected tingling sensation in her hand made her pull back. She clasped both hands together around her knee to stop herself from giving into the impulse to touch him again.

'Don't worry. I'm not ill. Not really. I mean, I'm on sick leave from work, but it's nothing.' He flushed. 'I've got burnout. It explains the exhaustion, anyway.'

'Does it?'

'I've been under investigation at work because of a treatment decision I made. It turns out that it was the right decision, but my career could be over anyway because of an administrative technicality.'

'I bet being investigated was tough.'

Rick gave a bitter laugh. 'Most people are innocent until proven guilty. But it doesn't seem to work that way for medical staff. God! Listen to me being all self-pitying. I'm sorry.'

'It's fine. You're allowed your feelings.'

'No, I'm not. Not when poor De... I mean, not when my patient is going through what he's going through. Anyway, I'm off work. Properly off, I mean, for the first time since I trained thirty years ago.'

'How's that going?'

'Honestly? I feel lost. I don't know what to do with myself. I feel like I'm walking through treacle all the time. Everything takes so much energy. I don't even know who I am without my career. And I feel guilty because...'

'Because what?'

He ducked his head, his voice low. 'The longer I'm off, the more I'm not sure that I want to go back.'

'Really? Why?'

He shrugged. 'I'm scared. It's daft. I'm not being struck off, which is good.'

'Struck off?'

'All GPs are on what we call the performers list. You can get struck off if you are found guilty of malpractice. And if you are struck off, you can't practise medicine.'

'Oh.'

'So, I haven't been struck off. And I'm glad about that. I really am.'

'But?'

'Now that I've stopped and I've had time to think about what happened, I'm not sure I'll ever be able to treat anyone again. I just don't trust myself.'

'I'm so sorry,' murmured Beth. She knew only too well what not trusting yourself felt like. The mountain of pain in his eyes made her want to throw her arms around him and tell him everything would be alright. Only, she didn't know if it would be.

'What if I get it wrong? The thought of doing a clinic makes me feel physically sick, then I start to shake and my brain turns to mush. It's life or death all day, every day. The smallest mistake can have catastrophic consequences.'

'Rick, you're ill. I'm not a doctor, but even I know burnout is serious. What has your own doctor said?'

'I haven't seen one. There's no need. I know the treatment.'

'You can't treat yourself. You didn't operate on yourself when you got your head injury, did you?'

'That's different. I'm not a surgeon.'

'Don't be obtuse.'

'I'm not.'

'What about your colleagues? Can they help you?'

'They've told me to keep my head down and rest up.'

'That's crazy. There must be more help available.'

A sudden rustle and then a loud cackle made Beth turn. Percy and the hens emerged from under the hedge and started scratching and pecking at the ground. 'You naughty creatures. You're not supposed to come though here.' Beth shooed the birds back through the hole. 'Goodness. Look at this.' She bent down to pick something off the ground and straightened up, a cigarette butt in her hand.

He opened his fist, revealing more than a dozen roaches. 'I was just clearing up.'

Disappointment crashed through her along with a mental collage of excruciating memories. Even her overactive hormones stopped promoting Rick's suitability and recoiled in alarm. 'Getting pie-eyed on weed isn't going to solve your problems, Rick.'

'What? No. They're not mine.'

That's what Trent used to say. 'This stuff is really bad for you, Rick. You must know that.' Scanning the ground, she saw yet more. 'Look at them all. How much are you smoking?'

'It's not me. There were a couple of teenagers up here. I just chased them off.' He sighed. 'You don't believe me, do you?' The sadness on his face stabbed at her gut. He got to his feet and started limping back towards the barn.

Beth hurried after him. 'I want to believe you, but I've been down this road before. I spent nearly a decade with someone addicted to drugs. Not to start with; he was clean when we first met, and charming and talented. Then he discovered weed and it changed him. I tried everything to help him, but it's a short but very slippery slide down to hard drugs. Trust me, Rick, wacky backy is not the answer to life's problems.'

He reached the porch and turned to look at her. 'I know that.'

He looked so earnest, but she couldn't allow herself to believe him. 'And quite apart from the health risks, just smoking by all those hay bales is stupid. Close to your outbuildings, not to mention my sheds and the stable block just over the hedge. It's all really flammable. Did you know that smoking causes more forest fires than anything else?'

'Beth. I promise you that I have never done drugs. Ever. And I certainly don't smoke. I get that you have history with this and I do want to talk some more, but right now I really need to lie down. Can we pick this up tomorrow and talk properly?'

She searched his face, wanting to believe him. 'Fine, you go and rest, but if we're going to talk about this tomorrow, we're also going to talk about you seeing a counsellor.'

He didn't reply.

She watched him stumble inside and close the door, and growled in frustration.

Why are things always so complicated?

Supressing the urge to drag him down to the village to see the GP – by the scruff of the neck, if need be – she headed back to the farmhouse. Only seconds later, she registered a sharp tang in the air that stripped the back of her throat.

Smoke.

A lot of smoke.

From somewhere nearby.

Thick and acrid. Scratching at her lungs. A dense, black plume billowed up from behind the stable block and the old dairy building.

Shit. The back garden.

There was only one thing it could be.

The shed.

Beth's feet started running before her brain was in gear. An anguished moan escaped. Tearing between the stable block and the farmhouse, she grabbed a bucket from a hook by the back door, yelling, 'Fire! Fire! Help! Where's Grace? Rose, Daisy, Jack, are you okay? Help!'

Thankfully, the water trough at the back of the stables was still full after the llampacas' recent visit. She filled her bucket to the brim and staggered towards the ancient black shed. The whole structure was engulfed in crackling, spitting, dancing flames.

The heat was too intense. Unable to get close, she had to fling the water from a few metres away. It arced onto the burning timber and hissed, but made little impact on the flames. Daisy appeared in her peripheral vision, battling to unravel a hose from outside the conservatory doors.

'Is Grace with you?' Yelling over the crackle of flames made Beth cough. Hot particles clawed at the back of her throat.

Daisy, her face grey with shock, shook her head.

Beth's eyes stung. 'Get that hose on. I'll fill more buckets. Don't get too close.'

Hurrying back to the trough, she called for help again, her voice little more than a croak. She returned to the burning shed with another bucket of water.

Rose arrived, tears streaming down her face. 'I rang the fire brigade,' she yelled. 'Jack's hooking up Charlie's hose to the standpipe in the field. Says he'll spray the shed from the other side. Keep it from spreading.'

'Good idea.' Beth coughed. 'Is Grace safe in the house?'

Rose's eyes widened. She shook her head. 'She was collecting eggs last time I looked.' She looked at the shed. 'Oh my God… what if…'

Beth froze. Her eyes darted to the red-hot flames. She dropped her buckets and ran towards the burning shed.

Somewhere, someone screamed. 'Not my baby! Not my baby. No. No. No!'

Before she'd taken more than half a dozen steps, Beth was knocked to the ground as something big and heavy landed on top her. She hit out at the weight holding her down and sobbed helplessly. 'Let me up! Please! Please! My baby's in there. My baby.'

Chapter 25

Rick held Beth's wrists as gently as he could. She continued to struggle, her mouth open in a silent scream.

'Stop fighting me, Beth. Grace isn't in the shed. She isn't in there. I promise you. Grace is safe.' Her terrified eyes locked onto his. The desperation in them tore at his heart. It was as if she couldn't process what he was saying. He put his mouth right next to her ear, so that she could hear him over the roar of the blaze. 'Beth. Listen to me. She's safe. Grace is safe. She's not in there. She's safe, I swear to you. She's at the barn with Paddy. I told her to stay inside and look after him.'

'She's safe?' Her voice was a hoarse croak. 'You're sure?'

'Yes. I'm sure. Now, can we get on with making everyone else safe?'

She gave a jerky nod. Rick scrambled to his feet, extending a hand to her to pull her up. Shielding her from the intense heat with his body, he steered her away from the angry red-hot inferno that made the skin on his back feel like it was melting.

'Let's keep going with buckets,' he shouted above the crackling. They staggered from the trough to the fire with heavy buckets, getting as close to the wall of heat as they could bear.

Beth gasped, pointing at specs of glowing ember flying into the sky. 'What about the thatch?'

'I don't know. Dampen everything you can. Try to stop it spreading.' Rick threw water as high as he could against the end wall of the stable nearest to the fire. It hissed as it ran down to the ground.

Sirens cut through the chaos.

'Oh, thank God,' said Rose.

Two fire engines steamed up the track, lights flashing. Suddenly, fire crew were everywhere, shouting instructions to each other.

Grateful to hand over to experts, Rick and Beth retreated towards the house and watched in silence. Rose wrapped an arm around Daisy's shoulders and they huddled together like dazed penguins. One of the fire crew, an older man with a silver goatee, approached. He was so slight in build that his bulky uniform coat looked like it was wearing him rather than the other way around. With careful deliberation, he unfurled a blanket and placed it around Beth's shoulders.

'Thank you,' she mumbled, clutching at it.

Hearing the tremble in her voice, Rick pulled her close, grateful when she didn't push him away. Instead, she leaned her forehead against his chest. Her arms crept around his waist and clung on tight. In spite of the circumstances, it felt good to be there for her. It had been such a long time since he'd had any meaningful human contact.

A name badge on the lapel of the fire crewman's jacket said: Brian Trenchard. 'Are you Barbara's Brian?' asked Rick.

Brian pushed his visor back from his face and grinned. 'The very one, guv.'

'Thank you for coming.'

He beamed. 'Wild horses couldn't have stopped me, not once I heard about this shout. Barbara would make mincemeat of me if I'd not come to check on the kiddies.'

Beth pulled back from Rick's embrace and, dashing a hand over her eyes, turned to Brian. 'Thank you. I… Sorry, I…'

Rick brushed at the tears tracking down Beth's cheek, but only succeeded in smudging more soot across her face.

'It's alright, luv,' said Brian. 'The worst is over. You're all okay.' A fat raindrop splattered onto his helmet. He looked up the darkening sky. 'You're in luck. That black up there isn't all smoke. Looks like that storm front is coming in. You can always rely on the forest to look after its own, you know.'

'It's the weather surely, not the forest,' said Rick.

'You think that, if you like.' Brian checked his phone. 'There's a month's worth of rain predicted to fall in the next twelve hours. No lightning expected. And the wind speeds have been downgraded from severe to moderate, so nothing to fan the flames. A good long soaking will dampen down anything that's still smouldering. Can't ask for better than that.'

Beth's heart gave a little bounce of hope in spite of her exhaustion. The dreaded storm, now a welcome ally. Who cares if the roof leaked, as long as it was still a roof.

'Do you know what started it?' asked Rick.

Brian puffed out his cheeks. 'That's the million-dollar question, isn't it? The watch manager, Jo, will be able to give you an idea. Look, over there, the one in the white helmet.' He pointed to a firefighter poking among the charred remains of the shed. 'The most common source of fire in the forest is careless tourists; smoking and barbeques and whatnot.' He gave them an encouraging wink and ambled off towards the fire engines.

Rick felt Beth stiffen and he turned to her, surprised to see her glaring at him. 'What's wrong?'

'I told you, smoking is dangerous.'

He tamped down a spike of irritation. *She's had a shock.* 'This wasn't me, Beth.'

She pulled further away from him. Her face rigid. 'I should go and check on Grace.'

'I'll go. You finish up here with the fire crew, then come and get her and Paddy when you're ready.'

Beth watched Rick go, confusion burning her belly. *Was she a fool to want to believe him?* Being in his arms had felt wonderful. Even so, the sensible part of her warned her not to get comfortable there.

The rain was getting heavier and the watch manager was heading over, carrying something blackened and twisted in a heavily gloved hand.

Rose crept over to stand next to Beth. 'What's that?'

Beth shook her head. Her eyes zeroed in on the watch manager's face.

'Hi, Mrs Hope. I'm Jo Tanner, Duty Watch Manager.' Jo pulled her helmet off, shook a dark, sweaty fringe from her eyes and smiled, white teeth stark against soot-smudged skin. 'It's all under control now. I suggest you keep back for a while. Let things settle. Whatever tool was plugged into this extension unit is the culprit.' She indicated the strange object in her hand.

A coil of electrical wire. A plug on one end. Some of the cord appeared in reasonable condition, but the remainder was a mess of wires and a bent metal stick surrounded by melted plastic.

It didn't make sense.

'We don't use anything electrical in the shed.' Beth looked from the item to the remains of the shed. 'Honestly, it's just storage; wood for the log burner, fuel cans for the mower, some old paint pots and... well... just stuff.' She scratched her head. 'What on earth is it?'

Jo turned it over in her hand. 'Looks like a soldering iron to me or something similar. Very dangerous to leave unattended.'

'I've never seen one before.'

'Me neither,' said Rose.

'Well, the extension cable ran from a socket in your stable, out through the side window and across the grass to the shed.' Jo gestured to the smouldering wreckage. 'And the fact that you had fuel and oil-based liquids like paint in there, plus all those logs, once the fire started, it wasn't going to stop. If we'd not got here when we did, you'd have lost the stable block, too – very possibly the house.'

'I don't understand,' Beth whispered, voice faint, legs wobbling.

Daisy's small hesitant voice came from behind Beth. 'It was me.'

Beth whirled around to face her. 'What do you mean, it was you?'

'It was an accident.' Daisy coughed, her throat sounding raw, and looked at the remains of the shed. Her voice dropped to a whisper. 'I was using a pyrography pen,' replied Daisy.

'A what?' said Beth.

'It's, like, for burning patterns onto wood. I got it online.'

Jo looked down at the item in her hands with interest. 'Hmm, pyrography. Yes, I know. Just like a soldering iron. Very hot.'

Beth's eyes went to the burned plastic mess, then back to Daisy. 'You almost lost us the house,' she whispered.

Daisy threw both arms out in defiance. 'I didn't do it on purpose, did I?'

Rage engulfed Beth. 'Oh good. I'm so glad you didn't do it on purpose. That makes everything alright then, doesn't it?'

'No! I was… I … oh…' Daisy burst into noisy tears. Rose wrapped an arm around her sister and led her away.

Jo's gaze went from Daisy to Beth. Putting her helmet back on, she patted Beth's shoulder. 'Why don't you go inside where its dry? Get cleaned up. Put the kettle on and maybe have a proper chat with her. We'll finish up here for you.' She walked away.

Beth's head swam, her vision was hazy and disjointed, and sound all woolly and indistinct. She willed herself to move, but her feet might as well have been encased in concrete for all the notice they took. She sank to her knees, her head in her hands. How much more could she take?

Chapter 26

Torrents of rain lashed Rick as he strode towards the barn, but he didn't care. Beth didn't believe him. Given her history, it wasn't surprising.

Grace stood in the open doorway, pale and frightened, staring out at the activity at the farmhouse. David's bear was tucked under one of her arms and Paddy sat at her feet. She scurried over to Rick and looped her free arm around his leg, pressing her face into his thigh.

Poor kid. None of this is her fault.

Tamping down his hurt and frustration, Rick smiled.

'Don't worry, Grace, everything's fine. Your mum will come and get you soon.'

Paddy sprang onto hind legs to paw at Rick's other thigh. The double assault nearly knocked him clean off his feet. 'Steady on, you guys, I'm all smoky and covered in dirt.'

'Yeah. You smell baaaaad.' Grace stepped back, her face scrunched up. 'Pooey!'

Rick laughed. 'Did you see the fire engines?'

'I saw two.' Grace bounced on the balls of her feet and

brandished two fingers at him in what would usually be considered a very dubious gesture.

Relieved to see some colour back in her cheeks, he ruffled her curls and gave the bear's ear a little tug. 'I see you've met Boo. He came all the way from London with me.'

'Paddy likes him. Don't you, Paddy?'

Paddy fussed at Rick's shoelaces.

'I'm glad. Boo needs a friend. He misses David.'

Grace opened her mouth and then closed it again.

'Want to know who David is?' asked Rick.

Grace nodded, her eyes round.

'He's my little boy, although he's a lot bigger than you.' Rick ambled over to the sofa and sank onto the cushions. 'David and Boo used to play computer games together. Want to try?'

He leaned over to the ZX console and inserted a simple game. A bright, jingly tune rippled through the air. 'Here. Watch that snowball roll down the hill and then press this button to make your penguin jump over it.' Grace clambered onto the sofa and settled Boo on her lap. Paddy whined and parked his bottom on Rick's foot. For a small dog, he was surprisingly hefty. Rick manipulated the controller and the penguin jumped.

Grace cackled with delight. 'Can I try?'

'Sure.' He handed over the controls just as his mobile rang.

Oops, I forgot to dismantle that.

Grace didn't take her eyes from the screen. 'Answer the phone, Rick.' She squealed as her penguin was joined by a seal and both little figures jumped in tandem.

Rick struggled from the cushions, eased his foot out from underneath Paddy's bottom and did as he was told. 'Hi.'

'Rick. Hi. Mark Freeman here again. We spoke before.'

'Hi, Mark.'

'We have a problem. Did you know your professional indemnity insurance only covers you for NHS work?'

'Yes, that's right. I don't do private work, so I've never needed the extra cover.'

'Right. Here's the problem. Dean was never officially registered with your NHS practice.'

'I know. The paperwork went missing before we could put him on the system.'

'Unfortunately, if he's not on your system, he doesn't technically count as one of your NHS patients. Ergo, he has to be considered a private patient and therefore...'

Rick's stomach felt as if someone had stabbed holes in it with a red-hot poker. 'Are you saying that I'm not covered for the court case?'

'I'm sorry. Yes I am.'

Rick's tongue felt too large for his mouth. 'Tell me you're kidding.'

'I wish I was. Unfortunately, it's not my decision.'

'But I don't... I can't... I... What do I do?'

'As a gesture of good will, we can continue to provide you with medical legal advice while the case is ongoing. And I promise, I'll do my damnedest to win for you. But if you lose, the company won't foot the bill for the damages. Whatever the settlement is, you'll have to pay it.'

'With what?' Rick's head was spinning.

Silence.

'I'll lose everything, won't I?' asked Rick, his voice barely louder than a whisper.

'That's very possible,' Mark said.

'And I won't be able to practice medicine again either, will I?'

'Put it this way, I couldn't possibly say what losing such a costly case will do to your insurance premiums. Look, let's not cross that bridge right now.'

Rick snorted, aware that Mark was trying to let him down lightly. The career he'd given his life to was finished. He'd have to start again doing something else. No doubt at the bottom of the ladder. He pulled his attention back to Mark, who was still talking.

'In some ways, given that any damages awarded will be specifically for Dean's ongoing care, you'd be better off if Dean was dead.'

'Don't say that. He doesn't deserve that.' Dean's face swam to the front of Rick's mind.

He is so young. He should have his whole life ahead of him.

'I'm only being realistic. It's harsh, I agree, but it might be kinder for him to die now, rather than hang on for years.'

'No. He's alive,' said Rick. 'And where there's life, there's hope.'

'If you say so.'

'Perhaps I should come back to London. If I could see him, I—'

'Absolutely not. I'm serious, Rick. If you do that, I can't represent you.'

'But—'

'No. Whatever you're doing to stay out of the papers, keep doing it. Cora Diamond is stirring up plenty of public animosity towards you. Don't give her any more ammunition. Keep your head down and don't pay any attention to any of the nonsense being spouted on the *Find Dr Death Podcast.*'

'The what?'

'I said ignore it. Just don't give them any clues as to your whereabouts. Watch your emails for updates from me. You'll have to surface for the first court appearance – you can't afford to miss that. We'll just have to take it from there.'

Rick stared at the phone after Mark rang off, feeling as if someone had just kicked both legs out from under him. He searched up the *Find Dr Death Podcast* and within seconds wished he hadn't. Ignoring the brash music from the computer game and Grace cheering on her growing collection of bouncy ice-bound creatures, he pulled his phone to pieces again and tucked it back in the kitchen drawer.

In more than two decades as a family GP, he had seen senseless tragedies like Dean's unfold before. They had all stayed with him. Every single one. A teenager who had got carried away at a pool party and dived into the shallow end by mistake. Two sixth-formers on holiday in Cornwall celebrating exam results by tombstoning off the cliffs to impress their friends when the tide wasn't high enough. Students at fresher's parties taking tablets offered by strangers. All young people with promising futures who had made impulsive, life-changing decisions that spun them off the rails into oblivion. Every single time, they hurt not only themselves but the people around them.

It wasn't possible to work within a community, as Rick did, and not see the fallout. He had supported countless broken families and shattered friendship groups over the years. But this time, he couldn't. This time, everyone thought he was the cause of the problem and he was helpless to do anything but ride this terrible roller coaster right to the bitter end.

A knock at the door pulled him back from a precipice of regret. Beth stood on the doorstep, soaked to the skin, her hair plastered to her head. The memory of how good it had felt to hold her close wandered through his mind.

'I'm sorry I implied that you started the fire,' she murmured. 'It wasn't smoking at all. It was Daisy.'

'I'm sorry to hear that, but, like I said, it was a couple of teenagers smoking, not me.'

She nodded, clearly preoccupied. 'Now I have to go and have a really difficult conversation with Daisy and I don't know what to say.'

'For what it's worth, I suggest you be honest. Try to be as calm and rational as you can, but tell her how you feel.' His arms itched to reach for her, to find a way to ease her sorrow, but he couldn't let himself. After the conversation he had just had with Mark, all Rick could offer was debt and notoriety. She didn't deserve that.

Maybe it's better to let her think I'm some weed-obsessed loser.

A heavy silence settled between them until a loud flourish of music rang out from the television and Grace squealed, 'No waaaay! A killer whale just ate my penguin.' She looked up and spotted Beth. 'Mummy, come and look at this.'

Beth scooped Grace into her arms. 'You were very brave coming to get Rick earlier. Did you know you saved the day? I'm so proud of you.'

'Muuum. You're all dirty and smelly.'

'I know. Sorry.' Beth gave Boo a gentle poke with one finger. 'Who's this you've got?'

Grace tucked the scruffy one-eyed bear further under her arm and set her mouth in a stubborn line. 'Boo is missing David, so he's playing with me and Paddy.'

'David?'

'Rick's little boy.'

'Oh! That's nice. But it's time to go now, so better put him down.'

'No, Mummy, pleeeease, I don't want to.'

Beth raised apologetic eyes to Rick.

He shook his head. 'It's fine. She can borrow Boo for a bit. David won't miss him.'

'That's kind. Thank you. Did you hear that, Grace? Boo can come with us to check on the others.'

The little girl wiped tears from her face. 'Can we come and play penguins again, too?'

'We'll see. Come along. Here, I brought your coat. It's raining.' After helping Grace into a waterproof, Beth glanced at Rick, her eyes wide and sombre. 'Thank you, Rick. I don't know what we'd have done without you today.'

He watched the two of them leave, his heart heavy. His warrior queen looked as if she carried the whole universe on her shoulders. A desperate need to protect her washed over him and he vowed that, in the short time he had before the court case, he would do everything he could to help. He wanted more than anything to be with her, but that couldn't be. When his life imploded, as it surely would, and very soon, he'd be damned if he'd take her down, too.

Chapter 27

After a long, hot shower, Beth ran a brush though her wet hair as her thoughts chased themselves in circles around her head. Rick had a son. A little boy called David. A son who no doubt had a mother. She threw the brush aside, quashing down the jealousy uncoiling in her belly.

Don't be silly. A good-looking fella like Rick is bound to either be attached or have a dating history. There'd be something seriously wrong if he didn't.

She sighed. He'd given no indication that he was attached to someone. Either way, she was a fool to read too much into one hug given in a moment of stress. No matter how delicious it had been. Her hormones jumped up and down and insisted it was not just any old hug. After all, she'd actually leaned on him and he'd let her. That had to mean something.

No. Don't go there.

She had to focus on the kids and the house and not get distracted. She pulled a soft blue sweater on over her jeans and went downstairs, the heavy drum of rain on the roof masking her footsteps. A bitter scorched wood smell hung in the air and – even though she'd scrubbed herself thoroughly, adding a generous squirt from her one remaining bottle of perfume – she was convinced she still reeked of smoke.

She paused at the lounge door to check on Grace, who was busy introducing Boo to the delights of Disney's *Frozen*. Moving on to the kitchen, she checked the bucket. No drips so far.

Daisy sat at the kitchen table, red-eyed, a pile of soggy tissues before her. Rose sat next to her. Jack stood at the window, hands in his pockets, his back to the room. He stared through thick ropes of water streaming down the window at a thin trail of smoke that continued to rise from the remains of the shed.

'Hi, Beth!' Rose poured a mug of tea from the pot on the table and nudged it in Beth's direction.

Beth sank onto a chair. A thick silence descended that she had no idea how to break.

Daisy sniffed and whispered. 'I'm sorry, Beth. Please believe me.'

The quiver in her voice tugged at Beth's heart and she watched Daisy crumple into a heap of heart-wrenching sobs, runny mascara and snot. It was impossible not to feel her pain. Beth lurched to her feet, rounded the table and wrapped her arms around the girl and held her tight. For once, Daisy didn't push her away.

'I know you're sorry, baby,' Beth shushed. 'I know. I'm sorry, too.'

'Mummy! Daisy is not a baby.' The outraged cry from the door made everyone look. Grace stood there, staring, open-jawed, Boo clutched to her chest.

Beth's laugh held more than a tinge of hysteria. 'Whether you like it or not, Grace Louise Hope, I am the mother around here and if I say you're my babies, then you're my babies. So, get used to it.'

Grace's mouth shut with a snap. She looked from Beth to each of her siblings in turn. 'Whatever,' she huffed and stomped off, slamming the door.

Jack sloped over to sit at the table. 'She gets more like Daisy every day.'

Daisy hiccupped.

Beth released her and sat back down. 'What were you doing, Daisy?'

Daisy released a juddering sigh. 'I was making something.'

'With that soldering thingy?'

Daisy nodded and grabbed a fresh tissue from the box. 'I got this kit off the internet. It draws patterns on wood. It's epic... well, it was, until it caught fire. I was making a nameplate for the door. You said you wanted one when you were fixing the bell the other day.'

Beth furrowed her brow. 'Here's the thing, Daisy. Why would you suddenly decide to make me something? You've never given me anything before.'

'Except a hard time,' snorted Jack.

Beth shot him a sideways glare. 'Not helping, Jack.'

Daisy sniffed. 'I thought I could show it to that lady in the craft shop. I thought it might prove I was crafty and...'

'And burn down the shed and nearly kill us all,' said Jack. 'Way to go, Dais.'

'Jack! Stop it,' admonished Beth.

He threw his hands up, all hurt innocence. 'Why're you getting cross with me?'

'I mean it, Jack. If you can't be supportive, keep your trap shut.'

'Fine!' He sank down in his chair and stared at the knotty grain of the tabletop.

Daisy's eyes shimmered. 'That metal thing was way hotter than I thought. I only put it down for a second. There was, like, this rough bit of wood that needed sanding. The hot rod thing touched some newspaper and smoke started, then it was, like, properly burning. This old rag on the table caught fire, too. Like, fast. I mean, really fast! Then it spread to the curtains and… and it was mega scary.'

Beth watched the teen's lips tremble, knowing there was more.

'So, like, Grace was outside. She was behind the shed. It was too hot to get past. Flames and smoke were pouring out of the door. I yelled at her to go the other way. To duck through the hedge, like, and run to the barn. 'Cos I'd seen you go over there. Then, I got the hose out. I thought, if I could get everything wet, I could stop it, but, like, the flames were on the roof by then and everything was on fire and… well… then you came.'

Beth rubbed her temples with the tips of her fingers and looked Daisy in the eye.

'I love you, Daisy.' The silence that greeted Beth's comment was deafening. 'The thing is, you've made it very clear you don't like me. Which hurts, by the way. You keep saying that I'm not your real mother, that you don't care what I think and I'm lame. To be perfectly frank, I've had enough. I know I'm not your mother. I'm not stupid. I'm not trying to be your mother. I just want you to let me look after you.'

Daisy bowed her head. She pulled at the scraggy tissue in her hands. Tears tumbled down her cheeks, dripping into her lap unchecked. Wiping her face, she sucked in a deep breath. 'I can't do that, because you'll leave.'

'Why do you think I'll leave?'

The teen shrugged. 'Everyone leaves. Mum left. I know she couldn't help it, because she died, but she still left. After that, Aunty B came for a bit and then she stopped. We see her in the village, but it's not the same. And now Dad's gone. And yeah, I know he's working abroad and stuff, but he could have stayed. He chose to leave.'

A small kernel of hope blossomed in Beth's chest. 'Is that why you give me so much grief? Because you think I'm not going to stick around?'

Daisy shrugged. 'Yeah. And also because you keep telling me I can't do what I want. Anyway, I don't care what Dad says on all his effing postcards, I don't think he's coming back.' Daisy looked at her siblings. 'I'm not wrong, am I? Well, am I?'

Beth and Rose exchanged a glance.

'There, see.' Daisy pointed at them. 'You two have been all huddled up the last couple of days, talking in whispers and... and... Oh. Come on! I'm not stupid. Something is going on.'

'Tell her, Beth,' urged Rose.

The weight of Jack's gaze landed on Beth, too. Her heart started to beat a wild rhythm in her chest. She wasn't ready for this.

'There's a lot of shit going down, Dais,' said Jack, 'and I don't believe the half of it. But if we tell you, you got to promise not to go off the deep end.'

Daisy scrubbed at her face with the remains of her tissue. 'What are you on about, J?'

Beth held her breath.

'For starters, Dad isn't sending the postcards,' said Jack. 'Beth is.'

Daisy's eyebrows disappeared up behind her fringe. 'Why?'

Rose leapt to Beth's defence. 'You got so upset after Dad left. Beth thought they would help calm you down.'

'What? Like I'm five or something?'

Rose shrugged. 'Then he sent, like, this really mean letter. Told her he couldn't bear to be near us kids because we remind him of Mum and that he wasn't ever coming back. And he stole the money Beth had saved to fix the roof.'

Daisy shook her head. 'He wouldn't do that.'

Jack glared at Rose. 'We don't know for sure that he stole it.'

'We do. He took it right out of the account. Without asking,' said Rose.

'But we don't know what's going on with him,' insisted Jack. 'Any more than he knows about stuff here. He might have borrowed it because he needed it.'

'We need it, Jack. Stop being thick.'

'Please stop it,' said Beth. 'Having a go at each other won't fix anything.'

Daisy was resolute. 'It's lies.'

'Show her the letter, Beth,' said Rose.

Beth blinked back tears and fumbled in her bag.

A heavy silence fell as Daisy read the letter, then she pushed it away. 'This is fake.'

Beth shook her head. 'It isn't.'

'You faked the postcards. You could fake a letter.'

'I didn't, though.'

'I don't believe you.' An icy cold hand took hold of Beth's heart at the quiet certainty in Daisy's voice.

'He was never that reliable, though, was he?' said Rose.

'Come on, Rose, he wasn't that bad,' said Jack.

'How many times did he say he'd come to something at school, you know, plays and stuff, and not turn up? Remember that competition you were in?'

Jack hunched down in his chair. 'You're talking bullshit, Rose.'

Daisy turned blank eyes on Beth. 'Are you going to divorce him?'

Beth nodded. 'When I can afford it.'

'See? I was right. Then you'll leave.'

'For God's sake, Daisy. I'm not leaving. This is my home. It's your home, too, for as long as you want it.'

'If she doesn't burn it down first—'

'Jack! Give it a rest, will you?' Beth sprang to her feet, took two strides to the dresser, grabbed the silver-framed photograph of Isla and shoved it into Daisy's hands. 'Look.'

Daisy stared at her mother's face, then back up at Beth. 'What am I looking at?'

'I've spent far too long thinking of your mother as this perfect ghost. A rival I can't compete with. But recently, I've been thinking that if I'd known her, I probably would have liked her. Everyone else seems to think she was really special.'

'She was wonderful,' muttered Rose.

'Then answer me this, Rose. How pissed off would she be at your dad for not sticking around to take care of you?' demanded Beth.

Jack gave a short laugh. 'She'd be bloody livid.'

'Yes, Jack, she would. And know what? I'm livid, too.' Beth looked at each of them. Daisy refused to meet her eyes. 'I'm not leaving, Daisy. Please believe me. If you can't let me take care of you for your own sake, then let me do it for your mum. I don't want to replace her. But if something ever happened to me, I'd like to think someone would be there for Grace. Someone to love her and put her first. Let me do that for you, Daisy, please?'

Several seconds passed. Daisy pulled her arm from under Beth's hand and stood up, still hugging Isla's picture to her chest. 'I'll think about it. I'm tired. I'm going to bed.'

'Please, I—'

'No! Just leave me alone.' The kitchen door slammed again.

'Are you really going to divorce him?' demanded Jack.

Beth sank onto a chair, her heart heavy. 'Yes, I consulted a lawyer about a month after he left. Apparently, divorcing someone when you don't know where they are is expensive and difficult, but not impossible.'

'But what if…' Jack shook his head. 'No, never mind.'

'What if he comes back?' Beth asked.

Jack nodded.

'If he does, I won't stop you seeing him, but I won't be his wife. And let's be clear on one thing, he won't be moving back in here. Assuming we can raise the money to save this place, of course.'

Rose suddenly slapped a hand to her forehead. 'The tents. Oh, Beth. The tents I picked up with Ethan.'

'What about them?' asked Beth.

'They were in the shed.'

'What tents?' asked Jack.

Rose tutted. 'Keep up, Jack. We're going to rent out the field for camping.'

'Are we? Why?'

Beth crossed the kitchen to look out at the devastation, the smoking hulk of the shed a stark reminder of how close they had already come to disaster. 'We've got to pay the mortgage and fix the roof, Jack. The money your dad took—' She held up a hand to pre-empt the protest that was already halfway out of his mouth. 'Whether he stole it or borrowed it is irrelevant. Without that money, we're in serious financial trouble.'

Beth listened as Rose explained her plan to her brother, her already low spirits sinking further. Her mobile vibrated in her pocket. What now? She swiped to accept the call.

'Hi, Beth,' came Jane's voice. 'Are you ready for that consultation?'

The last thing Beth felt like right at that moment was a therapy session, but she sure had plenty to talk about. 'Hi, Jane. Hang on a sec…' She turned to Rose and Jack. 'Sorry, guys. I have to take this. Can one of you check on Grace for me, please?'

Chapter 28

The storm had passed by 8am the next morning and the sun peeped out from behind a bank of retreating clouds, as if surprised to see that the world was still there. Rick armed himself with a strong cup of coffee and switched his phone on, determined to ring David.

I've left it too long already.

What should he say? What could he say? While he dithered, the handset buzzed with an incoming call. Without thinking, he accepted it.

A stranger's voice spoke. 'Dr Mahon? Do you have any comment on the Dean Markwell/Cora Diamond lawsuit?'

A beat passed as Rick struggled to process the question. 'Why can't you bastards just leave me alone?' He punched the red button, switched the phone off and threw it to the back of the drawer.

That was stupid. What if they recorded me?

It was exactly the sort of thing Mark Freeman had said to avoid. He should have just said no comment and hung up, or not said anything at all.

He dragged a thick fleece on and wandered out to check

on the llampaccas. With any luck, the fresh air would calm his jitters. The sound of someone chucking lumps of wood around came from next door. He'd promised himself he'd stay away from Beth, but it was only neighbourly to say hi.

'Hi. You alright?' he called over the hedge, the sharp smell of burnt wood making him cough.

Beth looked up from yanking at a section of blackened wood sticking out from the remains of the shed. 'Oh, Rick. Hi. Uh, yeah, I guess.'

Rick leaned over the hedge to get a closer look. 'You don't sound alright.'

'I'm not. Not really.' She brushed heavy-duty gardening-gloved palms against her jeans, leaving thick black tracks. 'Thank you, again, for yesterday. For helping with the fire and for looking after Grace, afterwards.' She tucked a stray lock of hair behind her ear, unaware that she was smudging soot across her temple, and gave the burnt plank of wood another ineffectual tug.

The air of sad exhaustion that surrounded her punched Rick right in the gut. 'Do you need a hand?'

'I can manage.'

'I know you can, but I'm in the mood to tear something apart right now. You might as well make the most of it.'

She looked from him to the stubborn piece of timber. 'Uh, sure, okay. Knock yourself out.'

'Give me a sec. I'll just sort the llampaccas out and then I'll be over.'

Ten minutes later, Rick arrived at Beth's side with a pair of gloves he'd unearthed from Charlie's tool store. He surveyed the wreckage and let out a low whistle. Charred boards poked up from the shed base like half-rotten teeth.

Black ash coated everything and rivulets of a tar-like residue containing bits of unidentifiable melted stuff seeped in all directions.

'Heck. What a mess.' Rick wasn't sure if he was talking about Beth's situation or his own. At least something could be done about a wrecked shed. Broken lives were harder to fix. He bent down to grab a large lump of burned something or other. 'Where do you want this?'

'My basic plan is to separate things into two piles; not salvageable and possibly salvageable.'

'Logical.' Rick looked around him. 'Is anything salvageable?'

'Some of the wood – the stuff that's not completely incinerated – can go in the log burner. I can't afford to waste it. I'm making a pile over there.' She indicated a small lean-to on the far side of the garden.

'And the rest?'

'Anything that can't be reused is going to the tip. There's a pile on the drive. A trailer is coming tomorrow.'

Rick nodded and set to, working all his recent frustrations out by twisting and ripping at sections of debris and hauling it away. From the corner of his eye, he watched Beth keeping pace with him. They cleared in silence, until Rick reached across for a wide upright panel of wood. Beth did the same and their hands collided. A shock wave of sensation rippled up Rick's arm and, although the only thing he wanted was to get closer to her, he stepped back and gestured for her to go ahead. 'Sorry.'

She tugged at the board, then grimaced. 'Actually, it's too big for me. Do you mind?'

He reached for the panel again.

'Can I ask…' She cleared her throat. 'No, it's… no, forget it.'

'No, go on.'

'I don't want to pry, but what's the real story behind that video? With your patient, I mean. I know what happened with the YouTuber.'

He gave the piece of wood a vicious yank. It broke away at the base.

Do I really want to go there? What will she think?

'You don't have to tell me. I'm not judging you. I mean, look at the total balls-up I'm making of my own life.'

He glanced over, noticing cute freckles beneath the soot smudges on her nose. 'You look like you're doing fine to me.'

'I'm not, though. Genuinely, I'm stuffing everything up. The roof probably still leaks; I know it didn't last night, which is a huge relief, but I've only patched it up temporarily. It needs a proper fix. I can't pay the mortgage. And I've no idea how I'm going to feed the kids if I can't get a job. I thought about setting up a campsite, you know, or a business of some sort. But that's a gamble. Am I just risking what little cash we have left? I don't know. All I do know is that I have to do something. That's me in a nutshell, Rick. Pretty useless.'

Rick stared at her. How she wasn't sobbing her heart out was beyond him. 'Do you know what I see when I look at you?'

'Oh dear. I'm not sure I want to know.'

'I see someone strong. And really brave.'

Pink spots appeared in her cheeks. 'I don't know about that.'

'It's true. You've had a lot of crap thrown at you, but you're still fighting. You said it was better to do something than sit around doing nothing. I admire that and I'm going to try and do the same. For what it's worth, I think that you can do anything you put your mind to.'

She blew out a long breath. 'Well, I have just escaped the whole house burning to the ground. I should probably count my blessings.'

He smiled. His warrior queen was back. Stubborn and opinionated as hell.

That husband of hers is a prize plonker for walking away.

'So, go on, I dare you,' she prompted. 'Tell me what's really going on with you. Give me you in a nutshell. What did you do that's got the whole world on your back?'

Rick threw a chunk of blackened wood onto a pile behind him. His instinct to preserve Dean's confidentiality had become irrelevant recently thanks to Cora's latest media blitz revealing all pertinent details. He was amazed that Beth didn't already know. 'I prescribed a drug – a standard treatment for depression and anxiety.'

'Why was that so bad?'

'I didn't know my patient was in the habit of scoring street drugs.'

'Ah.'

'Heroin added to the medication I prescribed caused acute heart arrhythmia and a massive stroke.'

'Did he die?'

'Not quite, but near as damn it. I'd never have given him that damn prescription if I'd had full access to his records.'

'Why didn't you?'

Rick sighed. 'It's a long story. Anyway, because he's moderately famous, the story hit the papers and there's been a massive pile-on on social media. I've been "cancelled".

Which seems to involve anyone and everyone having lots of fun ripping me and anything I've ever done to shreds. The upshot is I'm going to get sued for millions. And I'll lose. They'll take my apartment, probably the barn as well – everything. But worse than all that, I've lost my nerve as a doctor. The thought of seeing another patient sends me into a blind panic.' He scratched his head. 'Everything I've ever worked for is gone. And like a coward, instead of facing the music, I've been hiding here in the forest wondering what the hell to do.'

'I'm so sorry.'

Rick shrugged. 'It is what it is. Be honest, Beth. That's a bigger nutshell than you were expecting, isn't it?'

Beth smiled. 'That's the beauty of nuts. They come in all shapes and sizes. If ripping up what's left of my shed helps take your mind off all that, I'm glad.'

Captivated by the sparkle in her eyes, Rick's eyes drifted to her lips. All he had to do was lean in…

Beth's mobile rang. 'Oh! It's Daisy. I have to take this.'

Rick straightened. *That was close.* Reaching for a random hunk of debris, he watched Beth wander towards the house.

She suddenly stopped. 'Daisy, Daisy… *Daisy*, calm down. It'll be fine. All you have to do is be polite and enthusiastic and – oh, hang on. Just stay where you are, I'll be there in five minutes.' She hung up. Worry lines furrowed her forehead. 'Rick, I'm sorry. I have to go.'

'Problem?'

'It's nothing major, but Daisy's never actively asked for my help before and—'

'Say no more. Go. Don't worry about this lot, I'll sort it.'

'Are you sure?'

He waved her away. 'Go. Sort your daughter out. Leave me be. I'm having fun.'

She grinned. 'You're mad, you are.' The smile died on her face. 'Oh, Rick. I didn't mean that the way it sounded. You're not nuts. I mean…'

'I know what you meant. Anyway, you said you like nuts. Right?'

He laughed, watching her cheeks turn pink again. Making her blush was fun.

Chapter 29

Beth paced along the wide pavement outside Bits and Bobs, from the tables in front of The Coffee Pot all the way to the A-frame panels advertising fresh sausage and egg baps at the bakery. Checking her watch, she retraced her steps. *What's taking so long?*

Suddenly, the door burst open and Daisy emerged, punching the air in triumph. 'Yes!'

'You got it?'

'Of course I did. Why? Did you think I wouldn't?'

'No. Not for a second.'

'I can't wait to tell Sonya.' Daisy swiped her phone screen. 'And Lily and Sara. They'll be well jel.'

Beth made a shooing motion. 'Go on. Go tell the world how fabulous you are. Do me a favour, though, and grab Grace from preschool when she comes out? I want a quick word with Lucy.'

'Huh?' Daisy looked up from her phone. 'Sure.'

Beth made her way into the shop. Lucy, dressed head to toe in bright magenta, matching beads in her braids, handed over a dribbling Hazel.

'No wonder Daisy was terrified of you when she peered into the shop earlier, Lucy. You look like a superwoman. I take it Hazel is sleeping through the night now.'

Lucy's grin was smug. 'She is. And your Daisy is just what I've been looking for. Whatever you're doing with your teens, Beth, keep doing it. She's a credit to you.' She leaned closer and gave Beth a quick hug. 'I heard about the fire. Are you okay? Was there much damage?'

Beth's vision swam with unexpected tears. 'Not much goes under the radar around here, does it?'

'We could see the smoke from the village green.'

'It was an accident.'

'Of course it was an accident. Beth, honey. Don't be so defensive. Fire can happen to anyone, especially in the forest. People just want to help.'

Beth examined the rug at her feet, unable to trust her voice.

'You don't like letting people in, do you?' Lucy asked.

Beth lifted one shoulder and let it drop.

'Look, hun, everyone I've spoken to is simply relieved no one was hurt. Yes, they're talking about it, but that doesn't mean they're being nasty. If you give people a chance, they might surprise you.'

'Sure.'

'Right. Here and now, I challenge you to give people in this village a chance. That means next time someone offers you help, Beth, you have to say yes. Even if it's Barbara.'

Beth snorted. 'Like that's ever going to happen.'

'It will. You'll see. Say yes?'

'I left Rick smashing up the ruins of my shed this morning, does that count?'

'Rick?'

'My next-door neighbour.'

'Mr Gorgeous But Complicated?' Lucy grinned. 'Beth! You're blushing. Did something happen?'

'I think he almost kissed me.'

'You think?'

'Yes, I'm sure he was about to, but then Daisy rang and – oh! I don't know. I could be overthinking.'

'Do you want him to kiss you?'

'I shouldn't.'

'Meaning that you do.'

'There are so many reasons why it would be a bad idea.'

Lucy laughed. 'You totally want him to kiss you.'

'Maybe I do, but it isn't going to happen.'

'Why not?'

'I have too many other things to worry about right now.'

'Like what?'

'Like finding a way to earn a living.'

'Still no sign of a job?'

'I've filled in so many online applications, I could do it in my sleep. Speaking of which, I have an interview for an overnight shelf-stacking job in that big supermarket over at Deersleigh Park.'

'Overnight?'

'Yes. Two nights a week. Rose can watch Grace overnight and it'll be regular money coming in. Not much, but it's a start.'

'Didn't you say something about setting up a campsite?'

'Yes. I even filled in the application forms for the council, but…'

'But what?'

'There are bound to be objections. Lord Astley, for starters.'

'Lord Tosspot is always a pain.' Lucy scoffed. 'You can't let him stop you.'

'Even Barbara said she would object.'

'That doesn't sound like Barbara.'

Beth shrugged. 'I told you she didn't like me.'

'There must be more to it than that.'

'She said I'd be taking business away from the campsite at the bottom of the hill. Tara, is it?'

'Gosh. She's got a point. Tara's only just keeping body and soul together as it is.'

'I see that, I really do. But I just… I just don't know what else to do.' Beth sniffed and scrabbled in a pocket for a tissue as a wave of despair washed over her. 'We could lose the house.'

'I had no idea it was that bad.' Lucy frowned. 'Tell you what, why don't I pop up on Saturday? Tom can take the kids to see his mum, and you and I can have a brainstorming session.'

'That's kind, but you're already so busy.'

'Meh. You'd be doing me a favour. Much as I love my ma-in-law, she's driving me up the wall. Doesn't approve of women working when their kids are small and is more than happy to say so. Repeatedly. If you let me come and see you, you'll be doing your bit to preserve world peace.'

Beth dabbed at her eyes. 'Alright, come and have a cuppa and I'll give you a tour.'

'Great stuff.' Lucy beamed. 'Now, give me my baby back and be off with you.'

*

Stepping out of Bits and Bobs, a spring in her step at the prospect of seeing Lucy again soon, Beth heard her name called. Turning, she saw Barbara scurrying along the pavement. The older woman ground to a halt at Beth's side, wheezing.

'Oh my giddy aunt, my running days are definitely behind me. Beth. My dear. My Brian told me about the fire. You must have been terrified.'

'You'll be pleased to hear that all the equipment for the campsite went up in smoke, too.'

Barbara's eyebrows shot up. 'Did it? Oh, Beth, I'm so sorry.'

'Are you?'

'Of course I am. That's awful. I may disagree with your plan, but I don't wish you any harm. Tell me. How are the children?'

'They're shocked, but fine. Brian was wonderful.'

'He's a tower of strength, that man. Tell me, is it true it was an electrical fault?'

Beth nodded.

'Thank the Lord. I'm so relieved to hear that. No, please don't look at me like that. I'm not glad about the fire, just that... It's my niece's boys, Tyler and Kyle. They thought that they might have started it. The fire, I mean. Apparently, a whole gang of them have been hanging around up there, smoking and whatnot.'

Beth felt something squirm deep in her chest.

'My Brian tore a strip off them both, I promise you. They won't do it again. I'll send them up to apologise. Do me a favour, set them to work. I'm sure you could do with help clearing up.'

'But they didn't cause the fire.'

'That's not the point. They could have. They need to learn about consequences. Let them see fire damage up close and they'll never take risks like that again.'

'Fine. I will. Thank you.'

'Is there much damage?'

'Loads. I have a trailer coming tomorrow so I can take the first load to the tip.'

'Perfect, they can help fill it, then ride along and empty it, too. I'll tell them. They'll be no trouble. For all their stupid behaviour, they're nice boys, really. They know your Jack from school.'

'I can't pay them.'

'Good heavens! I don't want you to pay them. Sling them a biscuit from time to time, if you really feel you must.'

The thought of chucking Hobnobs out of the front door at two teenage boys made Beth laugh. Paddy would give himself a hernia trying to catch them first. Then she recalled Lucy's challenge to say yes. 'Thank you, Barbara. Send them up tomorrow morning and I'll put them to work.'

Chapter 30

The car park opposite the general store was deserted at 6am on Saturday. Rick pulled into a space, locked the car and jogged across the road. The smell of fresh coffee hit him as soon as he entered. Barbara was alone. Spotting him, she patted a large box on the counter next to her.

'Morning. Everything on your list is in here. Do you need anything else?'

'A black coffee to go, please.'

She filled a cardboard cup. As he tapped his credit card, Rick's eyes drifted to a bundle of newspapers on the floor. Cora Diamond's smile beamed up at him from the top sheet. He twisted his head to better read the headline.

Cora Diamond, new face of Hants FM.

'It's a shame, what happened to her lad,' muttered Barbara. 'But all the notoriety isn't doing her career any harm, is it?'

Rick forced a polite smile. 'She is highlighting the need for more child and adult mental health services, though, so maybe we should give her a break.'

'You're too nice for your own good.'

'Not really, just trying to find a silver lining. I'll just run this box out to the car and come back for the coffee.'

On his return, she brandished a small package. 'I nearly forgot; this came.'

'Ah! My new phone. With a new number. Hopefully, this one will stay private.'

'Are you getting harassed?'

'You could say that but I have to stay in contact with my legal team. I can't not have a phone.'

'Right you are. I'll expect your next list of groceries from a different number then. Just let me know it's you.' She came out from behind the counter to fetch the papers, grunting as she lifted them.

'Let me,' said Rick, taking them from her. 'Where do you want them?'

'By the rack near the door, please.'

He placed them where she asked. A magazine cover caught his eye. It was the sort of publication that featured people who claimed to have been abducted by three-headed aliens, who forced them to clean spaceship toilets. He yanked it from the shelf. 'Bloody hell, how can these two charlatans be getting an award?'

'Let me see.' Barbara flicked to the full article and read aloud. 'Social media commentators Sal and Ade up for an industry award for their innovative investigation of the #DrDeath story and the *Find Dr Death Podcast*.'

'Innovation? Lies and bullying, more like. I don't stand a chance in court, thanks to them.'

Barbara snapped the magazine closed. 'If there's one thing I've learned in life, Rick, it's that what you give out into the world, eventually comes back to bite you on the bum. Like my Brian always says, it's important to behave honourably yourself. Keep doing the next right thing. That way you can live with yourself whatever happens.' She put the magazine back. 'Don't give them a second more of your time or energy.'

*

Back at the barn, Rick set his new phone up, punched in Mark Freeman's number and stared out of the window at the llampaccas skipping and dancing in the back field in the sunshine as he listened to the ringtone.

Daft animals.

'Mark Freeman speaking.'

'Hi, Mark, it's Rick Mahon.'

'Rick, at last. You're a difficult man to get a hold of. You've not replied to any of my emails.'

'Sorry, Mark. It's been a bit difficult. There's just so much stuff coming in from journalists and social media... Look, take a note of this number, will you? It's new. I'm hoping to keep it private. You should be able to contact me directly on this.'

'Will do. What about emails? There are documents we need to send you. And you're going to have to think about coming back to London soon.'

Rick's heart lurched. He wasn't ready. 'When?'

'Not yet. Keep your head down a bit longer. But be aware, Cora Diamond's team are trying to get the first court date moved up to some time in the next few weeks. I'm not sure when. We'll need to go through some stuff. Make sure you're ready.'

Rick's chest tightened at the thought.

'It'll be fine, Rick. Sort an email account I can send papers to. We'll take it from there.'

The call over, Rick did as he was told. His fingers hovered over the phone keys, wondering if he should ring Sam at the surgery and see how they were all coping.

A knock at the front door made him jump.

Surely one call on a new line couldn't have given his location away? Perhaps paying for the phone with his credit card had left a digital trail. He rubbed his forehead. *That's paranoia. Get a grip.*

A second knock sounded.

Supressing an impulse to dive to the floor and crawl commando-style to hide behind the sofa, Rick got to his feet. It was pointless hiding. Barbara's Brian was right. The important thing was to be honourable and behave in a way that he could live with.

There were no reporters outside poised to thrust microphones in his face. Instead, two lanky teenage lads were larking about. One shoved the other off the porch step and sniggered. They looked vaguely familiar.

'Can I help you?' Rick asked.

Both boys immediately straightened and flicked greasy fringes out of their eyes. The taller of the two spoke, 'Nah, bud. Me and Kyle are helping you.'

The quieter boy nodded, sniffed and wiped the palm of his hand up his nose and into his hair.

'Helping me, how?'

'We're here to clear up.'

Rick looked closer. 'Hang on, I recognise you. You're the lads I chased off here yesterday. The ones smoking pot on my property.'

The two youths shuffled their feet, huddling closer together.

Kyle muttered, 'Sorry, man.' He nudged his friend. 'Told you he saw us, Tyler.'

'Do you have any idea how dangerous it is?' said Rick.

'Yeah. We've had the "no smoking in the forest 'cos it's causes fires" sermon twice already this morning,' grumbled Tyler.

'It's also bad for your health,' said Rick.

'Yeah. We got that lecture, too. Like I said, we're here to clear up. To make amends, like. Even though we didn't actually start the fire.' Tyler clearly thought they deserved a medal for altruism.

'Great, there's a whole pile of charred shed ready to go in a trailer next door. I'll show you.' Rick was halfway across the yard before he realised that the lads hadn't moved. Instead, they were staring at Tyler's mobile. 'Hey,' Rick said, 'you coming, or not?'

The lads looked from the phone to Rick.

'That's you,' said Tyler, pointing at his phone.

'Tyler, leave it,' muttered Kyle.

'What's me?'

'Doctor Death.' Tyler turned the screen towards Rick.

'Yes, that's me.'

'Woah, get away.' Kyle's eyes widened. 'You're Dean Markwell's doctor? You've actually spoken to Dean Markwell? For real?'

'I have.'

'No way.' Kyle shook his head. 'You mean it? Oh man! The D-Man's gameplays are epic.'

'Are they?'

'Yeah,' said Tyler. 'He's sick.'

'Yes, he is. He's very sick,' said Rick. 'Like I said. Drugs are dangerous.'

'Nah man. Not sick as in *sick*… well he is sick, like, but I mean sick as in seriously cool.'

Rick had nothing to say to that.

'Can I get a selfie with you?' asked Kyle.

Tyler shoved him. 'Don't be daft, mate. He's undercover.'

'Is he?' Kyle frowned. 'Why?'

Tyler rolled his eyes. 'He's the new guy Aunty B told us about. You know, Mr Extra Hush-Hush.'

Kyle looked Rick up and down, wide-eyed. 'You mean, he's on the list?'

This was getting surreal. 'Who the hell is Aunty B and what list?' asked Rick.

'Couldn't possibly say,' said Tyler. He mimed zipping his lips, locking them and throwing away a key. 'Don't worry, we won't rat you out. Wouldn't be worth the grief. Now, we clearing stuff up or what?'

Chapter 31

At the farmhouse, breakfast was getting out of hand. Daisy had woken up in a foul mood and was dispensing liberal quantities of sarcasm to everyone. Her most lethal barbs were all aimed at Beth. Clearly, the brief truce that had reigned in the immediate aftermath of the fire and her job interview was well and truly over. Beth was relieved to hear the knocker and hurried along the corridor to open the door.

'Hi, Lucy. Come in. Watch your step. The place is booby-trapped.' She kicked aside a pile of trainers, several school bags and a hockey stick. 'We're in the kitchen. Fancy a quick cuppa before I give you that tour?'

'Always up for tea, me.' Lucy bounced in, dressed in lime-green dungarees, her braids bound tightly back in a matching headwrap. 'By the way, did you know there's an old table, a chest of drawers and half a dozen broken chairs stuck in a hedge at the end of the lane?'

'You're kidding!' Beth glanced down the track. 'The phantom fly-tipper again. I'd better report it before Barbara has a coronary.'

Daisy's eyes grew round when she spotted Lucy. 'You checking up on me, boss?'

'I heard you were in charge of breakfast this morning. I thought I'd come see what you're like under pressure.'

Daisy's face turned the colour of chalk. 'I'm… uh… I'm—'

'Relax.' Lucy gave a merry laugh. 'I'm teasing you. I'm just here to see Beth.'

Jack was busy ploughing his way through a pile of scrambled eggs, his elbows out as if he was afraid someone might take it upon themselves to help him. He snorted. 'Ha! Dais, you got burned.'

Daisy fixed him with a death glare.

'Lucy is here to give me business advice,' said Beth. 'Rose's idea of a campsite is good, but it might cause problems for the lady down the road. I was hoping we could come up with another plan.'

Daisy scowled. 'I can't think of anything worse than camping. Why leave a perfectly warm, dry house to go live in a tent? It makes no sense.'

Rose leaned over Jack to grab an apple.

Jack nearly stabbed her with his fork.

'Relax, Jack. I don't want your food.' Rose bit into the fruit and chewed. 'I reckon there are loads of ways this place could start paying for itself.'

'Like what?' Lucy sat next to Grace, just in time to catch half a piece of toast as it slipped from Grace's hand. She passed it back to her with a grin. Grace giggled, chin dripping gruesome quantities of strawberry jam. She offered the toast to Boo, who sat in her old highchair, a yellow napkin tied around his neck.

'How about a B&B?' said Rose. 'The couple that run the Manor Hotel were in the Crashing Boar last week. They said they're fully booked this summer. They've a licence to hold weddings and that means loads of guests wanting to stay over. They haven't enough space. Perhaps we could put some up here?'

'The bedrooms here are full of us!' said Daisy. 'Or hadn't you noticed?'

Beth sank onto a chair next to Lucy. 'I don't like the idea of strangers in the house.'

'Posh guests need posh stuff,' Jack mumbled around a mouthful. 'Built-in bogs with their rooms and stuff.'

'That's true,' said Daisy. 'There's no way you can call this pile of bricks posh.'

'It's rustic,' agreed Lucy, 'but charming. The whole remote farmhouse setting is lovely, especially as you're not part of an actual working farm with piles of muck and machinery everywhere. If you spruce up the yard out front and make sure to keep it tidy, it'll look lovely. You could go for a traditional, low-tech, rural ambiance as your theme.'

'But where would we sleep?' insisted Daisy.

'What about the old stables?' said Jack.

'Stables? That sounds interesting.' Lucy put an elbow on the table and leaned in. 'Tell me more.'

Beth grunted. 'Don't get your hopes up, Lucy; it's just a big, grubby old space full of junk.'

'And 'piders,' added Grace. 'Big, big 'piders.'

Lucy gave Grace a wink. 'Big 'piders are the best, hon. I love big, grubby old spaces, too. You're going to have to give me that tour, Beth.'

'Come on then, but don't say I didn't warn you.'

*

Outside, Beth was surprised to see Rick loading scrap from the shed into the trailer.

'Morning, Rick. This is my friend, Lucy. Lucy, this is Rick.'

'Nice to meet you, Lucy.' Rick smiled. 'Beth, two random teenagers turned up at mine this morning. They said they're here to help clear up. I brought them over.'

'Tyler and Kyle,' said Beth. 'They're Barbara's nephews.'

'How come?' asked Lucy.

'You told me to accept help from her if she offered it. I followed your advice. I didn't expect them to actually turn up, though.'

The two lads scuffed their way across the drive from behind the stable, carrying a length of blackened timber between them. They dumped their load in the trailer and then shuffled to stand in front of Beth. Each nudged the other several times until, finally, Tyler muttered, 'We're sorry we were smoking.'

'Please don't do it again,' said Beth. 'And thank you for coming up to help out today.'

'S'alright.' Tyler gave a jaw-cracking yawn. 'Aunty B made us get up mega early.'

'Yeah,' grumbled Kyle, '9am on a Saturday.'

'Outrageous,' said Lucy.

'Exactly,' said Tyler. 'Is Jack around?'

Beth jerked her head towards the farmhouse. 'He's just finished breakfast. Go and find him. He can help, too.'

Tyler shoulder-barged Kyle hard enough to make him stagger. 'Race you.'

As they ran off, Rick turned to Beth. 'Is Barbara this Aunty B they keep going on about? It makes her sound like the boss of the New Forest criminal underworld.'

Lucy laughed. 'Half the kids in the forest call her Aunty B. She's connected to pretty much everyone, in one way or another. And *The Godfather* has got nothing on Barbara Trenchard.'

'She's way scarier than the mafia,' agreed Beth. 'Thanks for helping, Rick. I thought I'd take the first load to the skip later.'

'How?' He gestured towards the rear of her car. 'You haven't got a towing hitch.'

Beth groaned. 'I'm so stupid. I never thought.'

'We could use my car. You'll have to show me the way, though. I don't trust Tyler or Kyle's sense of anything, let alone direction. When you're ready, give me a shout.' He adjusted his work gloves, nodded and headed back to the ruins of the shed.

Lucy whispered, 'I see what you mean. He's gorgeous.'

'Lucy! Hush.'

'I only said he was good-looking. And I know you told me he was complicated, but I didn't realise he was quite that complicated.' She paused and examined Beth's face intently. 'You do know who he is, don't you?'

Beth reached up to unbolt the stable door. 'Yes.'

'Your sexy new friend comes with a whole truckload of baggage.'

'He's not my sexy anything. We're just neighbours.'

'Ha! You totally think he's sexy.'

'Give it a rest, Lucy. He has a young son.'

'They didn't say that in the papers.'

Lucy sounded so affronted that Beth had to laugh. 'And we all know how accurate the papers are. Anyway, my point is that I've no idea if he is attached to someone or not, but if he's got a kid, he might be.' She pushed one of the stable doors wide enough to allow them both to slip inside.

'You could ask him.'

'No, I couldn't. It would be too obvious. Now, come on. Focus. You wanted to see a big old space full of spiders. Here it is.'

Lucy's demeanour instantly became very serious. Beth watched her friend spin slowly on the spot, absorbing the interior proportions of the stables.

Built of brick to about waist-height, with upper walls consisting of thick overlapping wooden slats inset with high windows, all supported by thick oak beams, she had to admit she'd forgotten what an impressive structure it was – or would be, if it weren't for the alarming towers of boxes, bundles and general garbage stacked all around. Ancient spiderwebs formed fairy hammocks so substantial that whole armies of angry arachnids, wearing black bovver boots and biker jackets, could appear any moment to demand what the disturbance was.

'This is incredible.'

Beth snorted. 'Are we looking at the same thing? All I see is junk. There's no way I can rent this out as accommodation and I can't move the kids in here either. It's not remotely habitable.'

'No, but...' Lucy's keen gaze darted around the space. 'You're right, this isn't a traditional rental property, and even from a non-traditional viewpoint, it needs a lot of work.'

'That's what I said.'

'Yet, it's still a rentable space. It's well constructed and it appears watertight.'

'That's true.'

'It's very useable. Open and airy. Perfect for summer. Come winter, you might need to think about some sort of heating. Perhaps a log burner. They kick out a hefty radius of warmth, plus they're really atmospheric. With a good clear-out, some cleaning and lots of white paint and...' Lucy paused before finishing her sentence in a rush. 'Can I have first dibs on renting it?'

A horrible thought struck Beth. 'I won't accept charity.'

'It's not charity. I'm serious. Get this place up to scratch and I'll rent it from you. It won't be a huge sum, but it'll be a regular injection of cash and not at all seasonal like a campsite.'

Beth looked from Lucy to the cluttered space. 'What am I not seeing?'

Lucy stepped around a pile of boxes and wiggled through a narrow space between a stack of old chairs and what looked like battered tabletops, working her way deeper in to scan the far wall. 'I want to run proper craft classes. Somewhere we can do painting demos. I've always wanted to offer creative well-being courses, too. I genuinely think it will help people cope with the pressures of modern life. Everyone should make time to do something creative. Trouble is, most people don't know what the creative thing that works for them is, which is why you need some sort of well-being therapy centre to give them little tasters of what is possible. I reckon we could get arts council funding.'

'Really?'

'Yes, there's even the possibility of getting therapists on board, too.'

'You should talk to my counsellor, Jane. She'd love you.'

'Please give me her number.'

'What about the shop?'

'The shop is too small for what I have in mind. I'll still keep it in the village. The location is perfect for passing trade. But here, I can already see it. Therapy sessions alongside creativity sessions, where you can mix and match between different activities. Look at that big old barn door on its side over there. It's completely flat. Take the handle off it and lay it across a couple of trestles in this central section and you've got a massive worktable. And those four open stalls at the side? They'd be good for individual crafting groups or maybe a little crèche area. Parents could bring their little people along for soft play while they do some craft. Or... No, I'm sorry, I'm getting carried away.' Lucy turned to Beth, her eyes wide.

'So, you don't want to rent it?'

'I do. I really do. But as your friend, I ought to give you other options, not just the one I want. I mean, you could break the space down and rent individual stalls as artisan workshops. There are loads of local skilled arts and crafts workers wanting studio space. The light in here is perfect, with the high windows. Especially in summer. If you stand the main doors open, the whole place will be flooded with natural sunlight. There's room to store both equipment and finished products, too. You could even have exhibitions. Get connected with the Hampshire Art Week events. Beth, handle this right and you have a potential gold mine here! A mini gold mine, admittedly, because artists all have tight budgets, but still.'

'I don't know anything about art.'

'It's not that hard. And, anyway, the artists do the art, not you.'

'Why don't we run your well-being centre together?' asked Beth.

Lucy bit her lip. 'Are you serious?'

'Yes. I've got the space and you have the knowledge and contacts.'

Lucy thought for a moment. 'I need to work out the numbers and we'll have to set up an official partnership, but, in principal, I'm interested.'

'Then let's do it. I'll look into planning permission.'

Lucy waved an arm towards the end of the room. 'What's back there? I can't get to it, but I can see two doors?'

'I've never been back there. I've had enough to do staying on top of the house. I think the one on the right is a loo.'

'Useful.'

'I don't know what state it's in.'

'It doesn't matter. As long as it exists, we won't have the hassle and expense of getting builders in to dig drains and the like.'

'The other one leads to another storage space, I think. You can access it from the back garden as well. There's a second set of double doors, but they're bolted. I've no idea where the keys are. I've been meaning to get a locksmith out, but there's always something else I need to spend the money on.'

Lucy squeezed sideways through the jumble of boxes. 'Nearly there… Aha! Oh, bottom. It's locked and there's no way I can get to the other one. I wonder what's in there.'

Beth shrugged. 'No idea. I suspect more junk.'

'Want me to try to force it?'

'Oh no, please don't,' said Beth. 'We'll only have to repair it.'

Lucy gave in with reluctance. 'Fine. We can get to it later, once we've sorted this section out.'

'Let's go and work out what else we need to do to make this happen.' Beth turned for the door, a curious mix of nerves and excitement churning in her chest.

Chapter 32

Rick glanced in the rear-view mirror as he drove along the forest lanes. The three lads in the back of the vehicle, each plugged into headphones and nodding to different musical beats, periodically elbowed each other to draw attention to something on one of their mobiles. There was a lot of sniggering.

'I wonder what's so funny,' Rick muttered.

Beth looked over her shoulder. 'I have no idea, but they seem happy enough.'

'So do you,' said Rick. There was a definite spring in her step since she'd come out of the stable with Lucy.

'I am happy. I've had an exciting morning. Lucy reckons the stables would be great for a creative well-being centre. And the more I think about it, the more I think she's right.' She was literally bouncing with enthusiasm.

'Tell me more.'

'Well. We'll start with a craft-based initiative, offering a series of creative well-being activities, hopefully with art therapists and counsellors. Not just for individuals looking for mental health support, but for families and friends trying to rebuild connections after the pandemic.'

'Sounds interesting.'

'When that's up and running, we can add in extras.'

'Like what?'

'I thought we should make use of the countryside. There could be well-being walks through the forest and down to the coast. We could offer gardening projects and contact with the animals – the chickens and Pablo.'

Rick smiled. 'People could have supervised walks with the llampacas if Jack's up for running them. Getting Bert out regularly and socialising might stop him going AWOL.'

'That would be brilliant.'

Rick joined the line of cars turning into the municipal tip and inched around a central area filled with big metal skips looking for a parking space. 'What's your first job then?'

'We have to clear the stables. They are full of all sorts of junk. I'll put in a planning application for material change of use tomorrow.' The suppressed excitement in her voice was contagious, her words tumbling over each other.

'That's quick.'

'I really want this to work. No point hanging about.'

Pulling on the handbrake, Rick looked across into her dancing eyes. 'The old dairy building on my side of the fence is empty. Feel free to store junk in there, temporarily, if it helps.'

'Thank you. I'll take you up on that. I should probably ask you if you mind?'

'Mind what?'

'Having a well-being centre next door. It will bring more cars and people and stuff.'

'Not that many, surely.'

'Not crowds and crowds, but some. Although, I don't think it'll be particularly noisy.'

He laughed. 'I'm from London, Beth. I'm used to people, cars and noise. Admittedly, I've developed a bit of a problem with crowds recently, but if all the action is on your side of the fence, I should be fine. And, anyway, I won't be here forever.' Her face fell and he mentally kicked himself. The last thing he wanted to do was bring down her mood. Turning to the teens in the back, he said, 'Stir your stumps, lads. Time to empty that trailer. Make sure you check which container takes what type of material before you dump anything or the tip officer will tell you off.'

The sheer number of people milling around made Rick pause. They were all going up and down metal steps that lead to the ramps from which rubbish was thrown into big containers. He reached for his sunglasses.

I'll keep my head down and keep moving. It'll be fine.

They worked in harmony, clattering up and down the steps to dump junk, and the trailer emptied relatively quickly. Finally, Beth grabbed the last item, a wide sheet of plasterboard, and lifted it. She staggered.

'Can you manage that?' asked Rick.

'Of course I can.'

The flash of defiance in her eyes reminded Rick of when she'd stabbed him in the chest with a pointy finger. He backed away to give her room to manoeuvre and watched her struggle up the stairs, following a few steps behind. Just as she reached the top, a gust of wind threatened to sweep both her and the board off the walkway entirely. Rick dashed forward. Steadying Beth with one hand, he flipped the board over the rail and into the skip with the other. His sunglasses clattered to the walkway.

'You didn't have to do that,' said Beth. 'I was fine.'

'Sure you were, but I didn't want to have to climb into the skip to haul you out. I doubt the lads would notice you disappearing. Look at them.' Further along the walkway, Jack and Kyle were trying to rugby tackle Tyler into one of the other containers. 'Oi! You three! Cut it out.' Rick bent to pick up his sunglasses and caught an expression on Beth's face that he couldn't read. 'What?'

'Nothing. I'm just not used to people looking out for me.'

One step down from her on the staircase, Rick's eyes were on the same level as hers. She didn't look away. Neither did he and, without realising he was going to do it, he leaned in and dropped a kiss on her lips.

'Oh!' The blush that spread across her cheeks made him want to kiss her again.

''Scuse I,' grumbled a voice from behind. An older woman attempted to squeeze her aircraft carrier proportions past them. 'Some of us have stuff to do today.'

A short, spindly man bobbed along in the aircraft carrier's wake. 'Yeah, you two, get a room.'

Rick stepped away from Beth. She grabbed his T-shirt and pulled him back. 'Are you single?'

'Yes.'

'What about David's mother?'

'Anna? She left me eight years ago.'

'In that case.' She tugged on his T-shirt. He stepped closer. She tentatively touched her mouth to his.

Rick's whole world concertinaed. It felt like he only existed at those points where he touched her. All his noble plans to stay away evaporated. He wrapped his arms around her, pulling her close, and surrendered to electric sensations.

''Scuse I.' The aircraft carrier was back. They broke apart as the woman's bulk swept them ahead of her down the stairs. Rick held on to Beth's hand. The simple gesture felt natural and right.

'Hang on,' the aircraft carrier thrust her face towards Rick. 'Don't I know you?'

The fragile bubble of happiness around his heart burst. He dropped Beth's hand and turned away, shoving his sunglasses back on. 'I don't think so.'

'I've seen your face somewhere. For certain.'

'You're mistaken.' Rick's heart thumped in his chest. He could see Beth darting concerned glances at him.

The woman turned and bellowed, 'Gary, remember that bloke what showed us that photo?'

The man ambled over. He poked a finger into a gap between his shirt buttons and scratched his belly, deep in thought. 'Umm. You mean the one looking for that doctor fella?'

'Yes! Him. Where was it? I know. Ambleford. That was it. The day before yesterday. I never forget a face. It was definitely you.'

'He was mighty keen to find you and all,' said Gary.

'Right, thanks.' Rick nodded, nausea stirring low down in his belly. He called up to Jack, Kyle and Tyler, who were still busy wrestling each other on the walkway. 'Come on, lads. Time to go.' He was grateful that Beth stayed silent as she slid into the passenger seat. In the rear-view mirror, he could see the couple staring as he put the car in gear and pulled away.

Chapter 33

The atmosphere in the front of the car was thick with tension on the drive back through the forest to Ambleford. Beth hugged the memory of kissing Rick close. She hadn't wanted to stop; she'd felt fireworks in her head, down to delicious tingles in her toes. Her insides did a happy little tango. He was kind, generous and thoughtful, and if he could kiss her like that, he must genuinely care for her.

She stole a glance at him. That hunted look was back in his eyes, strain evident in tight lines at the corner of his mouth. Who could be looking for him?

Jack spoke up as they neared the village green. 'Can you drop us here? We're going to the park.'

Rick pulled in outside The Coffee Pot. The boys jumped out, slamming the doors far harder than necessary. Beth put a tentative hand towards Rick, stopping just shy of touching him. 'I think we need to talk. Will you let me buy you a coffee?'

He hesitated.

'Look.' She pointed to the empty tables and chairs on the

pavement. 'There's no one else here. If we sit outside, we can escape if we need to.'

After a beat, Rick killed the engine. 'I'd like that.'

Beth chose the table closest to the car.

Stacy, short and compact in a burgundy tabard with a badge that said: "*Smile, it might never happen*", bustled over armed with an iPad. 'What can I get you?'

'Black coffee, please.' Beth cast a glance at Rick. A small vein pulsed near his temple. He gave a small nod, but made no move to speak. 'Make that two, please. And a couple of Rose's cakes, if you have them.'

'Coming right up.'

They waited for their drinks in silence. On the green, a small group gathered. They wore matching yellow waistcoats and hopped up and down waving wooden sticks at each other.

'I've never seen real Morris dancers,' murmured Rick.

'They're rehearsing for May Day.'

A yelp of protest echoed across the grass as a stray stick connected with a delicate portion of Morris dancer anatomy.

Rick's smile didn't reach his eyes.

'What that woman at the tip said about someone showing your photo around, I can see it's upset you. Can you tell me why? I'd like to understand.'

Rick slumped down in his chair. 'I thought I was safe here.'

'Safe from what?'

'There's a podcast that comes out every couple of days or so. It's run by the two social media commentators that … anyway, it's dedicated to tracking me down.'

'How?'

'Asking for people to phone in with sightings.'

'You're kidding. Surely people have better things to do with their lives?'

'Evidently not. They chat about where I might be and how to flush me out. That sort of thing. It's nonsense, of course, but it's only a matter of time before they find me.' He kept his gaze trained on the dancers. Sticks had been thrown on the floor. A minor dispute was underway.

Stacy returned with a loaded tray. Beth decided to hit the problem head on. 'Stacy. Has anyone been asking questions in here recently, showing a photo perhaps?'

'There was a fella in a day or so ago. He had a photo with him. Hang on.' The empty tray under one arm, she pulled her iPad from the pocket of her tabard. 'Here, I took a screenshot.'

Beth leaned in. 'Of the man?'

'No. Of the photograph. See?'

Beth's eyes went from the screen to Rick. 'It's definitely you.'

Stacy looked at Rick, her eyes narrowing. 'Oh, yeah, so it is. Your hair is longer now, but it's you alright.'

'What did you tell him?' Rick's tone was flat.

'The truth. I hadn't seen you, had I?'

'Did he say who he was?' asked Beth.

'He left a card, but it got chucked in the bin while I was clearing. Sorry.'

'Rick, you've gone ever so pale. Are you okay? Have something to eat.' Beth pushed a cake towards him.

Rick ignored it. 'Stacy, did he speak to anyone else?'

'I couldn't say. It was mega busy in here. I doubt anyone paid much attention. It's not like he was offering a reward or anything.'

'If he comes back, can you let me know, please?' said Beth. 'You've got my mobile number. And can you not... well... not, you know?'

Stacy jerked her head at Rick. 'Not tell on matey boy here? Sure. No probs. I have a policy of never seeing or hearing anything. Customers don't come back if they think I'll gossip about them. Enjoy your coffee. Let me know if you want anything else.'

As soon as they were alone, Beth asked, 'Who do you think it was?'

'Paps, probably.'

'Paparazzi? I'd have thought you'd be old news by now.'

'That patient I mentioned, his mum is famous, too. Not so much before this. She had a bit part in Corrie and did a low-budget reality show, that sort of thing. But ever since this... well, she's never out of the papers and she's just been given this big radio show. Barbara said she thought she was using it to boost her career, but... I don't know.'

'What's her name?'

'Cora Diamond.'

'I've never heard of her.'

Rick snorted. 'I wish I could say the same.'

Beth sat back. 'I don't get it. You said your patient mixed street drugs with medicine you prescribed for depression. How come *you're* accountable?'

'It's a grey area. Paperwork proving my innocence went missing. It means Cora can take me to the cleaners. And with the exception of something else really big happening like aliens landing, it's a hot news item. A story that can run and run. You know that woman I'm supposed to have run over?'

Beth nodded.

'Well, she and her partner tricked their way into one of my clinics, but if it wasn't them, it would have been someone else. And my colleagues just…'

His voice broke and his distress made Beth's heart ache. 'What? What did they do?'

'They kicked me out. Not in so many words, but it was made very clear that they wanted me to disappear.'

'That must have hurt.'

He gave a bitter laugh. 'I've worked with them for over twenty years and they couldn't drop me fast enough. I couldn't take any more. I snapped and ran and the rest you know.'

'When you say you ran, what do you mean?'

Rick flushed. 'I didn't run exactly. I climbed…. out of a window.'

An uneasy sensation flooded her chest. 'You mean you disappeared? Just like that?'

'Yes, I… Why are you looking at me like that?'

A low buzz sounded in her ears. *What is it with men running away when things get tough?* An oily sense of disappointment slithered up her spine. 'That's what Paul did.'

'Paul?'

'My ex. He just disappeared. Next thing I got was a letter telling me it was all over and he was never coming back.'

Rick sat bolt upright. 'I'm not like Paul, I promise.'

'So you've contacted your family? They're not worried sick about you?'

He pulled a face. 'Not exactly.'

'Have you contacted anyone?'

'My indemnity advisors.'

'Your insurance?' Beth couldn't stop her mouth gaping. The memory of Daisy's distraught reaction to Paul's disappearance loomed large in her mind. Superimposed over it was a little boy, about the same age as Grace, wondering where his daddy was. 'What about your son? You can't walk away from a child without a word.'

'What? Child? No, wait…'

She sprang to her feet, jogging the table in her haste. 'I thought you were someone I could trust.'

'I am. Beth, you're not being fair.'

'Not fair is disappearing and not caring enough to put people's minds at rest.' Beth's heart pounded in her chest as if trying to spring free of her body altogether. 'What if that person showing your photo around is someone who loves you, desperate to know you're okay?'

'It's a reporter, I'm sure of it.'

'You don't know that.' She wiped away a rogue tear. 'But I know what it's like to be dumped and so do my kids – left behind like unwanted luggage because some man has decided he's had enough. I can tell you this: the people left behind always get hurt.'

Rick got to his feet, too, his expression solemn. 'I'm sorry Paul treated you and your children so badly. I would never abandon a partner or a child. David is a strapping twenty-two-year-old sous chef living in Italy. He rarely needs to chat with his old man. But you're right. I should have contacted him before now and I will. I promise.'

She dug a tissue from her pocket. 'I'm sorry. I hadn't realised how raw all that stuff with Paul still is.'

Rick came around the table and put a gentle hand on her shoulder. 'Shall I take you home?'

Her mind spinning with conflicting emotions, Beth picked up her handbag from the table. 'No, thank you. I'll walk. I could do with the fresh air.'

'We could both walk and I'll come back for the car later.'

She shook her head. 'I need time to think.'

'I don't like to see you upset.'

'I'm fine. Don't worry. I'll see you later.' She placed an apologetic hand on his chest for a brief second before turning on her heels and walking away from him.

*

Twenty minutes later, Beth was wishing she'd had the sense to wear more sensible shoes. Strappy wedge-heeled sandals weren't the best choice for hiking home from the village. Just south of Old Farm Lane, hot and sweaty, with blisters on blisters that made her toes scream, she paused to catch her breath. A wooden signpost marked the entrance to one of the many gravelled forestry commission car parks. She leaned on the post, easing her ankle straps away from red-raw skin, just as the sound of something smashing filtered through the trees. Peeking through a gap in the gorse bushes, she could make out a white van at the far end of the car park. Two deep voices carried clearly on the quiet forest air.

'Come on, Derrick. Get a bloody move on, 'fore someone comes.'

'Keep your hair on, Pete. Got a couple more of them chairs in 'ere. And that shelving unit.'

A loud grunt accompanied a thump.

Pete's voice came again. 'Come on. We've got to go.'

Beth took a moment to compute what was going on, but as soon as two and two made four, she scrabbled in her pocket for her phone. She crept forwards, filming as she went, just in time to capture Derek and Pete throw two black office chairs into the undergrowth, followed by a hideous purple bathtub.

They turned and spotted her.

Derrick cursed.

Pete leapt into the driver's seat and started the engine. 'Get in the effing van, man.'

Wheels spun.

Tyres crunched.

Gravel scattered like buckshot.

The van lurched forwards on a direct collision course with Beth.

She kept filming, her hands trembling. With only seconds to spare, she realised Pete wasn't planning to swerve. She stumbled back. The wing mirror clipped her arm. The whole world spun. Her arms and legs flailed. Something hard hit her head.

*

Black. All black. Beth shivered. She'd never experienced such intense cold before. Dragging a long, shuddering breath in, she coughed, then gagged. *What is that awful smell?* She forced leaden eyelids to open. Blurred brown splodges pulsated and then rearranged themselves into a more recognisable order. Mud. The bottom of a ditch. Stagnant water.

Ugh! Thank goodness my face didn't land in that.

Head throbbing, she pushed away from the slime and scum, trying to make her body cooperate. A sharp pain shot through her right shoulder. There was an alarming sensation of bone grinding against bone. The arm had no power. Her stomach heaved.

She inched her way out of the ditch, hampered by her waterlogged clothing. It took immense effort to get to her feet and stagger towards the road. Just as she reached the edge of the tarmac, she crumpled to her knees. Fiery pain shot through every cell in her body. One hand felt curiously warm. She looked down. Paddy was licking her wrist, his tongue rough. So, this was what she'd needed to do to get the grumpy old dog's attention. He nudged and nuzzled at her. Then he whined, sat back on his haunches and barked. Beth closed her eyes. Pain and nausea warring for supremacy. Paddy stopped barking, sprang to his feet and disappeared.

Was that it? Years of feeding him and walking him when Paul and the children couldn't be bothered, and what did she get in her hour of need? Thirty seconds of slobber and then he buggered off. Ungrateful mutt.

Her vision narrowed to a pinprick, as if she were gazing down a long, dark tunnel towards a distant light. Then the light went off and she slumped to the ground. The sweet smell of earth and grass registered only seconds before the empty blackness returned.

Chapter 34

Rick paced up and down outside the barn, not sure what to do. The physical pull to go and speak to Beth was like an immense magnet strapped to his middle, with her as the north. *I should never have let her go.* He had driven back from the village slowly, convinced he'd pass her. He'd planned to pull over and insist she accept a lift. But she must have cut through the forest to avoid him doing exactly that.

All seemed quiet over at the farmhouse. Percival strutted along the fence, giving Rick an ominous glare and fluffing his feathers with the pompous importance of a junior security guard in a brand-new uniform. Suddenly, an ear-piercing shriek tore through the air. Daisy galloped towards him in wellington boots that were far too big. Hair flying. Eyes frantic. She clutched the neckline of a long red dressing gown together with one hand and waved a phone at him with the other. She stumbled to a halt, her breath ragged. Words only decipherable between colossal gasps for air. 'Sorry… shower… emergency… Jack.'

'Is he hurt?'

'No… Beth…'

Stomach lurching, Rick grabbed the phone. 'Beth?'

'Rick, thank God.' Jack's voice was faint and crackly. 'Please help. Beth's hurt. I don't know what to do.'

'What happened?'

'She texted Rose to say she was walking up from the village, but she never arrived. Rose sent me and Paddy to look for her—'

'Hang on, back up. Beth left The Coffee Pot ages ago. Are you saying she didn't make it home at all?'

'No. I mean, yes. Paddy found her. Lying just off the road.'

'Where?'

'Down the lane. By the forest car park sign. She's unconscious, Rick. There's blood, like, everywhere, and...' The boy's voice broke. 'And I don't know what to do.'

'Stay calm. I'm coming.' A steely determination settled over Rick. 'Call an ambulance. But remember, whatever you do, don't move her.' Rick thrust the phone back to Daisy. He broke into a run, calling back over his shoulder, 'Is Grace somewhere safe?'

Daisy chased after him. 'She's watching telly. Rose took the car and went to Jack.'

'Good. Stay here and look after Grace.'

'But I—'

'Just do it, Daisy.' Rick didn't wait for her to answer. He was already starting his engine.

*

The sight of Beth's car parked on the verge told Rick he was in the right place long before he saw Rose and Jack crouched over a figure on the ground.

He leapt from the car. Paddy scurried over, barked urgently, then scampered the few paces back to Beth. The dog paused, then ran back to Rick and barked again.

'I get the message, Paddy,' muttered Rick. 'No need to do the whole Lassie thing. Give me a sec, I need some stuff.' He grabbed his medical bag from the boot of the car and an old picnic blanket.

Rose looked up, wringing her hands. 'She's hurt. I mean, really hurt.'

Rick glanced around. 'Any idea what happened?'

'No. We just found her here.' Jack chewed at his thumbnail. 'There's an ambulance on the way, but they said the traffic's bad.'

'She needs help now, Rick,' whispered Rose.

Rick tamped down on rising panic and tried to focus. *Think, man, think. Don't look at all the blood... Focus. Basics. Check for danger, then follow the A... B... C...*

He crouched beside her. 'Beth, can you hear me?'

No response.

'Beth, it's Rick. I'm here to help.'

Airway, clear. Breathing, steady. Circulation, there's her pulse – weak. Damn it, very weak. But still a pulse, so it's a no to full resus. He reached for her hand. 'Beth. Can you hear me, Beth? You're going to be fine. Do you hear? Can you squeeze my hand?'

Nothing.

Crap, crap, crap.

He took a deep breath.

Right. Assess injuries. Blow to the head, close to the temple. Deep cut extending into the hairline. Secondary grazing to the face. Possible neck injury, so can't risk the recovery position.

Watch the breathing. Steady the bleeding. Pressure. Yes, careful pressure. Keep her warm.

'You're doing fine, Beth.' He hauled his jumper over his head and draped it over her torso, tucking it up around her shoulders. Then he laid the picnic blanket on top. Moments later, Jack put his own hoodie on top, too, and Rose spread her jacket over Beth's legs and feet.

Rick shucked his T-shirt off. Grabbing hold of the hem with his teeth, he yanked off a section of fabric and made a pad to press over the biggest cut on Beth's head. He slipped his other hand under her neck to hold both her head and neck steady as he applied pressure to the wound. 'Beth, can you hear me? Beth? Come on, love. Stop lazing around out here. Time to wake up. You've got stuff to do. Beth?'

There. Her eyelids. A slight movement. 'Beth? Try again, love.'

Her eyelids fluttered and then both eyes opened. She looked at him. 'Blue,' she said.

'Eh?' Rick frowned.

'Blue... sky... blue... eyes... blue...'

'Blue, what?' It didn't matter that she didn't make sense, what mattered was keeping her talking. 'What else? Tell me, Beth.'

'Hair.'

'Are you saying my hair is blue?' he asked. *How hard had she hit her head?*

'No.' She gave a weak puff of laughter. 'Messy... your hair... Llampacca.'

Rick laughed, his relief at Beth's response overwhelming. 'I can't believe you're being rude about my hair.'

'She's just being honest with you, mate,' said Jack.

Beth gave another weak laugh, then gasped and closed her eyes.

'No, no, Beth, stay with me, stay with me,' said Rick. 'Beth, I… Damn it.'

'Listen,' said Rose. 'I hear a siren.'

Jack dashed along the road and waved to get the attention of the approaching ambulance.

Two paramedics emerged from the vehicle. One hurried over, pulling on a pair of plastic gloves. 'Hi, I'm Dev. Who do we have here?'

'This is Beth Hope,' said Rick. 'Multiple injuries. Serious head wound. She's breathing on her own. We don't know what happened. We haven't moved her.'

'Good work.' Dev carried out a brief assessment, calling to her colleague, 'Zaden, we're going to need a neck brace and a backboard.'

'Right you are.'

By the time Beth was immobilised and inserted into the ambulance on a stretcher, Rick was shaking.

Rose crept to his side. 'Is she going to be alright?'

He slipped a comforting arm around her shoulders, not sure what to say. Beth had never looked so small and fragile before. A lump formed in his throat. His warrior queen was broken and it was all his fault.

Dev jumped down from the back of the ambulance. 'Try not to worry. You did well. You've given her a fighting chance.'

'Of course he did,' said Jack. 'He's a doc—'

'I didn't do anything. Basic first aid, that's all,' said Rick. It was the truth, but how he wished he could have done more. 'Where are you taking her?'

'Southampton General.' Dev started closing the vehicle door and paused, looking at Rick. 'We've room for someone to ride along with her. Hold her hand. Are you coming?'

Rick wanted nothing more than to dive into the belly of the ambulance and hold Beth close, but he forced himself to step back. *It should be family.* 'Rose, you should go. You're next of kin.'

Rose's eyes swam with tears. 'I… yes, I… but what about Grace? And Paddy and the car and… and…'

'Jack and I will sort everything here. Don't worry.'

Jack scooped Paddy up into his arms. 'Message me when you know what's happening. And tell her… tell her from me she's got to get better. Yeah?'

Rose gave a shaky smile and climbed in to sit with Beth.

Rick watched the squat ambulance lumber off down the road and knew it was taking his heart with it.

'They've got their blue lights flashing but not the siren,' said Jack. 'They can't be that worried about her.'

'Come on,' said Rick. There was no point explaining to the lad that an ambulance with blue lights and no siren meant that it was carrying a dangerously ill patient. Someone they didn't want to alert to the seriousness of their condition. Sick with worry about his warrior queen, he gave Jack's shoulder a bracing pat. 'Let's get back.'

*

Daisy pounced on them before they were even through the front door, demanding, 'Where is she? What happened? Is she alright?'

'Calm down, Dais,' said Jack. He scooped Grace up into

his arms. 'It's okay, small fry. Rick turned into Super Doc, yeah? Beth is going to be fine. Isn't she, Rick?'

Rick felt the pressure of all eyes on him. He didn't want to lie, nor did he want the kids to see how worried he was. 'She's on her way to the hospital to get fixed, Grace. Rose went with her. She'll let us know what's going on soon.'

'See, Grace?' said Jack. 'Best thing you can do is watch all Beth's favourite Disney movies. Paddy will help you. Come on.' He carried Grace into the living room.

Daisy dragged Rick along the corridor to the kitchen. 'You'll go to the hospital, won't you, Rick? They'll listen to you. What with you being a doctor.'

Rick rubbed the back of his neck. 'Me going to the hospital might just cause problems, Daisy. I could get recognised; it could cause a stir and delay treatment for Beth.'

'How do you mean?'

'Don't pretend you haven't seen what's being said about me online.'

The red creeping up her neck told him she'd seen plenty. 'You can't let a bunch of deadbeats get to you. Most of them are just chasing clout.'

Rick's laugh was bitter. 'What does that even mean?'

'The YouTube stuff. The social media pile-on. It's all sheep shit. No one actually believes it. Or if they do, they're idiots. People just share stuff that's trending to get more followers and boost their own social media accounts. You can't let it stop you doing what you need to do.'

Rick slumped into a chair at the kitchen table. 'Fine. I'll go in as soon as we hear from Rose to tell us where she is. And even though I look like a tramp with all this hair, I'll do what I can.'

'I can fix your hair.' Daisy dived across the kitchen and rummaged in a cupboard for a set of clippers.

'Oh, I don't know—'

'We use them on Jack all the time. Come on, Rick. I'm always left babysitting while other people do the exciting stuff. Let me do something useful for once.'

She spoke with such fever, it felt churlish to refuse.

Minutes later, Jack called down the corridor, 'We got a film sorted, but we need snacks.' He ambled into the room, Grace and Paddy trotting behind him. 'Plus, I got a text from Rose... Oh, I say! Are you sure that's a good idea, Dais?'

Daisy was already carving a long strip through the thick springy hair on the top of Rick's head.

'Uh-oh,' said Grace.

Seeing the little girl's expression, Rick twisted in his seat and glared at Daisy. 'You said you knew how to do this.'

'I do. I've seen it on TikTok.'

'Beth cuts my hair.' Jack wrinkled his nose, his eyes locked on the top of Rick's head. 'She only uses the clippers at the back and round the sides. She uses scissors for the top.'

'Will you chill?' Daisy waved her phone in Rick's peripheral vision. 'YouTube demo coming right up. I got this.'

Rick took a deep breath and counted to ten.

Grace rummaged in the pocket of a coat slung over the back of a kitchen chair. She pulled out something pink and handed it to Rick.

'What's this?' He held up a scrap of glittery material. 'A unicorn beanie? You reckon I'm going to need this when Daisy's finished?'

Grace giggled. 'Come on, Paddy. We got a film to watch for Mummy.' She turned for the door, Paddy and Jack hard on her heels.

Chapter 35

Rick sidled up to the main reception desk in the casualty department. The hushed squeak of shoes on lino took him right back to his days as a junior doctor. The receptionist barely spared him a glance when he mentioned Beth's name. She pointed him towards a row of plastic seats on the far side of the room, where Rose sat alone, staring at the floor.

He slipped into the seat next to her. 'How are you?'

She looked up. 'What the hell happened to your hair?'

'Daisy thought I needed a tidy-up.'

'And you let her?' She frowned. 'Could have been worse, I guess.'

The main doors to A&E swished open and Lucy swept in. Her tall, slim frame was unmissable in bright yellow. Rick watched her search the room for Rose. Her gaze skipped to him and a look he couldn't fathom flitted across her face. She hurried over. 'Daisy told me what happened. Is there any news?'

Rose shook her head. 'They took her for an MRI ages ago.'

Lucy's gaze bounced to Rick. 'She left with you this afternoon? What the hell happened?'

'We stopped in the village on the way back to grab a coffee. She wanted to walk home. The next I knew, Jack was on the phone saying she was hurt.'

'Oh!' Rose said. 'That's the doctor.'

A young woman wearing a white coat and exhaustion like a second skin stood by the reception desk. Long, dark hair was pulled back into a loose bun and a stethoscope was looped around her neck. She scanned the crowded waiting area until her eyes lit on Rose.

'She's coming over.' Rose's voice rose to a high-pitched squeak as she half-stood, then sat back down. 'What if it's bad news? I can't... I can't...'

'Just breathe, Rose,' said Rick. 'Try to stay calm.'

The doctor stopped. 'Rose Hope?'

Rose stood. 'Yes.'

'I'm Dr Gunnar. Can you come with me, please?'

Rick and Lucy moved to accompany her. Dr Gunnar held up a hand. 'Just Rose, please. Beth is still in Majors. There's very little room.'

Rick and Lucy exchanged a worried glance.

'Majors?' asked Rose.

'It's where we stabilise the patients with more significant injuries before sending them to a ward,' said Dr Gunnar. 'Your mother is back from the MRI. She's conscious. I thought you might like to sit with her while we wait for the results to come through.'

'Oh, yes please.'

'Can you tell us how she is?' Rick asked.

'Without Beth's express permission, I can't divulge her medical information to you.' Dr Gunnar squinted at him.

'But you know that already, don't you? You are Dr Mahon, aren't you? Dr Rick Mahon?'

Rick nodded, his cheeks burning.

Dr Gunnar's gaze was impassive. 'You were in the news again this morning. That Cora Diamond lady is certainly persistent.'

'Rick treated Beth while we waited for the ambulance,' said Rose.

'He did a good job.' Dr Gunnar gave a brisk upward jerk of her chin. 'In all probability, Dr Mahon, your actions made all the difference. We're doing everything we can. Now, Rose, let me show you where she is.' Dr Gunnar turned on her heel and headed for the door.

'I wish there was something I could do,' Rick muttered.

'There is,' said Lucy.

'What?'

She looked troubled. 'Please don't take this the wrong way. You've just saved my friend's life and I owe you, but if you really want to help her, I think the best thing you can do is to sort your shit out.'

'I beg your pardon?'

'I'm not judging you. My fella's a doctor, too. I know there's way more to this thing than is being reported in the papers. And I wish you luck with it. I really do. But I'm worried that your situation will end up making Beth's life harder than it already is. The last thing she needs is more crap to deal with. And right now, you come with a big side order of crap.'

Rick ducked his head. 'I can't deny it. I've been trying to keep my distance, but it's too late. I've already fallen for her. She's the most incredible person I've ever met.'

'I agree. She's wonderful. And she really likes you, too.

Although she'll probably kill me for saying so. Under normal circumstances, I'd be over the moon for you both. You're perfect for each other.'

'But not right now.'

She shrugged. 'Maybe once the court case is over and things have settled, things will be different.' Lucy's phone buzzed.

Rick watched her scurry over to an alcove to answer the call. *She's right. As soon as I hear that Beth is out of danger, I'll go back to London. It's time I face the music.*

Chapter 36

Beth lay back against the pillows, groggy and confused. Her head felt as if it was packed full of soggy cotton wool. Her arm was strapped across her chest, her shoulder throbbing despite a hefty dose of pain medication. It was good to see the children and know that they were coping in her absence, but someone was missing. Her eyes darted towards the gap in the curtains that separated the area around the bed from the rest of the ward.

'Did you drive in by yourselves or did someone give you a lift?'

'Lucy brought us in,' said Rose. She sat next to the bed, with Grace on her knee.

Disappointment filled her at the thought that Rick hadn't bothered to visit. She focused on what Grace was saying.

'I've watched *Moana*, *Frozen* and *The Little Mermaid* for you and—'

'Shall we show Mummy the cake you made her?' Rose produced a plastic tub from her bag.

Grace pulled off the lid. 'It's got pink icing and glitter.'

'Wow, that looks delicious.' Beth's gaze drifted to Jack and Daisy stood at the end of the bed. Jack looked pensive. Daisy had her arms crossed. 'Is everything alright, you two?'

Jack shoved his hands in his pockets. 'How long are you going to be in here?'

'A few days, I think. They want to keep an eye on me because of my head.'

'And your arm?' He jerked his chin towards her shoulder.

'It'll heal, don't worry.'

He grunted.

Daisy scowled. 'Lucy is waiting outside. We're not all allowed in at once.'

Grace slipped off Rose's knee. 'Paddy wanted to come, too, but he can't because he is a dog.'

Rose stood. 'If we go out now, Lucy will have time for a quick chat before we go home.'

Grace grinned. 'Bye, Mummy. We'll come back tomorrow.'

'Bye, sweetheart. Thank you for the cake and for making me feel better.' Beth smiled at the older three, while resisting the urge to ask if they had seen Rick. 'Sorry I'm such a nuisance.'

'Huh!' snorted Daisy. 'I'll go get Lucy.'

Jack followed.

'Is Daisy alright, Rose?' asked Beth.

Rose shrugged. 'Daisy is just being Daisy. We all got really scared for you. Her, too, only she doesn't want to admit it. She'll be fine.'

Lucy tiptoed up to the bed as Rose left. 'Hi, I won't stay long. How are you?'

'Don't ask.' Beth groaned.

'Is it true you can't remember what happened?'

'Nothing after I left the village. Not until I came to, lying on the ground. Paddy was the first thing I saw.'

'That's weird. Does it feel weird?'

'It's a pain in the backside is what it is.'

'How do you mean?'

Beth's eyes filled with traitorous tears. 'I need to be getting on with setting up the well-being centre and sorting things out.'

Lucy tutted and gave Beth's uninjured arm a gentle squeeze. 'It can't be helped. The well-being centre will just take a little bit longer. We'll get there. I'll sort out the planning permission forms. I can bring them in here if you need to sign them. But other than that, you need to put all your focus on getting better. I'll help with the children. As soon as they discharge you, we'll get our heads together and come up with a plan for everything else.'

*

A week later, a full twenty-four hours after being discharged from hospital, Beth stood just inside the stables and stared at the piles of junk. With her arm still firmly strapped across her chest and likely to remain so for the foreseeable future, the idea of clearing the space seemed impossible.

She wandered out onto the drive and forced herself to take several deep breaths, trying to stop her gaze drift to the barn. The hollow sensation in her middle, the one that had materialised when Jack had told her Rick had packed up and gone without leaving a message, throbbed almost as much as her broken collarbone. It was like a permanent punch to the gut. How could one extremely annoying man cause so much angst? It was ridiculous. She had had a lucky escape. Rick clearly had a habit of disappearing whenever life got tough.

Forget him. Good riddance. I have enough to do without pandering to a... a... weak-willed Wolverine.

How come she missed him so darn much?

She stumbled over to the mounting block and perched on the edge just as she heard the throaty roar of a sizeable petrol engine. A Hell's Angel, all reflective sunglasses and fringed leather, steered a vintage wartime motorbike – complete with sidecar – across the gravel and pulled to a halt before her. A rounded figure in a pink boiler suit and a matching helmet with the visor pulled down sat bolt upright in the sidecar. It was such an unexpected sight that Beth began to wonder if she had taken too much pain relief. The Hell's Angel dismounted, helped his passenger alight, then hopped back on the bike and rode away. As the roar of the engine faded, the new arrival removed their helmet.

Beth hadn't thought it possible for her spirits to sink any lower. 'Barbara!'

'Beth.' Barbara slung the strap of her helmet over her forearm like a handbag and fluffed out her hair. 'Aren't you supposed to be—?'

'Resting? Yes, I know, but the bank isn't going to wait for me to heal. I don't see that I have any choice other than to keep going.'

'It's just as well Rose rang me, then. I can see I'm just in time.'

'Did she?' *Traitor.* 'In time for what?'

'To rescue you from yourself.'

'I don't need rescuing.' Even with her hackles up, Beth failed to inject the words with her usual degree of defiance. 'Please don't start on me, Barbara. I haven't the energy to fight you.'

'Excellent.' Barbara pulled a pink silk scarf from her pocket and tied it around her hair à la Audrey Hepburn. 'Because I am not here for a fight. I'm here to help.'

'Why? We don't even like each other.'

'We got off to a bad start. And most of that was me, I admit it. Call me what you will – bombastic, opinionated, a bloody-minded meddler. Believe me, I've heard it all and a lot worse besides, but I'll not stand idly by while another person is in trouble. Not if I can help.'

Beth didn't know what to say to that.

'You and I might not see eye to eye on many things, but I respect you. My Brian always says I've far too much energy for my own good – which is all to the good today, because I've the four limbs that the good Lord gave me and plenty of time on my hands. I suggest we get started.'

'Started with what?'

Barbara's eyebrows rose. 'How hard did you hit your head? I'm here to clear the stables for you.'

'That's incredibly kind of you, but it's a massive job.'

'Not to worry.' The older woman pushed the stable door wide and disappeared inside.

Beth lurched to her feet. 'What are you doing?'

'Letting the dog see the rabbit. Oh my… yes, I see. Never mind. The others will be here soon, of course.'

'What others?'

Barbara flashed her a wicked grin. 'I rounded up a posse. Aha. Look.' She pointed down the track. 'Here they are now.'

A yellow 2CV and a blue-and-white VW camper van picked a careful route through the potholed surface and parked. Reena emerged from the car and several crafty crochet members spilt out from the camper van, all chatting at once and asking Beth how she was feeling. The positivity and encouragement from all sides was overwhelming and so unexpected that Beth blinked back tears.

Barbara clapped her hands. 'Right, team. Our mission is to empty the stables. And Beth is going to rest like the doctor ordered.'

'But—'

'But nothing. Our help is conditional on you behaving. You get to sit and supervise. Nothing more. Reena, did you bring that comfy camping chair?'

Reena dashed forward with a canvas bag. 'Where would you like it?'

'Just inside the door. You'll be able to see everything from there while you direct us, Beth.'

In seconds, the chair was positioned. Grateful that she was being given the option to have some control over proceedings, Beth sat. She was in the hands of a monster, but she wasn't daft enough to refuse the help. 'Thank you.'

Barbara smiled. 'You're welcome. Now, try to relax. My Brian says you can't take risks with amnesia. Did the doctor say how long it might last?'

'Apparently, my memory could return at any time. Or never.'

'It'll come. My Brian says you need just the right trigger.'

Beth didn't dare suggest that Barbara's Brian might have watched a few too many medical dramas, but the rebellious thought tiptoed across her mind.

*

Several hours later, the majority of the working party sat in the back garden enjoying a rest and a well-earned cup of tea. Beth stood on the drive with Rose and Barbara, examining a series of organised piles.

'It's surprising how much of this stuff is actually useful,' mused Beth, waving her good hand at a pile of disassembled furniture. 'But why on earth are there so many tables and chairs?'

'No idea,' said Rose, 'but they've given me an idea.'

Beth narrowed her eyes. 'What?'

'A tearoom. We could sell teas and coffee and cake to the people coming to the well-being centre?'

'It's not a bad idea,' said Barbara. 'Another income stream from the same customers. Makes good business sense.'

Beth shook her head. 'I don't even have planning permission for the centre yet. I'm not sure I can cope with trying to set up anything else.'

'You don't have to,' said Rose. 'I'll do it. I applied for the licence to make food for the public for my cakes, like you suggested. This is just one step on.'

'I don't know. Where will people sit? I mean, yes, we have tables, but where do we put them? I've promised all the space in the stables to Lucy for crafting.'

'You've a huge patio out the back,' suggested Barbara. 'And a lovely view of the forest.'

'That's all fine and dandy when the weather is good, but what about winter? Or when it rains?'

'We could get an awning. Or if we start making money from the well-being centre, maybe we could build a log cabin. Please don't just say no,' Rose pleaded. 'I really want to do this.'

Beth rubbed her damaged shoulder. 'I want to say yes. I really do. But let me think about it. Just for a bit. In the meantime, what are we going to do with all this other stuff? Rick said… oh.' For a moment, she'd forgotten to miss him. She took a deep breath and forced her voice not to wobble. 'Rick said we could use his dairy to store stuff, but, of course, he's left now. Can I assume it's still alright to use the space?'

'Definitely.' Barbara's tone was brisk. 'After all, a lot of this stuff is still useable. It would be criminal to throw it away. It needs recycling and that will take time to organise. I suggest putting it on Freecycle or you could post pictures on the village Facebook page, marked for sale. Remember to put that buyer collects.'

The thought of organising that on top of everything else was almost too much for Beth.

'You've gone all white.' Rose steered Beth back towards her chair.

'My Finn's a whiz on that eBay thingy,' said Barbara. 'He could sell stuff for you. You can split the profit with him. Shall I give him a tinkle?'

Beth nodded. If Barbara's Finn could shift the junk on her drive, he was welcome to it.

*

An hour later, Lucy arrived and was impressed at how much progress had been made. With the stables clear, the posse started removing industrial-strength cobwebs and accumulated grime. Reena produced an ancient ghetto blaster and Shania Twain encouraged everyone to "Feel Like A Woman" at deafening volumes. Beth took more painkillers and filled in reams of council and funding paperwork on her laptop. The low growl of an engine cut through her concentration. A large, rusty van pulled up. Two gangly young men got out.

'Finn.' Barbara put down her broom and hurried over. She threw her arms around the taller of the two, squeezing so tight that Beth feared bones might break. 'You came. And you brought Ramesh, too. How wonderful.' Ramesh endured a similarly effusive greeting.

Finn, Beth learned, was Barbara's youngest grandson and Ramesh, his boyfriend. In their early twenties and currently between jobs, they were surprisingly enthusiastic about flogging random stuff on the Internet and made short work of transferring salvageable items from the junk piles into the back of their van.

Beth shook her head in wonder as she watched the vehicle bounce its way back down the track. 'I had no idea so much could be sold on.'

Barbara shook cobwebs off her feather duster. 'My Brian says it's all about timing. You need to be able to store stuff while you wait for the right person and the right price. Finn's parents have several outbuildings he can use. A lot of forest properties do. You'd be surprised what people around here have tucked away out of sight.'

Barbara disappeared around the side of the stable.

Beth caught Lucy's eye. 'She makes it sound like there are dodgy deals going on all over the New Forest.'

'Perhaps there are. She's in charge of the village post office, don't forget. She has access to all sorts of information.'

Beth snorted. 'Barbara Trenchard, our very own Don Corleone.'

Lucy giggled. 'Head of the Grandma Mafia. I'm telling you, she should be running the country, not the village shop.'

'Hush, Lucy, she'll hear you.'

'Relax. I'm sure whatever she's up to is totally legit.' Lucy nodded towards the stable. 'The good news is we're almost done in here, ready for painting tomorrow.'

'We're painting tomorrow?'

'You're not painting anything tomorrow. And neither am I. Barbara has arranged for some of the local Explorers pack to drop by. They need to take part in a voluntary community project for some badge or other. This fits the bill.'

'And the paint?'

'Don't panic. It'll be cheap; a single layer of basic whitewash, not Farrow and Ball. George has some end-of-line stuff at the hardware store. He said we can have a nice fat discount.'

Beth nodded and sank down into her chair. Her arm ached. Her head throbbed. Her gaze drifted across to the barn for what felt like the millionth time.

Chapter 37

London

Rick had spent over a week holed up in his London apartment, waiting for news on Beth's progress from Rose. Once Rick knew that his warrior queen was well enough to be discharged from hospital and was even making progress on her well-being centre project, he felt able to move forward with his own issues.

Stood outside Five Oak Surgery in the growing dusk, he could feel his heart thudding in his chest.

Stop dithering. Just go in.

Clinic had finished for the day. The door was locked. It was the only way to stem the constant stream of patients arriving. A physical full stop, indicating the transfer of overnight care to the out-of-hours team. Inside, however, Rick knew his colleagues still had hours of work ahead of them, catching up on phone calls, referrals, prescriptions and making sure that the day's care decisions were fully implemented.

He pulled out his key and inserted it in the lock.

Stood in the empty reception, he heard Gita's voice coming from the back office. 'Did I hear the door? Sam, have you forgotten to lock up again?'

'No way, I definitely... Chuffing hell!' Sam dropped the glass of water he was carrying. It bounced on his shoe, sending a wave of liquid up his trouser leg, before rolling towards Rick. 'Rick! You're alive.'

'Last time I checked.' Rick bent to pick up the glass.

'What's going on? Oh!' Gita stopped short at the sight of Rick.

'Hi, Gita.'

'You're not dead.'

Rick shoved his hands deep into his trouser pockets. 'Definitely not dead. Thought about it. Decided against it.'

She threw her arms around him. Rick wasn't sure which of the two of them was more surprised. Equipped with a well-developed no-nonsense attitude to life, Gita didn't hug people, especially not professional colleagues. 'Why the hell didn't you answer my emails? No, don't answer that. I don't care. I'm just glad you're okay.' She stepped back and glared at him. 'I'm sorry. You do know that, don't you?'

'Sorry for what?'

'For that morning. The way I handled things. When I told you to leave, I didn't mean it the way it must have sounded. I was genuinely trying to think of you, not just the business. I don't think that came across.'

'No, it didn't.'

She tucked her chin down, her mouth tightening. 'Well, like I said, I'm sorry. But I am also really cross with you.'

'Why?'

She tutted. 'For jumping out of a window, for starters. And then for going dark on me. I've been worried sick. Michaela has, too. But we couldn't call the police because that would just make things worse for you because everyone would think you'd cracked up and then you'd lose your licence for ever.' She grabbed his arm. 'Come on. Come through to the back. Sam, get him a drink and don't let him leave. Sit on him if you have to. I'm getting Michaela.'

'I'll keep him away from the windows,' muttered Sam.

Before he knew it, Rick was parked on a stool in the staffroom while Sam clattered cups in the sink.

Gita returned, towing Michaela by the hand. 'See? Look, love. I told you. He's back.'

Michaela stopped just inside the door and stared at him. Tall and slim, with greying brown bobbed hair and kind eyes behind round, gold-rimmed glasses, she looked like a tired, mildly surprised owl. Rick was shocked to see how gaunt she'd become in only a matter of weeks.

Sam placed three steaming cups of tea on the small table. 'Right, you three, get your chops round those. I'm off to sort out today's scripts.' He closed the door behind him when he left.

Silence fell.

Eventually, Michaela spoke, 'Are you good?'

Rick dipped his head a fraction. 'I wasn't, but I'm getting there.'

'And the window? What were you thinking?'

Gita grabbed the biscuit tin and shoved it under Michaela's nose. 'He wasn't thinking.'

Michaela rummaged in the tin and pulled out a custard cream. 'As escape routes go, it was fairly ingenious, I suppose. The number of times I've wanted to disappear halfway through clinic. It never occurred to me to hop out the window.'

'It was pretty undignified, if I'm honest. I wrecked a

perfectly good suit. I vote we swap the roses for something less prickly.'

'Noted.'

'I didn't plan it, you know. I just snapped. I had to get away. I'm sorry I left you in the lurch.'

'You did more than that.'

'Michaela! Don't—'

'What, Gita? Don't tell him what a total cock-up he caused?'

Rick lurched to his feet, his heart racing. He paced over to the window.

'You planning to jump out again?'

'Michaela! Stop it or so help me… Rick, she doesn't mean it.'

Rick looked from one to the other. He'd worked with them for more than twenty years, been best man at their wedding. He'd never seen them at odds before.

'Fine, I'm sorry.' Michaela sighed and held up both hands. 'She's right. I don't mean it. I know Gita made a hash of telling you to take a break. And I'm sorry if you thought we didn't want to help you. We did. We do, but…' She didn't seem to know how to go on.

'You've got to want to help yourself.' Gita finished for her. 'Not stick your head in the sand like you usually do.'

'What's that supposed to mean?'

'You push yourself too hard. How many times have I asked you to slow down and take a break so you don't burn out? You don't take any notice. You were running on empty way before the Markwell case.'

'I thought I could handle it.'

Michaela reached for another biscuit, muttering, 'That's because you're an arrogant prick.'

'Michaela! Don't.'

'Don't what? Don't tell him the truth? I don't know which is worse. Him sodding off in the first place or him thinking we wouldn't want to help.' Michaela looked at the biscuit as if she didn't know what to do with it, then chucked it back in the tin. 'Do the last twenty-five years mean nothing to you, Rick? I thought we were friends.'

'We are.'

'Well, newsflash, friend. We're all struggling. The whole bloody NHS is struggling. We're holding this practice together on a wing and a prayer. Do you know how hard it was to find a locum to cover your shifts?'

Rick shook his head.

'Bloody impossible. And don't get me started on how much it's costing. There aren't enough doctors and those that are out there can pick and choose where they want to work. Why would they come here? I wouldn't. I'd go to Cornwall, work part-time and spend the rest of the day surfing. Even in winter. I'd prefer to freeze my tits off there than slog my guts out in London for a grumpy-arse business partner who doesn't trust me.'

Gita nearly spat out her tea. 'Michaela!'

'I'm sorry,' said Rick.

There was a long pause. Michaela scrubbed at her face with a tissue. 'I'm sorry, too. Anyway, having said all that, we actually have a much bigger problem on our hands.'

'Michaela.'

'Stop saying "Michaela" like that, Gita. He needs to know.'

'But he's ill.'

Rick held up both hands. 'Stop arguing. Please. Both of you. What do I need to know?'

Michaela leaned back against the wall. 'You're not the only one who's going to get screwed over by Cora Diamond. As your business partners, Gita and I stand to lose everything, too.'

'I don't understand.' Rick looked at Gita for confirmation.

She refused to meet his gaze. 'It's true. If you lose your case, whether you like it or not, you're going to take us down with you.'

Chapter 38

New Forest

It was relatively warm for a Saturday in early April. White candyfloss clouds skated across a baby-blue sky. Chickens skipped across the drive, fluffing their feathers out, clearly delighted to have made it through the winter once again. A gaggle of teenage Explorers, dressed in borrowed overalls, arrived bright and early, keen to slap paint around. Beth insisted that whitewashing was something that she could do one-handed. She soon realised how exhausting it was and felt grateful when an alert came in on her phone, giving her the perfect excuse to sink into the camping chair on the drive and check her emails. Paddy immediately parked his bottom on her foot as if keen to keep her there.

She double-clicked on a message from the council, all eager anticipation, and then groaned. 'This is a disaster.'

Lucy hurried over. 'What is it?'

'Lord Astley has objected to our application for planning permission.'

'Blast. Although it was to be expected. He's always difficult with local businesses. It might get passed anyway, though. He's only one person.'

'One person, who's the largest landowner around, with fat fingers in all the local pies. The other objections probably come from his cronies. I bet there will be more.' Beth willed the tears that were gathering to go away. 'What if it's rejected?'

'Then we'll appeal.'

'How long will that take? And there's no guarantee an appeal will succeed.'

'Come on. We're not defeated yet. Where's your fighting spirit?'

Beth shook her head, a rising thickness in her throat making it impossible to speak.

Lucy perched on the mounting block and crossed her arms. 'There's clearly something else bothering you. Spill.'

'You sound like Daisy.'

'Daisy reliably informs me that "spill the tea" means "what's the gossip?"'

Beth tried to let the wave of jealousy Lucy's words triggered wash past her. She was glad Lucy and Daisy were getting on – of course she was. Her own relationship with the girl remained as snarly as hell and she was beginning to think it was never going to improve.

Oblivious, Lucy continued, 'So, come on. What's going on?'

'It's stupid, I know, but I really miss Rick,' she blurted out. 'I mean, *really* miss him. I didn't realise how much he meant to me until he kissed me.'

'Woah, woah, woah. Back up. He kissed you? When?'

'When we were at the tip.'

'And?' Lucy stared at her, eyes like satellite dishes.

Beth's face grew warm. 'It was nice.'

'Only nice?'

'No. Way more than nice. It's been a long time since…' She looked down at her hands.

'Go on.'

'Since someone held me. You know? Like they cared. It felt so good. And now I miss him. But how can I miss him? He's no better than Paul.'

'Why do you say that?'

'Because he's gone. Without a word. He just upped and left. You don't do that to people you care about. It just shows how little I know about him.'

'Have you Googled him?'

Beth stiffened. 'Why would I Google him?'

'Duh, so you know what you're getting into. I know you're at least a decade older than me, Beth, but you're not a dinosaur. People Google other people all the time. For all sorts of reasons. And most definitely if they fancy them.'

'Well, they shouldn't. It's rude.'

Lucy's lips set in a grim line. 'Do you really miss him that much?'

Beth's gaze slid across to the barn, then she dragged it back and gave herself a stern (internal) talking to. 'Yes.'

'Then you should know it's probably my fault he left.'

'How come?'

'I told him that you didn't need his complicated situation making your life more difficult than it already is.'

Beth felt anger spark deep inside. 'That wasn't your call to make.'

'It is a bit actually, but I swear I was thinking of you. Not me.'

'I don't understand.'

'You're trying so hard to get this place going, building a business, and if he's not careful, it could all get tarnished by association.'

'What are you talking about?'

'All the publicity, the negative social media.'

'Don't be silly. Social media is kids' stuff.'

'Grow up, Beth. It's life stuff. Whether you chose to engage with it or not, it's out there and it influences things. See for yourself.' Lucy tapped on her phone and held it out. 'Here. This is what's on X at the moment.'

Beth took the handset and read, then scrolled and read some more. 'Oh my... Jack said it was bad, but... this is horrible. Why do people say stuff like this?'

'That is only a fraction of what's out there,' warned Lucy. 'Rick is a hot potato right now. From a business perspective, it could be very damaging to be associated with him.'

'That's a terrible thing to say.'

'It's a realistic thing to say.'

'We should be helping him, not turning our backs.'

'I'm not saying I believe what's being said,' Lucy said. 'And I wasn't trying to drive him away. I just wanted him to be careful not to drag you into it.'

Beth shook her head. 'He deserves so much more than that. No wonder he went back to London.'

'I know. I'm sorry. But maybe it's for the best. He's got to face it all some time.'

Beth glared at Lucy. 'When I told you about the big, shitty thing I was dealing with, you told me to let people help me and things would get better.'

'I know I did, but—'

'And you were right. Okay, my problems are still here,

but things are better. Noisy, crazy and daft, but better.' Beth sniffed. 'I don't feel lonely anymore. And even though things aren't fixed yet, there's this light at the end of the tunnel – a dim one, but it's there.'

'I'm glad.'

'Rick is trying to handle something awful, too. And he's alone and he shouldn't be. He's got us. Or maybe not you, but he's got me. Only he doesn't know he's got me, because you told him to sod off. Oh, Lucy, what am I going to do?'

A sudden high-pitched squeal and flurry of footsteps came from inside the stable. Beth wiped tears from her eyes in time to see a teen dash onto the drive, chased by another brandishing a loaded paintbrush.

Lucy cursed under her breath and got to her feet. 'Look, I'd better sort this lot out, but, listen, tell me what I can do to fix this thing with Rick and I'll do it.'

'Take me to London.'

'Are you serious?'

'Deadly.' There was another squeal and more teenagers running with paint. 'Not this instant, but as soon as you can. I'd go myself if I was fit to drive, but I'm not. And there's no way Rose will agree to me taking the train. Please, Lucy. I have to see him.

Chapter 39

Rick spent the next few days working his way through legal papers for the upcoming court case and generally helping out at the surgery with non-patient-facing jobs. By arriving early in the morning, well before the start of clinic, and staying late in the evenings, he successfully avoided drawing any unwanted attention to the fact that he was back in town. On Friday, Sam stuck his head into the back office just as Rick looked up from filing blood test results.

'There's a Beth Hope in the waiting room for you, mate.'

'What is she doing here?'

'Don't ask me. Ask her. I'm busy. Michaela's running behind and the natives are getting restless.'

'Can I do anything else to help?'

'Yes,' said Sam. 'Talk to your friend. I'll send her in. And if you're making tea, I'll have two sugars.' He was gone before Rick could respond.

*

Rick jumped to his feet when Beth walked into the room. She looked pale and fragile, with a huge bruise on her forehead of a mottled yellow-green. It was all he could do not to pull her into his arms. He'd missed her so much it was a permanent physical ache.

'So, this is your staffroom,' she said.

'It is. Grab a seat.' Rick looked around, seeing the eclectic collection of tatty furniture as if through her eyes. 'Sorry about the mess. It's only tidy in here if we've got a CQC inspection.' With the surgery operating at full pelt all the time, there was rarely an opportunity to down tools and sort out the décor. Any refurbishment tended to focus on clinical areas and rooms with a high patient footfall. The staffroom never got a look in. He filled mugs with hot water from the kettle at the little kitchen unit crow-barred into a corner.

'CQC?'

'Care Quality Commission. Ofsted, but for doctors.'

'Oh.'

'The rest of the time we're run off our feet with only seconds to grab coffee and stuff.' He placed a cup of tea on the coffee table in front of her and retreated to lean against the kitchen counter. 'How did you get here?'

'Lucy gave me a lift. She'll be back in a bit to take me home.'

'Why did you come?' The words were out before he could stop them. They sounded so blunt, but he needed to know.

'Lucy showed me the horrible comments about you online. I know you mentioned them before, but I had no idea how bad it was. I wanted you to know that you're not on your own with all the horrible stuff that's going on.'

'You could have called. Rose has my number.'

She hunched her shoulders. 'I'm rubbish at talking on the phone. I needed to do this in person.'

'It's good to see you.' She couldn't possibly know how good.

'Can I ask…? I mean, there are laws against saying stuff that isn't true. Can't you sue for libel or something?'

'With hindsight, maybe I should have done. Only, I was afraid it would perpetuate the story. I was hoping it would all settle down.'

Beth struggled to her feet and paced towards him. 'Come back to the forest. Let me help.'

'I can't. It's kind of you, but—'

'I'm not being kind. I thought we were friends.'

'We are, but you need to go. I'm serious, Beth. You can't be around me.' The flash of pain in her eyes was awful, but he needed to make her leave. He turned his back on her. 'My situation will cause problems for you.'

'I don't care about that.'

Rick slammed his cup down. 'You should care. I can't protect you. I'm going to lose this case. There will be massive damages awarded. Crazy numbers. They'll take everything I have.'

'You don't need to protect me.'

'Yes. I do.' Desperate to touch her, he closed the gap between them and cradled her head in his hands, staring into her eyes. 'You are the most incredible person I have ever met.'

A small frown crinkled her forehead. 'You must have met some crummy people.'

'Don't do that.'

'Do what?'

'Don't put yourself down. You're amazing.'

Her smile wobbled. 'You're pretty wonderful, too, you know.'

How he didn't kiss her there and then, he didn't know. He released a huge sigh and stepped back, releasing her. 'I won't drag you into this.'

'You're not dragging me anywhere, Rick.'

'You don't understand. They won't stop with just me. They'll go for everything. Any asset linked to me. My apartment, the barn, my savings – everything. Damn it, even my friends aren't safe.'

'What do you mean?'

'This surgery is an unlimited liability partnership. Michaela and Gita are equally liable for... for...' He swallowed, hardly able to say the words. 'My friends could lose their home because of me.' He glanced around the room. 'This place will go, for sure. God knows what'll happen to our patients.'

'That's monstrous.'

'It is what it is. And while they can't get you financially, being associated with me will damage your business. You need to stay away from me.'

'I don't think I can do that.'

'I need you to. Please.'

There was a long silence.

Then, Beth spoke, 'It's your patient's mother bringing the case, isn't it?'

Rick gave a short bitter laugh. 'Yes. I'm beginning to think that Barbara might have been right about her. She said all the publicity wasn't hurting Cora's career. Even Jack said she was chasing clicks.'

'Meaning what?'

'Doing stuff to raise her profile, get people to like her social media stories, that sort of thing. If she is, it's working. She wasn't particularly famous before, but she is now.'

'If that's true, then it's awful,' agreed Beth. 'But are you sure that's what she's doing? Have you spoken with her?'

'I've never met her. My lawyers have advised me to stay away.'

'So, everything you know about her is second-hand or hearsay.'

'Meaning what?'

'Well – I'm just playing devil's advocate here – you don't really know what her motives are. You're judging her based on what the media says, just like all those other people are judging you.'

'Beth, come on. She's suing me for millions.'

'She might not know what else to do.'

'I don't follow.'

'If any of my kids were that ill, I'm not sure I'd react logically. And if there was no chance of recovery, I'd want to scream my pain from the rooftops. If the court case and all the media attention give Cora a platform to do that, she may not be thinking about the fallout. The collateral damage to you and everyone around you might genuinely not have occurred to her.'

'I don't think that's the case.'

'But, Rick, remember you told me you had a rugby injury when you were the same age as Dean? You said you were in a coma for a month.'

Rick rubbed his scarred eyebrow. 'So?'

'How did your mum react?'

'My mother is nothing like Cora Diamond.'

'Answer me this, if this was any other patient – forget the legal situation and all of that – what would your instinct be telling you to do?'

Rick already knew the answer. 'I'd go and see them. To find out what I could do to help.'

'Why aren't you doing that this time?'

'A lot of people, who have my best interests at heart, are telling me not to.'

'Do you always do what you're told?'

Rick laughed. 'As a doctor, yes. We have to conform. There are so many rules; CQC, NICE guidelines, professional revalidation checks, continued professional development. Working for the NHS is not like being in a medical drama where the maverick doctor does something totally left field and saves the day. Real medicine… no, real life doesn't work like that. The consequences are too high. So yes, professionally, I do what I'm told, because that way I can help the most people.'

'If it wasn't for people telling you to stay away, would you have contacted Cora?'

'Yes, but my hands are tied. I can't risk making things worse for everyone else.' Rick spun on his heels and stalked to the window to stare out at the rain-lashed car park, his thoughts already jumbled without Beth adding to them. He watched an orange Mini turn off the main road as if pursued by the hounds of hell and skid to a halt. The driver performed an erratic three-point-turn, missing several parked cars by a whisker, and stopped in the designated no-parking zone right outside the surgery entrance.

A muted ping sounded in the room. Beth unzipped her

bag. 'Lucy's here. Rick... I... Here's the thing, you once told me that it was better to try something and fail, than not try at all.'

He turned. 'Did I?'

'Yes.'

'I think I was giving you back your own advice from when you were up on the roof.'

'It doesn't matter if you were. We're both right.'

'Are we?'

'Yes. Look at it this way. You say that you will lose everything. Right?'

'That's what my lawyer says.'

'Then what have you got to lose? Sod conforming. You're an honourable person. You acted in good faith.'

Rick laughed softly. 'Barbara told me once that Brian said when you're in a difficult spot the only thing to do is the next right thing. That way, you can live with yourself.'

Beth grinned. 'Well, if Brian says it, it must be true. Go and see Cora. Tell her. Give it one last throw of the dice.'

'I'll think about it, but I need you to do something for me.'

She crossed the distance between them, her eyes full of hope. 'Anything.'

It was breaking his heart to say this, but he had to. 'I need you to break off all contact with me. No, don't shake your head. I mean it. If I am going to survive what is coming, I need to know that it can't impact badly on you and your family. You're too important.'

Her eyes filled with tears, but he held firm.

Her phone pinged again, breaking the deadlock, and she nodded. 'Fine. I'll stay away for now. But please, Rick, don't let it be forever.' She leaned up and pressed a kiss to his lips and hurried from the room, taking all the sunshine in the world with her.

Chapter 40

The trip back to the forest washed Beth out completely. She spent most of it trying not to cry, while overthinking the whole conversation with Rick. She shouldn't have opened her big mouth about Cora. What the hell did she know about his situation? By the time Lucy dropped her back at the farmhouse, she was mentally and physically exhausted. Rose bustled her off to bed with a hefty dose of medication and threatened to set Barbara on her if she didn't go to sleep immediately. The next morning, she was stiff and sore, and didn't feel as if she'd slept at all. Stumbling downstairs, headachy and puffy-eyed, she found Barbara, Lucy and Rose in deep discussion across a kitchen table littered with the remnants of breakfast.

Rose shoved a cup of tea and a plate of buttered toast in Beth's direction. 'Are you feeling better?'

She nodded, even though it was a lie, aware of a tense undercurrent in the room. 'What's up?'

'It's the planning permission,' said Rose.

'More objections?'

Rose nodded.

'Maria has let me down,' said Barbara, her lips compressed into an ominous line.

'Lord Astley refused to withdraw his objection, did he?' asked Beth.

'He always was a slippery little toad,' said Barbara, 'even when we were children. If only I had something on him, I'd force him to back down.'

'Aunty B!' Rose's giggle was uneasy. 'Are you saying you'd blackmail him?'

'If need be.' Barbara's grim expression made Beth very grateful they were on the same side.

'By the way,' said Rose, 'the kitchen inspector is coming today. At one.'

'You're kidding.' Beth's gaze swept over the accumulated chaos. Layers of coats lurked on chairs; bags and shoes were abandoned just inside the back door; junk cluttered surfaces; piles of dirty crockery waited for someone to discover that the dishwasher could be emptied and restacked. Beth knew that the rest of the house wasn't much better. 'What time is it now?'

Rose checked her phone. '10.10am. Chill, Beth. We've got this.'

Beth failed to smother a whimper.

'That's why I'm here,' said Barbara. 'Cleaning is just the thing to take my mind off slimy weasels.'

Lucy grinned. 'I'm here to pitch in, too. While you were sleeping, I dropped Jack and Daisy to the bus stop and took Grace and Hari to preschool. Hazel is with my ma-in-law for a couple of hours. So, I'm all yours.'

'Grace!' Beth's hand went to her mouth. 'Oh, I'm such a bad mother. I didn't even notice she wasn't here. My head just isn't working properly.'

'You've been doing too much,' said Rose.

'Go have a sleep,' said Lucy. 'And don't worry. When you come down, this place will be gleaming.'

Beth's head was pounding. She gave in, took some painkillers and went back to bed.

*

Two hours later, she came back down the stairs to a house she barely recognised. The hall, stairs and landing were tidy. The floors gleamed. Padding into the kitchen, she was tempted to go out and come back in again, just to make sure she was in the right place. All the surfaces were clear; the general detritus of family life had been swept away as if it had never existed. 'It's like a show home in here. I'm scared to touch anything.'

'You just missed Lucy,' said Rose. 'She went to pick up Grace and Hari. Barbara is in the utility room, ironing a tablecloth. I'm just getting her a drink. Do you want one?'

'Only if it won't make a mess.'

'We had a major clear-out while we were at it,' said Rose. 'I hope you don't mind.'

Beth laughed. 'It was well overdue, if you ask me. What have you done with everything?'

'Stuff we need to keep is all dumped in the bedrooms to be sorted later. Rubbish got put in Barbara's camper van. She's going to take it to the tip tomorrow.'

Barbara came out of the utility room. 'I won't be dumping it in the hedge like the phantom fly-tipper, I can tell you.'

'Oh!' A bizarre dizzy sensation took Beth's breath away and her legs wobbled. She shot her free hand out to steady herself.

Rose grabbed her arm. 'Beth, what is it?'

Beth blinked. 'I… uh… I don't know.'

Rose tutted. 'Sit down. I knew you shouldn't have gone to London yesterday.'

Beth sat. Something pushed at the edge of her mind. Something she couldn't quite grab onto. 'There's something I… oh no. It's nothing.'

'You've overdone it, haven't you? I told you—'

'No, no. It's not that. I remembered something.'

'About your accident?' Barbara's excitement cut through the fog in Beth's head. 'My Brian said that would happen.'

'It was only a brief flash.' Beth concentrated. 'No. It's gone again.'

'What was the trigger do you think?' asked Barbara.

'Um…' Beth racked her brain. 'You were saying something.'

'About the fly-tipping?'

'Yes. That was it. I got this sudden head rush… like a picture. Fly-tipping. How strange. I… Oh.' Beth felt her jaw go slack. 'Oh yes. Oh my goodness. Yes.'

'What?' Rose's eyes widened.

'I need my phone.' Beth looked, but the counter where she'd left it was bare. 'My phone. Rose, where's my phone?'

'It's here.' Rose passed over the handset. 'Why?'

'I'm not sure, but…' Beth hit play on the last video she'd recorded. Barbara and Rose crowded in close. Silent tears tracked down Beth's cheeks as they all watched in stunned silence.

An arm slipped around her shoulders and Rose hissed, 'The bastards. They just left you. You could have died. I nearly lost another mother.'

'Can I see that again?' Barbara watched the whole video through twice. 'Is it possible to zoom in? When the van comes close, I think I recognise the driver. Yes. I'm sure of it. That's the Dixon boy.'

'Are you sure?' Rose checked the footage again. 'You're right.'

'The other one will be his dopey cousin. They're renovating the cottages over past East Field for... Heavens above!'

Beth sat forwards. 'What?'

'Those cottages belong to Robert Astley. They're working for him.'

'No way,' said Rose. 'Are you saying he's the phantom fly-tipper?'

Barbara shook her head. 'I wouldn't have thought he'd be that stupid, but the Dixons certainly are. Come to think of it, the last time this sort of thing happened, they were working on another Astley property.' Barbara started the video again. 'There. I'd recognise those awful kitchen units anywhere. They're definitely from the Astley cottages.'

'It doesn't make sense,' said Beth. 'The Astley estate is loaded. They can easily afford to get rid of their rubbish legally. Why would he risk fly-tipping?'

Barbara shrugged. 'I doubt he knows anything about it. In all probability, the Dixons are taking the money for a legal disposal, pocketing it, then forging the paperwork.'

Rose wiped her eyes. 'We have to call the police.'

'No, let's not,' said Beth.

Barbara stared at her aghast. 'Why ever not?'

Rose was outraged. 'We can't let them get away with this.'

'I've no intention of letting them get away with anything,' said Beth.

Barbara gave her a keen look. 'What's going through your head?'

Beth paused, wondering if she had the guts to follow through with the idea that was currently formulating. *Yes, I absolutely do.* She'd told Rick that it was better to try something rather than do nothing. 'Barbara, can you get me through to speak to Lord Astley?'

'I can. That's assuming he's at home, of course.' Barbara stabbed a number into her mobile and put it to her ear. 'Maria, hello. Sorry to disturb you. I need a favour. There's someone here who needs to speak to Robert. It's important. Might you persuade him to come to the phone and give her five minutes, please? Thank you.' There was a pause. 'Ah. Hello, Robert. Mrs Hope from Hope Farm would like a word.'

Beth took the phone. 'Hello, Lord Astley.'

'What do you want?' His supercilious tone made her hackles rise.

'I've got some information here that you're going to want to get out in front of.' She stalked over to look out of the kitchen window.

'What?'

'I have a video of your staff illegally dumping waste.'

'What are you talking about?'

'The Dixons are dumping junk from the East Field Cottage renovations.'

'I don't believe you.'

'I'm happy to send you a copy of the footage. It's definitely your rubbish. I have one witness already who will swear to it. I'm sure there are others.'

'What witness? No, don't tell me, it's that witch Barbara Trenchard, isn't it?'

'It isn't someone you can bribe to keep quiet, if that's what you mean. The problem is that this video footage not only shows the Dixons illegally dumping waste, but also shows them running me down as they tried to escape.'

'Why should I care? I didn't run you over.'

'I know that, but it won't look very good for you if you can be linked to this, will it? You know what social media is like these days. Mud sticks. A local lord connected to a hit-and-run on a poor defenceless mother. A mother whose business application he is on record as objecting to. Think about it.'

'You're bluffing.'

'Am I?'

There was a silence and then, 'What do you want?'

'Drop your objection to my well-being centre and, while you're at it, get your friends to drop theirs.'

'And if I do?'

'I'll tell you where the waste has been dumped and give you time to get it cleared up before I go to the police. I'll even trim the video to remove any footage that incriminates you.'

'Why would you do that?'

'Like you say, it wasn't you that ran me over. If you never intended for the waste to be dumped, that waste is then removed and I have my well-being centre, why would I want to make your life difficult?'

'Hmm.' There was a lot of huffing and puffing from the other end of the line. 'You know that's blackmail, don't you?'

'It depends how you look at it. I prefer to call it giving a neighbour a chance to do the right thing.'

'I'll remember this.'

'Good.'

For a brief moment, Lord Astley sounded like he was swallowing wasps. 'Tell me where the waste is. I'll get it picked up.'

'I'll tell you when my planning application is approved.'

'That could take ages.'

'I'm sure there's something you can do to speed things along. Now, do we have a deal?'

'We do. You'll be hearing from me shortly.'

The line went dead. Beth turned back to the others.

Rose's eyes were out on stalks. 'That was… that was…'

'Very impressive,' said Barbara. 'Well done.'

Beth laughed, relief swamping her. 'I was winging it. Do you think he'll actually do it?'

'He'd be daft not to.'

'You are going to go to the police though, aren't you?' asked Rose.

'I'll have to find out who to speak to, but yes. Once we get the planning application and the waste is gone, I'll make some calls.'

'Angelica,' said Barbara. 'That's who you should speak to.'

A loud knock sounded and Rose leapt to her feet and headed for the front door, calling over her shoulder, 'Oh yes! Angelica. Good idea.'

'Angelica?' asked Beth.

'My cousin's girl,' said Barbara. 'Police officer. Southampton CID. She'll know who to pass it to.'

'Sounds perfect. Thank you, Barbara. What would I do without you?'

Rose returned, a slim white envelope in her hand. She looked like she'd seen a ghost.

'Rose?' Beth asked. 'What is it?'

'I had to sign for this.' Rose handed over the envelope.

Beth's stomach lurched. It was addressed to her in very distinct, uneven, block capitals.

Chapter 41

'I can't believe you've persuaded me to help you do this, Rick.' Gita's voice was an octave higher than normal. She pushed her glasses further up her nose and peered over the steering wheel. 'Michaela's going to kill me when she finds out and I daren't think what she'll do to you.'

'I know. Thank you for setting it up.'

She glanced across at him, then back at the road. 'It will only make things worse.'

'I have to try. I have to know that I did the right thing. It's the only way I can live with myself.'

'And going to talk to Cora Diamond, the woman who hates you most in the world, who'll probably slag you off in the papers five minutes after you leave, is the right thing?'

'I think so.' He'd not been able to get what Beth had said out of his mind. 'If Cora genuinely wants to improve medical services for people like she says she does, then maybe I can persuade her that destroying the surgery isn't going to help. She can take me to the cleaners, but hopefully I can get her to leave Five Oaks out of it.'

'I bloody hope you know what you're doing,' muttered

Gita, pulling up at a set of metal security gates. 'We're here. Call me when you're done.'

*

The flashy, modern, metal-and-glass monstrosity on the banks of the Thames was exactly the sort of apartment block Rick had always imagined a celebrity would own. The heady scent of beeswax polish and lilies filled the approach to the security desk, making even the air he was breathing seem exclusive. The guard removed dark glasses and give him a hard stare.

Rick straightened his suit jacket. 'I'm here to see Ms Diamond.'

'This way, sir.' The guard stood and padded across the marble floor to a lift. He gestured for Rick to enter the small space and then followed him in as the doors slid closed.

Rick hated lifts at the best of times. The movement made his head feel impossibly heavy, and taking each breath became harder and harder. Moments before full-on panic set in, the upward motion stopped and a soft ping sounded. Rick almost fell out onto a small landing before a shiny chrome door.

The guard knocked and then opened the door. 'Dr Mahon's here, Ms Diamond.'

A disembodied, husky, soft voice replied, 'Thank you, Zac.'

'I'll be downstairs if you need me.' Zac gave Rick another hard stare and left.

Rick stepped onto soft cream carpeting and found himself in a huge open-plan space. Floor-to-ceiling French windows ran the length of the room, leading onto a clear glazed balcony overlooking the Thames. Momentarily stunned by the view, it took Rick a moment to register the woman in the white trouser suit near the far wall. She was smaller than he'd imagined. A brisk breeze skipped in through the open casement and toyed with her long blonde curls. She wrapped both arms around her slim frame as if trying to hold herself together. Thrusting her chin out, she said in a soft husky tone, 'The elusive Dr Mahon. We meet at last.'

He approached, stopping a few feet away. 'Elusive?'

'Maybe cowardly is a better word. More fitting for the man who destroyed my son's life and then ran away.'

Rick stiffened. 'I didn't leave of my own accord. You ran me out of town.'

'I did no such thing.'

'You and your social media buddies hounded me out.'

Her forehead creased. 'What social media buddies?'

'Don't give me that.'

'Dr Mahon, I am genuinely baffled.'

'If that's true, and I seriously doubt it, then check out The Sal and Ade Show on YouTube. Or, better still, listen to the *Find Dr Death Podcast*. You can get daily updates from all the random people taking it upon themselves to track me down and discover my hideout. I'm sure you'll find it very satisfying.'

'That has nothing to do with me.'

'Every time you speak out on TV or get interviewed in the papers, there's an upswing in vitriol aimed at me.'

Her mouth tightened. 'I had no idea.'

Rick gave a bitter laugh. 'The stupid thing is despite the abuse, I don't want you to stop speaking out. If you can improve the provision of better mental health facilities, then you have to keep going.'

'You agree with me?'

'Of course I do. You have a platform. You might actually do some good with it. I'd just prefer not to be public enemy number one while you're doing it.'

There was a silence as she appeared to digest what he had said, then she uncrossed her arms. 'Why did you come?'

'I came to ask how Dean is?'

'Better late than never, I suppose.'

'And I also came to ask if…'

'If what?'

'If you could see your way to letting the surgery off the hook in whatever settlement gets reached in court? I'll find whatever compensation you win, somehow. But, please, for the sake of the patients and my colleagues, don't destroy Five Oaks.'

She didn't answer. Instead, she turned on her heel and walked away.

Rick sighed. It had been worth a try. He headed for the door.

Her voice stopped him in his tracks. 'I thought you came to see Dean.'

He spun back to face her. 'He's here?'

'I couldn't bear to see him in hospital. I thought he should be back in his own apartment, surrounded by all his things.' She waved an arm at the three huge flatscreen TVs that made up one wall, with vast couches set around a glass coffee table before them. 'Somewhere he can see or, at least, hear his computer games. I thought it might help. I'm rubbish at playing them for him and that probably drives him round the bend. Or it would if he… if… I… They say that hearing is the last thing to go.'

'It's true.'

Cora pulled at a section of the wall opposite the screens. It concertinaed back on smooth runners to reveal an additional space with yet more windows overlooking the river. A figure lay in a hospital bed, a bank of life support equipment nearby. Dean. A man dressed in scrubs was checking monitors. 'Pat. This is Dr Mahon. He's come to see Dean. You can take a break while he's here, if you like.'

Pat nodded a greeting and left.

Rick approached the bed. Dean wore Pac-Man pyjamas. His hair was brushed neatly away from his eyes. Wires snaked from his chest to the ECG. A blood pressure cuff gripped his upper arm and an oxygen monitor was clipped to his finger. 'He must be stable or they wouldn't have allowed him home. That is really good news.'

'I'm told he's doing as well as can be expected, but he's completely non-responsive.' Hopelessness dripped from Cora's voice.

'I wish there was something I could do.' Rick laid a hand on Dean's arm, but immediately pulled back as Dean's skin twitched. 'Sorry, mate, are my hands cold?' Rick rubbed his hand together and then stopped. 'Hang on.' He looked at Cora. 'When you say he is non-responsive, do you mean he's not responding to anything at all?'

'That's what I've been told.'

'Are you sure?' Rick frowned and laid his hand on Dean's arm a second time. The skin twitched again. 'Can you remember exactly what the doctors said?'

'Shall I call Pat back?'

'No, let him have his break. It's probably nothing.'

'Why? What did you see?'

He watched the ECG trace. 'He reacted to my cold hands, but it's very minor and that might not be a new response.' Rick's medical instinct took over as if he were slipping on a favourite old coat that had hung forgotten in a cupboard for far too long. He pulled a pen from his inside pocket and took hold of Dean's middle finger. 'Sorry about this, mate.' He pressed the tip of the pen down hard onto the nail. Dean's hand jerked.

Cora cried out. 'Stop. You're hurting him. Why would you do that?'

'It's a standard test to check awareness.'

She pushed him aside with the fury of a lioness protecting her cub. 'I was a fool to let you anywhere near him.'

'You saw his hand move, though, didn't you?'

'You made it move. You're just trying to derail the court case.'

'I didn't. And I'm not. I promise. Just because he responded doesn't mean he will wake up. And even if he does, he will still need care. I fully expect you to go ahead with the case and take everything I have, but that's not important right now. Cora, Dean responded.'

She frowned, her eyes going from Rick to Dean and back again. 'What do I do?'

'Ring his medical team. If they told you that he's completely non-responsive, then something has changed. Ask them to repeat the cognitive awareness tests.' He pulled a piece of paper from his pocket. 'This is my new mobile number. Please don't give it to the press. Call me, day or night, if I can ever do anything for you or Dean.' He placed the card on a nearby table and left.

Chapter 42

'It's not fair. Why can't we stay and see Dad?' Daisy asked for the fourth time in less than five minutes. She leant one hip against the Welsh dresser in the kitchen, crossed her arms and scowled.

Beth, one arm still in a sling, was busy encouraging Grace to work out how to do up the big buttons on her favourite unicorn coat. 'I agree, Daisy. But you read the letter, same as I did. He said he wants a meeting with me here, today, at two, and that if any of you kids are here, it won't happen.'

'Is it me or is that, like, weirdly controlling?' asked Rose.

'Very weirdly controlling,' agreed Beth.

'I don't want to see him, anyway,' muttered Jack. He pulled a sausage roll from a packet near the back of the fridge, sniffed it, then crammed the whole thing into his mouth.

'We could hide upstairs and surprise him,' said Daisy. 'And then, when he sees us—'

'If you want to take the risk that he won't turn around and leave, then be my guest,' said Beth. 'I'm past caring what he wants anymore.'

Rose handed Jack half a baguette stuffed with cheese and steered him towards the door. 'I care. Daisy, we talked about this. We'll let Beth and Dad talk, then we can see what happens after that. Now, come on, I'll buy you a hot chocolate at The Coffee Pot.' She picked up the car keys and dangled them in Daisy's face.

Daisy glared at Beth and pushed away from the dresser. 'Okay, fine, but we're only giving them an hour, then we'll be back.'

'Good,' said Beth. 'I'll look forward to it.'

*

Twenty minutes later, there was a firm rat-a-tat-tat on the knocker.

Beth paused on the way to open the door. The delicate perfume from pink stocks in a vase on the windowsill helped to steady her nerves. She was grateful the house was still tidy after the kitchen inspection. The thought of Paul judging her, thinking she'd fallen apart without him, made her skin feel like a thousand ants were crawling just under the surface.

A petite, pretty, blonde woman, who looked to be in her early thirties and was dressed in floaty, white linen layers, stood on the doorstep. 'He's not coming,' she said, her South American drawl making her sound as if she'd just stepped off the set of *Gone with the Wind*.

Beth scanned the driveway. A low-slung, dark-green, soft-top sports car was parked at a jaunty angle near the stables. 'I'm sorry, what?'

'Paul,' the woman said. 'He's not coming.'

'Oh, and you are?'

'Rachel. May I come in?'

Beth stepped back from the door and gestured down the corridor towards the kitchen.

Rachel walked through the kitchen and on into the conservatory. 'What a beautiful room. Paul told me how much he enjoyed designing it.'

Rachel's languid way of speaking was beginning to get on Beth's nerves. 'I think the real credit goes to his first wife, Isla.' *Why is this woman here? Who is she?* 'Did he also tell you about the children?'

'Not until a few weeks ago, but they're part of the reason I'm here.' She crossed to a wicker sofa that afforded an excellent view of the garden. 'May I sit?'

Beth nodded.

'Will you join me?' Rachel asked.

Beth didn't like being invited to sit in her own house, but she couldn't very well continue to lurk in the doorway. She sloped over to an armchair. 'Why are you here?'

'Paul asked me to come. He's had a tough time. He's been travelling all over the place trying to find himself and ended up in India. That's where we met. At an ashram. We bonded over yoga and spiritual healing.'

Beth eased the sling where it pinched at her neck. 'Right.'

'He wants a divorce.'

'Why hasn't he come to ask me himself?'

'He doesn't want you to think there's any chance of you getting back together.'

'Arrogant sod!' It had been a while since Beth had fantasised about throttling her husband, but her palms were starting to itch.

'Yes, he is a bit, but that's part of his charm. Don't you think?'

'That's a matter of opinion. So, are you and he…?'

'We are,' replied Rachel, holding up her left hand, a wide, satisfied grin spreading across her face. 'He popped the question a few weeks ago. British men are so romantic.'

Beth's gaze lit on the diamond adorning Rachel's ring finger and her eyes narrowed. It was huge. Several thousand pounds' worth of huge. Not enough to fix a roof, mind, but still, the timing was suspicious.

'We'd like to get married before the baby comes.' Rachel placed a protective hand on her slim midriff, her expression unfocused and dreamy. 'We're going to settle in Washington. Paul's going to take a job with my law firm. It's going to be wonderful.'

'And you're not remotely concerned that Paul has already abandoned four other children?'

'He won't do that to me. I have an ironclad prenup. He wouldn't dare.'

'Oh good,' said Beth, half hoping Paul would attempt to leave Rachel. The prospect of her tearing him limb from limb was unexpectedly appealing.

'So,' prompted Rachel, 'the divorce?'

'Are you here as his lawyer or his fiancé?'

'Both.'

'Then you're negotiating on his behalf?'

'Yes.'

Beth paced over to the French windows and stared out at the smooth, creamy travertine patio slabs. 'Here's the thing. I'm glad Paul didn't come today. He's saved me the trouble of running him off my property at the sharp end of a shovel.'

'I beg your pardon?'

'I have more important things to think about than a useless husband. He can have his divorce.'

'Alrighty, that was easier than I exp—'

'Not so fast.' Beth held up a finger. 'I have conditions.'

'Such as?'

'He has to pay for it. All of it. And he has to cough up the child maintenance he's missed.'

'That sounds fair.'

'And,' said Beth, as if Rachel hadn't spoken, 'he'd better start making regular emotionally supportive contact with his children because – even though I think he's a prize prat – they love him.'

'That is also reasonable.'

'There will also be a discussion about the two hundred thousand pounds he stole from me.'

'What?' Rachel looked as if she'd accidentally swallowed a fly.

'In fact,' Beth gave a humourless smile, her gaze moving down to the ring, 'make that two hundred and ten thousand pounds.'

'I don't understand.'

'I'll send you the paperwork and the bank statements that prove it. And, finally, he'll have to sign full custody of Grace over to me. She won't be popping over to the States for a visit any time soon.'

Rachel didn't respond.

'Then, and only then, will I agree to a divorce. Let me know when the papers are ready for me to sign and then you can have Paul with my blessing. I'll show you out.' Beth swept from the room, her head held high. She opened the front door and waited. 'Goodbye and good luck. You're going to need it.'

The future Mrs Hope the Third shot Beth an uncertain look before heading over to her car and driving away.

Beth glanced outside before closing the door and spotted a familiar figure leaning against the gate to the llama field, petting the animals. Her heart started tap-dancing. Grabbing a fleece, she hurried over.

'Rick. You came back.'

He turned and smiled, but it didn't reach his eyes. 'I know I said that we should stay away from each other, but something happened and I, well, I really needed to see you.'

It was only as he said the words that she realised just how much she had needed to see him, too. She placed a gentle hand on his arm, enjoying the warm tingly sensation that the contact triggered. 'What happened?'

'I went to see Cora yesterday.'

'Oh! How did it go?'

'I might have made things worse.'

'Oh God, Rick. I am so sorry.'

'Why are you apologising?'

'Because I suggested you go.'

'Hush.' He pulled her into his arms. 'It was good advice. I'm glad I went. I feel so much better about it all.'

The delicious feeling of being held close by him jarred with her concern. 'Tell me what happened.' She listened intently as he told her about Dean potentially responding to stimulation.

'So, you see? You were right to tell me to go. I needed to see them both. And Cora... well, in some ways, I think she needed to see me.'

'I can see why she'd be upset if you caused Dean pain.'

'Yes, I agree, but it's a standard test for pain responses. His doctors will do the same if they reassess him.'

'And this response is a good thing, yes?'

'Yes. It's a really good sign.'

'Does it mean he will get better?'

Rick shrugged. 'It's possible. How much better, I can't say. Some people recover completely and others never progress at all. It's really up to Dean and his medical team now.'

'What are you going to do?'

'There's nothing I can do, apart from wish them well. I'll spend the next couple of weeks here. I've come to rely on forest life more than I ever thought possible. If I can stay under the radar here for a bit longer, I'll make the most of the peace and quiet before going back to London and all hell is let loose by the court case. After that, this place will probably be sold.' His eyes scanned the barn and the field. 'I've no idea where I'll go.'

Beth gave him a small squeeze. 'Come to us – in whatever way, shape or form makes you comfortable. I mean, of course, we have to think of the kids and go slow and everything, but… and we can be just friends, if that's what you want. Or, maybe, in time, we can… I … well… hmm.' She felt her cheeks go warm. 'I'm sorry. I'm not making much sense. I don't really know what I mean. I just don't want you to leave.'

Rick slid his hands up to take her upper arms in a gentle grip, gazing intently into her eyes. 'You are a very special person, Beth. Under different circumstances, I would be delighted to explore whatever this is between us – working around what the children need, of course. But the way things stand at the moment, I have to say no. My problems can't become yours.'

'But—'

'You have already done enough. Without you, I'd have fallen apart weeks ago. I won't be like Paul. I am not going to make my financial burden yours.'

'You're not—'

'If I can't clear this whole messy situation up and come to you with a clean slate, or if there is any chance that you or your kids might get hurt by association, then I'll keep away.'

A huge chasm of loss at the thought of his leaving opened before her.

His mobile phone pinged. He released her and checked his screen, then cursed. 'A message from an unknown number.'

'Could it be David?'

'Possibly. I still haven't been able to get hold of him. I'm getting quite worried about him, to be honest. I'd better check.' He put the device to his ear.

Beth watched his eyes grow round as he listened to the message. 'What is it?'

'Cora wants to see me.'

'When?'

'Monday afternoon.'

'So you have a few days before you have to go back.' A few days in which she could change his mind about leaving for good. 'Well, if you're stuck for something to fill your time, come over and see what we've done in the stable. We're painting what Barbara calls a "Muriel" on one of the walls. Well, Lucy is painting it and the rest of us are colouring in the bits she tells us to, but it's surprisingly relaxing.'

'I might just do that. A bit of art therapy is just what I need.'

They might have stood there staring at each other for hours, but the sound of a car heralded the children returning.

Daisy leapt from the car and stormed across the gravel. 'Is Dad still here? What did he want?'

Jack skidded to a halt behind his twin. 'Is Dad coming home?' He threw Rick a challenging glare. 'Or did he see you with Rick and change his mind?'

Rick stepped back and shook his head. 'I wasn't here, mate. Whatever is going on with your dad, it has nothing to do with me.'

Rose arrived carrying Grace, with Paddy scuffing over the gravel behind her.

Daisy scowled at Beth. 'Well? Is Dad coming home or not?'

Beth shook her head. 'I'm sorry, Daisy, but your dad didn't come. He sent a… a friend.'

'What? Why?'

Resisting the urge to glance at Rick, Beth said, 'He wants a divorce. He's moving to America—'

'What?' Daisy's howl of outrage tugged at Beth's heart.

'He wants to stay in contact with you. His friend said he will be calling you about it soon. There are just some things he needs to sort out first.'

'No! That's not fair. That's just so… *not fair.*' She spun on her heels and ran back towards the farmhouse.

Jack glanced from Daisy's retreating back to Beth and then to Rick, before dashing after her.

Rose gave Beth a sad smile before turning to Rick. 'Hi.

You came back. It's nice to see you.' She passed Grace to Beth. 'I'll go and see if I can talk to them.'

Beth held Grace close. 'I'm sorry your daddy didn't come, Grace.'

The little girl looked more confused than distressed and wriggled to get down. 'Can I go and play with the penguins?' she asked Rick.

Rick laughed. 'If your mum says that you can.'

Without bothering to see if Beth agreed, Grace was off like a shot. Rick touched Beth's arm. 'It sounds like there's been a fair bit going on here while I've been away. Would you like a cuppa? You don't have to talk, but if you'd like to, I'm all yours.'

If Rick was so set on leaving, Beth was damned if she'd pass up the opportunity to spend time with him.

Chapter 43

The following Monday afternoon in London, Rick was surprised not to be escorted up to Dean's apartment like he had been before. Instead, Zac merely waved an arm towards the elevator with an unsettlingly cheerful greeting. 'Hi, Doc. You know the way, don't you?'

Up in the apartment, the concertina wall had been reinstated. There was no sign of any medical equipment and no sign of Dean. Cora strode across the thick carpet towards him. 'Dr Mahon. Thank you for coming.'

'I was glad to be invited. How is Dean?'

'He's—' A short soft ping sounded in the room. Cora frowned. 'Damn it, that's the lift. They're early. I was hoping for more time.'

'Who's early?'

Her tone suddenly became urgent. 'Dr Mahon, will you trust me?'

The back of his neck prickled. 'I don't understand.'

'Please, there isn't time to explain, but please trust me.'

'Explain what?'

'I'm about to receive some guests.'

'Would you like me to leave?'

'No, quite the contrary, you need to be here for this, but… Dr Mahon, I'm sorry, I was going to… oh never mind.' Cora picked up a black folder from the coffee table and turned towards the entrance hall just as that soft ping sounded again.

The door opened. 'Ms Diamond,' called Zac. 'Your guests have arrived.'

'Thank you, Zac. Please show them in.' Cora flipped her hair, encouraging her curls to tumble over one shoulder. She seemed different from the woman Rick had met last time. Harder, more in control. A worm of suspicion stirred in his belly. Then, Zac ushered the last two people Rick ever wanted to see again into the room.

Sal and Abe.

There was suddenly not enough oxygen in the room.

Cora exchanged noisy air kisses with the arrivals. 'I am glad you could both join us.'

Rick steeled himself not to react.

Sal shot Rick an evil grin. 'Dr Death. We meet again.'

'Yo, dude.' Abe waved his camera at Rick. 'Hang on a mo. Lemme start rolling. The fans will want to see this little showdown.'

Aware that Zac was blocking the door, Rick looked from the YouTubers to Cora and then over at the balcony.

Sal snickered. 'You're four floors up, Ricky, babe. No jumping out of windows today. We got you.'

'Let's not get ahead of ourselves.' Cora's tone was brisk. She opened the black file, drew out some papers and placed them on the coffee table with a pen. 'Legal formalities first. You need to sign these consent forms for the right to film the first time that Dr Mahon and I appear on camera together. Remember? We talked about this. You and I will both film this little discussion and then you and Abe get forty-eight hours to release your scoop before I go public with footage, too.'

'Yeah, yeah. Abe, you first.'

Abe lowered his camera and scrawled his name. Sal did the same.

'Excellent.' Cora tucked the papers away.

Rick cleared his throat. 'I—'

Cora shot Rick a look. 'Don't worry, Dr Mahon. I'm only interested in recording the truth here. The forms state that footage can only be used if it's shot in one continuous piece. No editing allowed. None of us wants anyone to claim that it's been altered.'

Sal tutted. 'Can we get on with it?'

'Of course.' Cora gathered up the papers and handed them to Zac.

'Is he staying?' asked Abe.

'He's here to make sure everyone... how shall I put this?' Cora looked meaningfully at Rick. 'Behaves themselves.'

'Good idea,' said Sal, shooting a sideways glare at Rick. 'Don't want Dr Death cutting up rough.'

'Can I start filming already?' whined Abe.

'You can,' said Cora. 'I'll start my cameras, too.' She picked a remote up from the coffee table, pointed it towards the huge screens on the wall and pressed a button, saying to Rick as if there was nothing untoward happening, 'I mentioned Dean's obsession with gaming technology, didn't I? There are cameras everywhere in this room. To record him playing, as well as his reactions, and so that he could explain his strategy to his fans. I never thought I'd ever find them useful.'

Rick's eyes darted around the room, sweat trickling between his shoulder blades. *Bloody hell. There really are cameras everywhere.* One over the main screen, one on the wall to the right and one over the door. There was even a small one on the coffee table. Little red lights indicated that all were recording. Rick's eyebrow twitched. He pressed shaking fingertips to his scar. *I am totally screwed.*

'Ready?' asked Abe.

'No comment,' muttered Rick.

'Not you. He means her,' hissed Sal, waving a hand at Cora. Then, without missing a beat, she turned a beaming smile towards Abe's camera. 'Here we are again, fans. Sal and Abe discovering the real truth behind all the big celeb stories. Just for you guys.' She turned towards Cora. 'I can't believe I'm here with the wonderful Cora Diamond, mother of the tragic D-Man. And, big scoop, fans, I'm also here with the villain of the piece, Dr Death. That's right, folks. Bet you didn't expect that. Everyone out there trawling for sightings for the *Find Dr Death Podcast* can relax. The man of the moment is right here.'

Abe panned his camera from Cora to Rick, then spun it around to face himself and gave a big smile and wave into the camera lens, saying, 'I'm here, too, folks.'

'Abe,' hissed Sal, 'not now.'

'Sorry.' Abe focused back on Sal and Cora.

Sal pinned a fake smile back on her face. 'Cora, I understand there's something you want to give to the doctor responsible for Dean's tragic situation.'

'I hope it's a smack in the mouth,' muttered Abe.

'Abe, come on,' Sal snapped. 'Remember, we can't edit this.'

Abe stuck his tongue out. 'But I do hope it's a smack in the mouth. An action shot will look great.'

Sal glared at him and then turned back to Cora. 'So, Cora, what is it you want to give Dr Death?'

Cora, reaching into her folder and pulling out some papers, replied, 'I'd like to give him these.' She held the papers out to Rick.

Rick didn't move. A curious sense of detachment washed over him, as if he were watching a play he had no part in.

'What are they?' Sal's tone was belligerent.

Cora held the papers up, making sure that all the cameras got a good shot of them. 'These are the missing temporary resident forms from Dr Mahon's medical practice and the accompanying consultation notes, too. They prove Dr Rick Mahon did exactly what he said he did. He warned Dean that mixing the medicine he was being prescribed with heroin could be fatal.'

'Wha…' Sal looked closer. 'No way. They must be fakes.'

Cora shook her head. 'They're genuine. I assure you.'

Sal's eyes darted from Cora to Rick and back again. 'What are you saying?'

'I'm saying that Dean is responsible for his situation. Not the kind doctor who tried to help him. It's bad enough that you've repeatedly twisted things I've said in interviews and misquoted me, and tried to big yourselves up using my son's illness.'

'Now, wait a min—' Sal frowned.

'No, you wait. You've played a huge part in hounding Dr Mahon out of his home, away from his job and the patients that need him. These papers prove he is innocent. You should be ashamed of yourselves.'

'Let me see them…' Sal lunged at Cora.

Zac darted forward. 'Stay back.'

Sal stopped.

'What you and Abe have done is immoral,' said Cora. 'Worse than that, it's evil. Destroying a person's life for entertainment, for clicks; growing your social media following through scandal and lies. You're monsters, both of you.'

Sal looked as if she might be sick.

'What's going on?' Confusion clouded Abe's gaze.

'Shut up, Abe. And for God's sake, stop filming, will you?'

Abe tightened his grip on his camera. 'You told me not to. We signed, remember?'

Sal rubbed a hand over her face. 'Just let me think.'

'What is going on, Abe,' said Cora, 'is that you and Sal are about to deliver a major scoop to the world's social media.'

'Really?' Abe gave a big smile. 'That's great, isn't it, Sal?'

'Don't be so thick, Abe. She's going to destroy us.'

'Not necessarily,' said Cora. 'I'm giving you a chance to make this right.'

Rick rocked back on his heels, watching the interplay between Cora and Sal.

Sal's eyes narrowed. 'How?'

'You've got two hours to put together and upload a post exonerating Dr Mahon. Publicly apologising to him for everything you've put him through.'

'But… we can't… our award…'

'You claim that your channel uncovers the truth. Well, you've just been given the truth. Contrary to the papers you signed, I will allow you to edit the film, but only if it is edited to tell a positive story about Dr Mahon. Do you understand?'

After a pause, Sal nodded.

Cora continued, 'I suggest you make this post a really good one, Sal. Because if I don't like what I see, I'll release my footage from this afternoon.' She pointed to the four cameras around the room in turn.

'You can't do tha—'

'I can. And I will. You've given me the right to do exactly that and much, much more. Always read things before you sign them. I promise you that if I'm forced to post anything at all, I'll do it properly. It will go everywhere – social media, the papers, the radio, both in the UK and around the world. Trust me, you don't want me to do that. Or do you?'

'No,' Sal mumbled.

'I didn't think so.'

'I don't understand,' Sal wailed. 'Why are you doing this?'

'Taking drugs isn't cool. Dean made a mistake and paid a heavy price, but it was his own fault. People need to know that. If I can stop even one of his followers from copying his example, then I will sleep easier.'

Sal stared at her in shocked silence.

'You have two hours. You'd better get a move on, hadn't you?' Cora indicated the way out. 'I'll be watching.'

Rick watched Cora as Sal and Abe disappeared out into the hallway. The sound of the lift doors closing reached them and she sagged, as if her legs could no longer hold her up. Sinking onto the nearest leather sofa, she reached for the remote and turned off the cameras, then leaned back. Her eyes closed. 'It's done.'

Rick stumbled over to a couch, too. 'Uh. Do you mind telling me what the hell just happened?'

She opened her eyes. 'With luck, I've just restored your reputation. Or, at least, I've started the ball rolling. I honestly had no idea what was happening to you. I mean, I knew there was some social media nonsense going on, but I had no idea of the extent of it until you told me. Plus, in my defence, I genuinely believed you hadn't warned Dean about the dangers of mixing street drugs with the medication you prescribed.'

'Where did you find the consultation papers?'

A hoarse voice, rusty from lack of use, came from behind. 'I gave them to her.'

A frail figure in a wheelchair emerged from behind the sliding doors.

Rick lurched to his feet. 'Dean!'

Chapter 44

Beth couldn't help wondering what was happening between Rick and Cora. The few days that Rick had stayed to help out at the well-being centre had been wonderful. He'd cleared gutters, moved tables, cleaned windows and helped to paint the "Muriel". The sight of him chatting to Barbara's posse and teasing the children had warmed Beth's heart despite the perpetual undercurrent of anxiety that nagged at her. When he set off for London, he had hugged her for a long time before pressing a hard kiss to her lips. She could tell that he wasn't planning to return. Every moment since had felt slow, heavy and exhausting, and she had to force herself to stick to her usual routine, ignoring the impulse to crawl under her duvet and never come out.

At midday, she stood outside preschool, waiting to pick up Grace. A message came in from Lucy.

A bit snowed under in the shop. Please can you bring Hari over, when you get Grace? Thanks.

As Beth sent back a reply to agree, she saw an email arrive. Opening it, she read the contents with rising excitement.

One-handed, she scooped up the plethora of bags, coats and finger paintings that Hari and Grace scampered out with, and then carefully herded them across the road to the craft shop. The bell jingled overhead – a bright echo of her delight. Lucy was at the far end of the room, pricing ribbons. Beth hurried over. Grace was hard on her heels; Boo under one arm, Hari in hot pursuit.

'Guess what, Lucy? No, never mind. I can't wait for you to guess. The planning permission came through.'

'Yay!' Lucy gently danced her around in a little circle before releasing her. 'That's great news.'

'We passed the kitchen inspection, too. Although that means I now need to have a conversation with Rose about the tearooms.'

'I think she's onto something. You'd have a customer base from the well-being centre, as well as people walking up from the village and the campsite at the bottom of the hill.'

'I know, I just don't see how we're going to house it properly. I mean, when the weather is fine, we can use the patio... but maybe we should use the conservatory as well. It's just not very big. Maybe I'm overthinking.'

Lucy quirked one eyebrow. 'Maybe? I think you're well past the overthinking stage. You look like you might go into orbit any second. Take a deep breath. It's going to be fine.'

'We don't know that, though, do we? If only we had a space we could dedicate to it.'

'It will sort itself out. Let's just enjoy the good news about the planning permission coming through so quickly. Lord Astley must be spitting pips at having to use his influence on your behalf.' Lucy laughed. 'Barbara pretended to be shocked, but I could tell she was impressed at the way you handled him. Remind me never to get on the wrong side of you.'

'Don't be ridiculous.'

'If we've got permission, we can start advertising initial crafting sessions. It won't take long to get the main section operational. We could have our first trial run in a couple of weeks.'

'As soon as that?' A buzz of excitement ran through Beth.

'Daisy is handling social media. She can start marketing the courses. We need an opening ceremony, maybe a barbeque or a party of some sort. Take pictures and videos, hopefully with lots of people smiling. Have a ribbon to cut or something. It's a shame we can't get someone famous to do the honours.'

'That's a good idea.'

Lucy pulled out a pack of coloured card and some thick marker pens. 'Let's make some posters.'

Beth eyed the pens as if they might bite. 'I'm not the creative one, remember.'

'I'll write out the first poster, then you can copy me. It'll be easy. Look, Grace and Hari are already on it.'

Beth smiled at the sight of the two children pulling pens from the pack.

'What else is on your list?' asked Lucy.

'I have to sort out the loos at the back of the stable. They've not been used for yonks.'

'Not by yourself, surely? You're better than you were, but you've still got to take it easy.'

'Don't worry. Rose won't let me do anything strenuous.'

Lucy pushed the top back on her pen. 'Leave the loos until tomorrow – I'll pop up and help. I can get someone to cover me here for a couple of hours.'

The bell jangled again, this time with an alarming sense of urgency, as the door crashed back on its hinges.

Rose dashed in. 'Beth. There's a guy in The Coffee Pot asking about Rick.'

'What guy?'

'I don't know. Reena's getting ever so cross with him.'

Lucy moved towards the door. 'Come on. Before Reena uses her taekwondo on him. The last thing we need is her dislocating another elbow.'

'Ouch, poor Reena. I bet that was painful.' Beth helped Hari off his chair as Grace grabbed Boo, and they all hurried after Lucy.

'Not for Reena, it wasn't.' Lucy broke into a run.

*

At The Coffee Pot, Stacy was attempting to mediate between a tall, dark-haired, rumpled-looking stranger and Reena. 'Now, come on, you two. Settle down. You're disturbing my customers.'

Reena ignored her. 'Whoever you are, young man, you'd better not be here to cause that lovely Rick Mahon any trouble.'

'I'm not,' said the stranger. 'Where is he?'

'I'm not telling you that. We respect people's privacy around here.'

'Please, I just need to find him.'

Beth had the vague feeling she'd seen the man before.

She put a hand on the older woman's shoulder. 'It's okay, Reena.' She turned to the man. 'Who are you? What do you want with Rick?'

But the stranger wasn't listening. Instead, his eyes had fixed on something just behind her. 'Boo!'

A smile transformed his face and Beth knew exactly who he was.

'David.'

*

Rick had just left Cora and Dean when his phone rang. Even though his mind was reeling from the events of the afternoon, when Beth's name flashed across the screen, he didn't hesitate to answer. 'Hi. Is everything alright?'

'I know you didn't want to... I mean, you said you wanted to stay away from me, and I don't ... well.'

The hesitation in her voice made him want to kick himself. 'Beth, it's fine. You can always call me if you need me. What's the problem?'

'It's not a problem. David is here.'

'What?'

'He turned up in the village. You said you were worried about him, so I thought you'd want to know.'

'Yes. Definitely. I've been trying to call him. Is he alright?'

'I think so, he's just exhausted.'

'Can you put him on?'

'He's asleep. I was making him a cup of tea and he just nodded off.'

Rick checked the time. 'If I set off now, I can be with you in a couple of hours. And Beth?'

'Yes?'

'Thank you.'

*

For once, the route out of London was clear. Rick made excellent time back to the forest. He didn't stop to knock on the front door of the farmhouse; he just walked straight in. 'Is he still here?'

Beth hurried towards him. 'Yes. He's in the lounge. I think he's still asleep. Apparently, he drove over from Italy to look for you a couple of weeks ago, after he got wind of that awful podcast. He knew you'd inherited Charlie's place, but he didn't know the address. He's been combing the New Forest, showing your photo to everyone, trying to find you.'

Rick groaned. 'Gita said he phoned the surgery ages ago, but that they couldn't tell him anything because they didn't know where I was.'

Beth pulled a face. 'I should warn you. He's quite angry. It's probably best to let him sleep.'

The door to the lounge opened and a sleep-rumpled David appeared.

'David! I've been so worried about you.' Rick stepped forward, arms outstretched in welcome, but stopped short at the glower on his son's face.

'You've been worried about me?' David crossed his arms. 'I'm not the one who disappeared off the face of the earth, Dad.'

'I know. I'm sorry.'

'What the hell were you playing at?'

Paddy whined. Out of the corner of his eye, Rick saw the little dog creep towards Beth.

She leaned down to the cowering pooch and gave him a reassuring pat. 'Let's go through to the kitchen, Paddy. We'll find David and Rick a snack. Hungry people get grumpy. Grace, come out from under there and give me a hand.'

Grace scrambled out from under the stairs and peered around her mother's legs, her eyes darting from Rick to David and back again. 'Is he telling you off, Rick?'

'He is, but you know what?'

'What?'

'I deserve it. I was thoughtless and I upset him.'

'You'd better say sorry,' Grace whispered. 'Then he can say it's alright.'

'Good idea.' Rick turned to Beth. 'Thanks for your help and for the offer of a snack, but I think David and I should take this discussion over to the barn.'

'If you're sure.'

'I am. Perhaps… if you don't mind… Could you and I catch up tomorrow?' She might not want to, given how adamant he'd been about staying away. 'There are some things I'd like to tell you.'

'Yes, that's fine. Tomorrow.' Her eyes were wide and solemn.

Rick rubbed the back of his neck and turned back towards his son. 'Shall we?'

David nodded and glanced at Beth. 'Thank you for your hospitality.'

*

Rick led the way, his hands shoved deep into his pockets. 'I'm very sorry, David. I should have contacted you when things first started to go pear-shaped.'

'Why didn't you? If I'd known you were in trouble, I'd have come back.'

'I didn't realise it was going to get as bad as it did. Plus, you've got your own life. You don't need to babysit your old man.'

David nudged him with his shoulder as they scrunched across the drive towards the barn. 'It's not babysitting. It's caring.'

'I know. And, anyway, I did call eventually. Not straight away, admittedly, but when I did, you didn't pick up and it wouldn't let me leave a message. And then, after that, it wouldn't connect at all.'

David pulled out his phone. 'When? Look. There's not a single missed call on here from you. And you haven't responded to my emails or social media messages either.'

'I had to get a new number and a new email, and I've closed my social media accounts down. I was inundated with calls and messages from journalists and other people wanting comments.'

'Oh, I've had a lot of those, too. Persistent sods. At first, I turned off messages and then I blocked unknown numbers.'

'Might you have blocked me, too? My new number, I mean.'

'It's possible.'

'You're right, though, son. I should have called sooner, but I didn't know what to say. I've been too ashamed.'

'Ashamed? Of what?'

Rick's voice was suddenly hoarse. 'Being a failure.'

'You're not a failure, Dad. You're my hero. You always have been.'

Rick dashed a traitorous tear aside. 'I'm sorry.'

'It's fine. I'm here now.' David clapped him on the back. 'What can I do to help? Do you need me to come to court?'

Rick took his keys from his pocket and unlocked the door. 'There's not going to be a court case.'

'How come?'

Rick gestured into the barn. 'Come on. I'll explain everything. I've had a very eventful day.' He looked over at the farmhouse. As soon as he had caught up with David, he couldn't wait to go back and see Beth properly. He had so much to tell her, but that would have to wait until tomorrow.

Chapter 45

The next morning, Beth glanced over towards the barn. Rick's car was still there, so at least she knew he hadn't disappeared back off to London. There was no sign of movement, though.

Hopefully, Rick and David had sorted out their differences. What if he had changed his mind about coming over?

Full of pent-up energy, she decided that tackling the loos in the stables was better than pacing up and down obsessing about whatever it was that Rick had said he wanted to tell her. She armed herself with a bucket full of cleaning products and released her conflicted emotions on the toilet bowls. The ancient porcelain had a crackled patina but was functional, thank heaven, and the pipework was sound. A cocktail of limescale remover, bleach and elbow grease soon worked wonders. Sharp chemical fumes made her head spin and she opened one of the high-set windows to take a grateful breath of fresh air.

After scrubbing the sink within an inch of its life, she turned her attention to the eight-legged tenants watching her from overhead. Manipulating a long-handled broom one-handed wasn't easy, but by wedging the base of it under her sling, she persuaded the spiders to abandon their long-held lodgings one-by-one.

Grace arrived munching on a jammy slice of toast, with Paddy at her side. She scrambled on top of a large wooden packing case under the window. 'Watch out, Mummy,' she cried, pointing at a black shape scuttling across the floor. 'Big, big, *big* 'pider.'

Beth suppressed a horrified squeak and stepped out of the grumpy arachnid's way. 'Thanks, Grace. Well spotted.'

'Morning all.' Rick appeared behind Grace.

'Excellent timing.' Beth grinned a welcome, her insides skipping up and down with delight at the sight of him. 'How are you with spiders? Any chance you can reach those big cobwebs up there?' She waved at the thick silvery ropes stretching across the ceiling.

'Shouldn't you be taking it easy?'

'I'm fine. Lucy and the rest of the gang will be here soon. I wanted to get started while I had the energy.' She bent down and opened the built-in unit under one of the sinks. 'Oh my. There's so much crud under here.' Her eyes lit on something tucked at the back of the first shelf. 'What's this?' she said, reaching for it. A hazy squirm of recognition wriggled in her brain, but she couldn't quite place it. Rising to her feet, she showed Rick a small stuffed animal attached to a key ring with three keys of differing sizes hanging from it.

Rick squinted at it. 'Is that a donkey?'

The tired, grim-looking stuffed animal did look a bit like Pablo. Footsteps sounded in the corridor.

Rose arrived armed with yet more cleaning products. 'Beth, what are you doing?'

'This is nothing to do with me, Rose,' said Rick.

'Traitor!' said Beth. 'I'm fine, Rose.'

'Rose,' called Daisy, appearing in the doorway. 'I need… Oh!' Her eyes locked onto the scrap of grey fabric in Beth's hand. She scowled. 'Where did you get that? Have you had it all along?' She demanded. 'I might have known you'd do something like this. It's those bloody postcards all over again, isn't it?'

Rose grabbed her sister's arm. 'Daisy, calm down. Give her a chance to answer.' She threw Beth an apologetic look. 'Where were the keys?'

Beth held them out. 'Under the sink. I literally found them a few minutes ago.'

'It's true,' said Rick. 'I saw her.'

Daisy snatched them. She cradled them against her chest as if they were precious. 'OMG, I can't believe we found them.'

Rose leaned closer. 'Are you sure it's them?'

'Yes. No. I don't know. Jack will know. Where is he?'

'In the back garden. Come on,' said Rose. The two girls hurried from the room.

Beth exchanged a mystified look with Rick. 'What's got into them?'

He shrugged. 'Only one way to find out.' He sat on the edge of the packing case. 'Come on, Grace, hop on for a piggy-back ride. We'll go and see what all the fuss is about.' Grace needed no further invitation. Beth hurried after him, almost tripping over Paddy, who was keen not to be left behind. As they spilled out of the stables, they ran into Barbara and Lucy on the drive.

'Where are you off to?' asked Barbara.

'I have no idea,' said Beth. 'Something is up with the children.'

Barbara and Lucy followed Beth as she rounded the stables into the back garden, just in time to see Daisy hand Jack the little donkey and ask, 'J. Are these Mum's keys?'

'Beth found them in the old bogs. We didn't think to look there, did we?' said Rose.

Jack touched each key in turn. 'That looks like her car key, that's the one for the front door and...'

'Is that the one, do you think?' Daisy's voice was breathless with excitement.

'The one for what?' asked Beth.

Rose glanced up. 'After Mum died, Dad packed up all her stuff and locked it in the back section of the stables.' She waved a hand towards the padlocked rear doors. The huge double doors were an identical set to those at the front, except these were covered in ivy because they'd been out of use for so long. 'We've been looking for the key ever since.'

'You never said. If I'd known getting in there was important to you, I'd have called a locksmith out ages ago.'

'Yeah, right,' sneered Daisy.

'I would,' insisted Beth. 'You should have your mother's things. It's not right to keep them from you.'

Rose hushed her sister before she could say something else. 'There's a lot of stuff we never said, Beth. And, anyway, locksmiths cost money.'

The unprecedented activity in the garden, so early in the morning, was gaining attention. Pablo slunk over from the vegetable patch. Gengis, Percy, the hens and Lady Muck edged closer. The llampacas peered over the fence, a squad of gangly cheerleaders, all long eyelashes and big hair, shoving each other out of the way to gain a better view.

Jack rammed the key into the massive padlock. It turned with a little persuasion. The rusted bolt and the ropes of ivy put up more of a resistance, before giving in and allowing the huge stable doors to finally swing wide.

'Wow!' exclaimed Jack.

'Oh my!' said Beth. The space was stuffed to the brim. There were several long, thick wooden poles, similar lengths of rolled canvas fabrics, and countless bags and packages haphazardly piled up.

'What is all this?' asked Rose.

Jack stepped inside, examining the contents closely. 'Damned if I know.'

Rick gently slid Grace to the ground. He picked up some paperwork resting on top of one particularly large bundle. After a quick glance, he handed it to Beth.

She read and gave a surprised laugh. 'It's a tipi.'

'A what?' asked Rose.

'A modern version of a Native American wigwam,' said Rick.

Jack scratched his head. 'That's random, even for Mum.'

'Not that random, actually,' said Barbara. 'Isla was quite keen on them. She showed me a picture once.'

'According to the date on these, she bought this a few weeks before she died,' said Beth. A thought struck her. 'Barbara, do you remember telling me that Isla wanted to start a donkey sanctuary? Might this have something to do with that?'

'Possibly. She talked a lot about raising money by holding events up here, so maybe.'

'And might that also be why there were all those tables and chairs in the main section we've just cleared? And what about that huge packing case we found full of cups and saucers and things?'

'Again. Entirely possible.'

Rose gave an excited squeal. 'Mum might have wanted to run a tearoom up here for her donkey sanctuary. Just like I want to for the well-being centre.'

Beth smiled. 'She might. Either way, I think your mum just gave us one of the best presents ever. This thing is huge. We could pitch it, off to one side of the patio. It would definitely work as a covered space for your tearoom.'

'It'll be like a piece of Mum is still here with us.' Jack's voice was low, almost a whisper.

'We could even name it after her,' said Daisy, tossing Beth a mutinous look.

There was silence. It seemed to Beth that the children Isla had never intended to leave behind were holding their collective breaths and waiting for her to react. Whatever she said next had the power to make or break her relationships with all of them.

'I...uh...' It was strange. She didn't feel threatened by Isla's memory anymore. The poor woman hadn't been perfect. Beth wasn't perfect either. She was just a mum trying to do her best. Her eyes went from Rose to Jack and, finally, to Daisy. A wide smile spread across her face. 'Know what, Daisy? Naming the tipi tearoom after your mum is a great idea. Let's call it Isla's Lodge. It will be a vital part of the well-being centre, keeping everyone fed and watered. An important part of everything we do, all day, every day.'

Daisy squealed and flung her arms around Beth, barely able to contain her emotions. 'Thank you, Beth. Oh! Thank you. Thank you.' She burst into noisy tears.

Beth suppressed a wince of pain as her damaged collarbone objected to being squashed. She patted Daisy on the back with her good arm, then eased back to pull a tissue from her pocket and mopped the torrents of water cascading down the teen's cheeks. Broken bones notwithstanding, she wouldn't have missed her first proper hug with Daisy for anything in the world. 'It's all right, sweetheart. It's all right.'

Jack shuffled over and patted Daisy on the back, too, while shooting Beth a quick smile of gratitude.

Beth grinned back. 'All we need now is to work out how to put a tipi up.'

Daisy released her. 'Can we do it now?'

Jack examined the papers. 'These look like assembly instructions. They don't look that complicated.'

'We'll have to make sure we do it right. If it collapses on anyone, they'll sue us,' said Lucy.

'You know who you need?' said Barbara.

'Your Brian?' asked Beth.

'Good Lord, no, he'd be utterly useless at this sort of thing. Couldn't put a four-piece jigsaw together. He's not butch enough either. No, my cousin's daughter, Luella, is the woman you need.'

'Is Luella particularly... er... butch?' A vision of a gilt-clad wonder-woman striding across the farmhouse lawns flitted through Beth's head.

'No, she's tiny. She's a structural engineer, knows about buildings and all those pesky health and safety shenanigans. And, with a bit of luck, she might even lend you Dennis.'

'Dennis?'

'Her husband. He retired two months ago. Now, he is butch. Built like a brick privy.' Barbara nodded with satisfaction. 'Just the job. It'll be good for him to have something to do other than prop up the bar in the Crashing Boar all day.'

'That's true,' agreed Rose. 'Him, Wilf and Barry. They're always in there.'

Barbara snapped her fingers. 'Good thinking, Rose. Wilf and Barry could help, too.'

'I don't know, Barbara,' said Beth. 'Do we really need a bunch of drunken layabouts raising our tipi?'

'Ha!' Barbara hooted with laugher. 'They aren't alkies. Although, come to think about it, Wilf might be borderline. They're just retired and bored. Give them something useful to do and they'll be happy as Larry. In fact, Larry might help, too. You can give them all beer afterwards to say thank you.'

'Well, if you're sure.'

'Trust me, Luella will keep them in line. Scariest woman in the forest, she is.'

Beth's eyes bugged at the thought that anyone could be scarier than Barbara.

'Let me sort out some public liability insurance for the centre and then we could have a tipi raising party,' said Lucy. 'Make it part of our opening event for the well-being centre.'

Daisy clapped her hands. 'That's a great idea. We could have a ribbon for someone famous to cut, too.'

Jack scoffed. 'Where would we get someone famous from?'

Rick coughed. 'I might be able to help with that.'

Beth saw a frown dance across Lucy's brow. 'With respect, Rick,' said her friend. 'I know you want to help, but I'm not sure that you'll bring the right sort of notoriety to this.'

Rick laughed. 'I didn't mean me. I was thinking more of Cora Diamond and, maybe, if he's well enough, perhaps Dean Markwell.'

'You're kidding.' Jack's eyes were as big as dustbin lids.

Beth's breath caught in her throat. 'He's recovered?'

'Recovering rather than recovered. It's going to take time, but he is doing well. There are official announcements about it set for this afternoon. If you could keep it under your hat until then, I'd be grateful.'

'Dean Markwell? Here?' muttered Jack. 'That would be epic.'

'That is good news, but I thought they were suing you,' said Lucy.

Beth watched the interplay between her friend and the love of her life.

Rick shook his head. 'Not anymore. And this is exactly the sort of project they are both keen to support. Something that promotes mental health and well-being, especially if you are involving qualified therapists as part of the package.'

'We have one counsellor already confirmed.' Lucy glanced at Beth. 'Jane agreed to be involved.'

'I knew she'd like the idea.' Beth grinned. 'She'll be awesome.'

Lucy dropped her gaze. 'Rick, I… wanted to say that I… I am sorry for what I said to you at the hospital. I was trying to—'

'To look out for Beth. I know. And you had a valid point.'

'But perhaps I didn't say it as well as I could have.'

Rick waved a hand. 'It needed to be said. Let's forget it.'

'I will, if you will. Thank you. Now,' Lucy clapped her hands, 'I think we have some work to do.'

Beth let out a breath she didn't realise she was holding. 'Actually, Lucy, I think it's time I took a break.'

'Are you feeling all right?' asked Rose.

'Yes, perfectly fine, thank you. But I'd like to take half an hour to go for a stroll with Rick.' Beth felt her face grow warm as a sudden wave of shyness swept over her. What was wrong with her? She'd just effectively asked the most popular guy in school out on a date in front of the whole class. What if he didn't want to come?

As if she sensed Beth's concern, Lucy did what any good friend would under the circumstances. She backed her up. 'Good thinking. You need a break and taking Dr Rick with you in case you come over all faint from overwork is an excellent plan. We'll finish up in the loos while you are gone and sort out the party. Come on, Barbara. Kids, you're with me.'

*

Ten minutes later, walking sedately under the trees, her good hand resting in the crook of Rick's elbow, Beth couldn't think of a single thing to say. His tall, strong, solid presence at her side made her insides do mini somersaults.

'It's wonderful news about Dean,' she said. 'And the court case, of course.'

'I won't lie, I am relieved about the lawsuit. However, the important thing is that Dean is getting better. It turns out he took the consultation papers when he realised that the information would go onto the central NHS database. He didn't want his mental health battles being leaked to the press, damaging his reputation and his YouTube following. And then he had a bad spell. His mood dropped and that's when he scored the street drugs that lead to the accidental overdose. He blames himself. He feels really guilty that I got caught in the crossfire, when all I did was try to help him.'

'And he told you all that yesterday?'

'He did. And that awful YouTube couple got totally burned by Cora.'

'Really?'

Rick nodded. 'I should be ashamed of myself for enjoying the memory of them squirming, but I'm not. You were right about Cora, by the way. She didn't realise how far reaching the consequences of what she was doing would be for me or my patients.'

A niggle of jealousy at the way Rick spoke about Cora stirred in her chest. She forced herself to find something positive to say. 'It sounds as if she is trying to undo some of that.'

'More than that. She and Dean want to use the profile around the case to really make a difference for young people's mental health and they've asked me to join them.'

It was wonderful to hear Rick sounding so enthusiastic. Beth couldn't help feeling sad at the thought that this was something else that would take him away from her.

Who am I kidding? There is no way he'll stick around if he gets his old life back. Especially if the glamorous Cora is a part of the package.

Her chaotic, complicated existence in the forest could never compete with London. 'I am glad for you,' she murmured.

Rick blew out his cheeks. 'I'm not sure it's really me, though. I mean, I fully support them. And will happily play a part in their campaign from a back seat, but...' He looked up at the tree canopy. 'I've missed all this so much. I've decided I'm going to make my home here. In the forest. I'm going to drop my hours at the surgery. The locum whose been covering for me is lovely and will be a great addition to the team. It means I'll commute up to London a couple of days a week for clinic, but, the rest of the time, I'll be here.'

'Really?' She hardly dared to let herself hope.

'Yes, the space, the greenery, the peace. It's wonderful.' He grabbed her hand and gave it a gentle squeeze as he stopped walking and turned to face her. 'I missed you most of all.'

Beth stared up at him, barely able to breath. 'I missed you, too.'

He pulled her closer, his bright eyes gazing intently down into hers. 'Say if you want me to stop.'

Beth stayed silent, her heart's inner gymnastics reaching Olympic gold medal standards.

'Beth, I'm out of practice with any sort of romance, but...'

'But?'

'I'm just going to say it. I think I'm in love with you... no...'

'No?' The disappointment was too much, like a cannon ball to the chest.

'No, not I think... I know... I know I'm in love with you.'

'I never thought I would ever say this to anyone again, Rick. I'm in love with you, too.'

'I don't know how we're going to work this around the children, but we'll take it slow for them. Let's just enjoy spending time together and take it as it comes.'

'Sounds perfect to me.'

He leaned in and pressed a gentle kiss to her lips.

The world stood still.

Oh... my...

Warm and soft and...

Beth's legs melted. She sank into his embrace, her heart singing with joy. This time, everything was perfect. Complicated, messy and utterly bonkers, but still perfect.

When their lips broke contact, Beth couldn't stop grinning. She slid her good arm around his waist. 'So, you didn't decide you fancied Cora Diamond instead, then?' She had to ask. If her Wolverine was choosing her over someone rich, famous, gorgeous and nice like Cora, she wanted it stated in plain English.

Rick tipped his head on one side, his eyes narrowing. 'Now you come to mention it, she's a fine-looking woman.'

'Oi!' Beth poked him in the ribs, relieved when he laughed.

'I'm kidding. She's genuinely a really lovely person. You'd like her. And I'm looking forward to working with her, but she's no warrior queen.'

'No what?'

'That's what you reminded me of when I first saw you trying to fix your tyre. And then again when you yelled at me for scaring the cows. You looked like a warrior queen. Utterly magnificent. So damn cross, all red curls and flashing green eyes. I was terrified and smitten at the same time. I've not been able to get you out of my mind since.'

'I thought you looked like Wolverine when I first saw you – but then, when you scared the cows, I'm afraid I just thought you were a prat.'

'Oh, I am a prat sometimes.' He bowed his head and kissed her again. 'But I'm a prat who's going to be sticking around, if that's alright with you.'

'Hmm. I think that's alright, but you'd better kiss me again to help me decide.'

Prat or not, he was an excellent kisser.

Acknowledgements

This book would never have seen the light of day if it weren't for support from a large cast of experts. In no particular order, I would like to thank:

Claire McGowan, who also writes as Eva Woods (author of *The Lives We Touch* and many other wonderful books that I sadly don't have room to mention). Claire mentored me during the early development phase of this story. I shall be eternally grateful for her guidance and all the great writing advice she shared.

Emma Haynes, director of the Blue Pencil Agency (www. bluepencilagency.com), has been so supportive. The Blue Pencil online tutorials and in-person writing workshops offer an incredible opportunity to meet other writers and learn the craft of writing.

Jenny Kane (author of *The Mill Grange Series* and more) for patient editing, practical writing advice and some much-needed encouragement.

Emma Darwin, author of *The Mathematics of Love* and *This is Not a Book About Charles Darwin,* for her awesome writing craft tutorials. If you're a writer, check out her blog, *This Itch of Writing.* It's packed with useful information.

Sophie Beal of Cadence Publishing, for beta reading the manuscript when I was feeling particularly disillusioned. Your encouragement and advice made all the difference. Who knew that a chance meeting with you at the Bournemouth Writing Festival would lead to regular coffees and far too much cake (is there such a thing?) while we chat about books?

The wonderful Elane Retford and Sarah Snook from www. iaminprint.co.uk for putting on so many amazing resources for authors and being such a source of inspiration, practical help and reassurance. It has been wonderful working with you as a host for The Writing Sphere and as part of the I am in Print Bristol Writing Festival team.

Fiona Mitchell, author of *The Maid's Room* and *The Swap*; Frances Merivale, author of *The Exceptions*; and John Merivale for completing so many constructive reading reports and editorial reports on the various drafts of this manuscript.

All my fellow writers in The Writing Sphere community for their encouragement and shared wisdom and, in particular, Dr Lucy Andrews for an incredibly useful beta report.

The Book Guild Team for responding so positively to my manuscript and giving this story a chance to be heard, and Kate Baker, author of *Maid of Steel* (and also The Book Guild

Author Ambassador), for replying to random questions about all things writing with such patience.

My children, who have put up with far too many burnt offerings, thanks to me having an idea and scurrying off to write it down just seconds before dinner is supposed to come out of the oven.

And finally, Steve, the most patient man on the planet. Thank you for understanding, for believing in me and helping to make this book a reality. This wouldn't have been possible without you.

A note from the Author

Thank you for coming on Beth and Rick's journey with me.

I hope you enjoyed sharing their story as much as I enjoyed creating it.

The village of Ambleford and all its residents have become very dear to me. So much so that there is a second book in the Forest Families Series coming soon. If you would like updates on that, please subscribe to my newsletter via the link on my website. www.alicegmay.com

Alternatively, if you would like to comment on your visit to Ambleford, please consider leaving a review. All feedback is most welcome.

And now, I am going to disappear back into my writing cave to find out what shenanigans Barbara Trenchard and her gang are getting up to next...

Wish me luck. I think I am going to need it.

Love
Alice

Instagram: @alicegmay

YouTube: @alicegmayartandbooks

TikTok: @alicegmayartandbooks

Facebook: AliceMayAuthor

Twitter: @AliceMay_Author

Website: www.alicegmay.com